By Any Other Name

Also by Laura Jarratt

Skin Deep

By Any Other Name

LAURA JARRATT

First published in Great Britain in 2013
by Electric Monkey, an imprint of Egmont UK Limited
The Yellow Building, 1 Nicholas Road, London W11 4AN

Text copyright © 2013 Laura Jarratt
The moral rights of the author have been asserted

ISBN 978 1 4052 5673 5

48090/1

1 3 5 7 9 10 8 6 4 2

www.electricmonkey.co.uk
www.egmont.co.uk

A CIP catalogue record for this title is available from the British Library

Typeset by Avon DataSet Ltd, Bidford on Avon, Warwickshire
Printed and bound in Great Britain by CPI Group

EGMONT

Our story began over a century ago, when seventeen-year-old
Egmont Harald Petersen found a coin in the street. He was on
his way to buy a flyswatter, a small hand-operated printing
machine that he then set up in his tiny apartment.

The coin brought him such good luck that today Egmont has
offices in over 30 countries around the world. And that lucky
coin is still kept at the company's head offices in Denmark.

For Holly Hughes, who encouraged me to write

Holly

They told me to pick something unobtrusive, then they handed me a book of baby names and a cup of hot chocolate from a machine, and they left me there in the white room.

The cup was beige plastic. The chocolate tasted powdery. I stored these points away for later, as a memory of rebirth. The first moments of my new life: plastic and powder.

Strange that I should save that memory to take forward into the future, out of all the thoughts I could have had but didn't. All those feelings that should have been welling up inside me, bursting out . . . But I didn't feel anything. Numb from my skin to right down deep in my core. My senses concentrated and focused instead on just three things – a beige cup, the cheap chocolate drink and a baby names book.

I picked up the book and thumbed through the pages. Names in alphabetical order, names with meanings, names I knew, names I'd never heard of. How to pick? Nothing that would stand out, nothing that would link me to the past — those were the instructions.

The past. As if everything that had gone before this moment was buried already.

Rebirth . . .

I read through the book until the words blurred and blended into one long muddle and every name sounded the same.

In the end, I chose Holly. Because it was December.

Chapter 1

The removal men manoeuvre the sofa through the front door and disappear inside the house. Dad's voice shouts directions to them. The late February wind gusts up the hill so I fold my arms to keep my jacket closed.

There's no fence around the garden. It feels exposed, as if anyone can walk right up to the windows and look in. The door is made of frosted glass, which is even worse. It'll be like living in a fish tank, on display to everyone, and I don't want to go inside.

The house itself is ugly. Apart from the too-big windows, there's a pointless wood-plank effect that starts halfway up the wall and continues to the roof. It's hideous. The upstairs windows stick out of the eaves like they were put in as an afterthought. The drive is full of weeds where the tarmac is crumbling.

I survey the house next door from the pavement. It looks tidier than the one we're moving into, but the garden is gravelled over and dotted with stupid stone ornaments, including a giant mushroom with water fountaining out of a hole on the top. OK, riiight . . . a fountaining mushroom. Mum is so going to shudder when she sees that.

Dad's voice drifts out of the front door again as the removal men come out and go back in with a mattress. The open door beckons me to go inside and explore, but I don't want to. I don't want this scruffy house on a nowhere street in a dot-on-the map village to be home.

This isn't my home.

But neither is the place we lived before the fifth of December last year. Not now. Because there is no before. That's when I became Holly Latham, aged fifteen years and ten months.

Down at the bottom of the hill of identical, ugly, semi-detached houses, a bunch of figures in school uniform appears and walks up the hill towards me. I check my watch – quarter to four and school's out.

They get closer. The first group are about my age and I step on to the drive to let them pass, pretending to stare over the roofs of the houses to the hills on the other side of the village. OK, so maybe now I do want to go in through that open door, to hide. I can feel their curious eyes on me.

I try to block them out. I can see most of the village from here. There's a cut-through to the high street and there's more shops than I expected. The church spire towers up over the black-and-white timbered cottages in the old streets, while the sprawl of the school lies on the outskirts, down the hill and in among fields dotted with sheep.

People *choose* to live here?

The country's all right for holidays, but what do they do here day after day? There's something missing, something that unsettles me, makes me jittery. It's the heartbeat of the place. The fast, excited, racing *lub-dub* of the city is subdued into a slow, dull, measured thud here.

I hate it already.

Out of the corner of my eye, I see the first group has gone past, disappearing round the corner into a rabbit warren of cul-de-sacs. Some younger girls, maybe eleven, walk by and I take the chance to study their uniform because I'll be wearing it next week. Black trousers, white polo shirt, black sweatshirt with a small school badge. Unobtrusive. Just like I'll be.

They move on and the street goes quiet again. I breathe out and relax, letting out a *pffft* of tension. The front door stares at me, challenging me – am I too chicken to go through it? It's waiting to swallow me up.

No, not yet. I'm not ready to be the person who lives here. Not quite yet.

There's a last, lone figure beginning to trail up the hill. He's not in uniform . . . oh no, wait . . . he is. No sweatshirt, that's what confused me. But his polo shirt has the school logo on it. His arms are bare despite the wind, but he's got headphones jammed in his ears and his hands are stuffed in the pockets of his school trousers. He slouches along as if he isn't aware that the skin on his arms is goosebumped and mottled purple with cold. Black hair flops over his face and his head is down, staring at the pavement, so I'm safe watching him. Metal glints in his ear and his eyebrow. Does this school allow piercings or did he put them in when he left? The black Converse All Stars he's wearing certainly wouldn't be allowed at my last school . . .

. . . But that's a code violation. An unauthorised memory access. Holly isn't allowed to think about the time before Holly came to be. That's how I choose to play it, how I make this craziness work and keep away the fear always present at the edge of my mind.

The boy glances sideways as he passes, walking in the middle of the road as though he can't be bothered to cross properly, and he catches me looking.

Dark, hostile eyes in a pale face glare at me. Eyes so hostile that I take a step back, even though I'm annoyed with myself for doing it. Then his head ducks down again and he's gone round the corner.

'Freak,' I mutter after him.

But he's unnerved me enough to make me brave the house. To walk slowly up the drive, to take a deep breath, to step inside. I let it swallow me whole.

Chapter 2

I go into the kitchen and Dad brushes past me with a box. 'Make the removal men a cup of tea, would you? The stuff's over there.' He nods to the counter and carries the box through to the dining room.

'How do they take it?'

'I don't know. Ask them.'

He's unpacking plates from the box and putting them on the table so I follow the sound of footsteps on the bedroom floor above to find the removal men putting our wardrobes back together. One's younger than the other and pretty cute in a rough-edged kind of way, but Holly Latham doesn't flirt. She doesn't do anything to draw attention to herself, so once I know that they both want milk and two sugars, I go back downstairs without smiling at him or checking to see if his eyes follow me.

Dad's still unpacking at speed. 'Give me a hand when you've made the tea. Your mum just texted. She'll be here in an hour because Katie's fretting so we need to get a move on.'

I make the tea and Dad never says a word about all the time I wasted outside when I could have been helping him. I feel a surge of gratitude for that and for him not asking why I was lurking out there so long. Maybe he knows. Maybe he feels the same. I take the tea up to the men and then grab the box nearest to Dad and begin to unpack too.

It's nearly an hour before the removal men finish, even with both of us helping. The van has barely got down the hill before Mum's car comes into view.

She looks tired as she pulls up. Katie's grizzling in the back seat. 'How's she been?' Dad asks as Mum gets out. The answer's obvious but he asks anyway.

'Difficult.' Mum goes to open the back door to get Katie, but Dad stops her.

'I'll do it. You've had her all day. Take a break. Look around the house – see if you're happy with where we've put the furniture.' He leans into the back to unclick Katie's seat belt and he talks quietly to her.

It's the first time Mum's seen the house. She scans the outside and her lips purse. Her eyes move on to next door and I know the exact moment when she sees The Mushroom because she winces the same way I did. When I snigger, her mouth quirks upwards and she gives me a push towards the door. 'Get inside before they see you.'

She knows I won't last long. We fight with each other to get through the front door before it's too late. I don't make it and she pulls me inside as I fall about laughing.

'Where *have* we moved to?' She leans against the wall, her eyes streaming. 'That dreadful toadstool . . . oh, Lou – *Holly* . . .'

We stop laughing as if someone has slapped us. Mum broke the rules: never, ever call me Louisa. Even inside the house that matters. My skin goosebumps like that boy's in the street.

Dad brings Katie in, doing her robot walk where she moves her left arm and leg together, then her right, and he has to stand behind and steer her shoulders. My sister's tall for eight years old and she's got startling corn-coloured hair. You read that description in books, though you never see it on people you know, but Katie's really is like ripe corn. I realise again how hard it is for her to be inconspicuous. Katie makes us far too traceable and the goosebumps rise on my flesh again.

She's making one of her noises. I think it's her robot noise, though it sounds more like a strangled scream. Dad hurries her in and shuts the door.

Katie jerks free and runs past us, chasing from room to room and letting out a shrill squeal in each one as she explores. We stand in the hall and hold our breath as she stomps up the stairs. Her feet thump on the floor above . . .

There's a louder squeal, excited, and then it goes quiet. We wait . . . then we hear a happy giggle and Dad breathes out. 'She's found her room.'

We trail upstairs. Katie's lying face down on her duvet cover with the pink ponies and she's snuggling her big fluffy rabbit. The rabbit isn't allowed out of her room. Ever. Her other teddies are, even the cuddly monkey she's had since she was born, but that rabbit has to stay put. That's a Rule.

'You did her stars!' Mum points at the ceiling. Katie rolls on to her back and looks up at the luminous net of stars and planets. It's an exact copy of the one she used to have in our old house.

'Great Bear, Cassiopeia, Andromeda, Canis Major,' she recites, pointing at each in turn.

Dad smiles and pats her head. 'Yes, angel, that's right.'

'However did you put them up so quickly? And get them all in the right position? It took you ages the first time.' Mum shakes her head in amazement. We all know Dad has got them right because if even one of the plastic shapes was a centimetre out, Katie would notice. She can't tell the time, but she remembers exactly where every star should be.

'I made a tracing of the original and transposed it on to the ceiling when we got here, while the removal men were dropping the covers down on the carpets. I thought it would help her realise this place is permanent for us — our forever place, not like the last two — then she might settle quicker.'

'An angel's got to have stars to sleep among,' Katie chirrups.

Dad only said that once to her, on the day he first put the stars up on her old bedroom ceiling, but she latched on to it and says it over and over.

He grins and kisses her. I slip out and go downstairs to carry on unpacking. The fewer boxes there are when Katie comes down, the less likely it is that she'll freak out. It's bad enough that her routine's been broken again, and Mum's had the worst of that today, but it isn't over yet. There'll be crying fits eventually. A lot. Like there was the last time and the time before that.

This is supposed to be the final time and I hope so. It's only a few months till my GCSEs. It has to work here. We told the Witness Protection Liaison Officer that. We can't go through moving Katie again.

At least she has her stars back now.

'Boo-Boo!' she shouts as she runs down the stairs, and she hugs me. We can't stop her calling me that, her version of Lou-Lou, no matter how hard we try to teach her to say

12

Holly instead. I hug her back and hold her tight — after what happened last year I'm grateful I still have the chance to hug her at all.

Chapter 3

It was a horrible, wet November night and my mood matched it. Rain pounded down, soaking my hair, running in little rivers down my neck. I shifted my violin case from one aching hand to the other.

Hate walking home. Hate walking home in wet weather especially.

The puddles were lit up orange under the street lamps. I tried to dodge the worst of them, but it was like playing hopscotch. I should've brought an umbrella, but that would have just been something else to carry in addition to my PE kit, violin, schoolbag, Tasha's birthday present.

'Skin's waterproof,' Dad would say if he was here, as he did every time he dragged us out in the rain on family holidays. Mum laughed at me when I grumped at him about it once I got old enough to care about looking sodden and bedraggled.

'Skin might be waterproof,' I muttered at the rain, 'but that won't keep me warm when you soak me through.' A gust of wind blew water into my mouth so I ducked my head down further, shifting my grip on my violin case as the handle slid through my wet fingers.

A crappy day. It started badly. I forgot my maths homework and got yelled at – Mrs McPherson spitting, literally, about GCSE failure staring irresponsible 'gurrrllss' like me in the face. Then I got a ton of English coursework back to redraft. And I was dropped from the hockey team for Saturday because I still had a sprained ankle from the match two weeks ago. The only thing that hadn't been a disaster was that Tasha loved the birthday present I bought her: a pamper kit of bath bombs and body butters, and a silver and crystal charm for her bracelet.

But everything else had been crappy. Stupid day, miserable weather and miserable, stupid me.

I kicked a splash of water up from a puddle, then wished I hadn't as a cold gush filled my shoe. I shifted the violin case back to my right hand and struggled to adjust my bag because the corner of my maths textbook was digging into my back. My toes squelched in the wet shoe and the rain battered down harder on the pavement, laughing at me.

Tasha was eating out with her parents tonight. We weren't

allowed to party on a school night so we had to wait until the weekend to celebrate her sixteenth properly. Although my coursework mountain had put a dampener on that. What a sucky year! Still, suckier things than exams and coursework had happened this year . . .

Every time I thought of the summer and Katya, I shivered. Was it when I remembered her that I heard the splish-splash of another pair of feet? Or did the sound trigger the memory? I wasn't sure, but I was suddenly aware of someone walking close behind me.

When I turned the corner into Green Street, I paused, listened . . .

Splish, splash . . . following me.

Before the summer, I wouldn't even have glanced over my shoulder. But that was before. Before Katya. Now I did look back. There was a man in trainers, his hood up to hide his face.

I walked faster, my sprained ankle twingeing a little at the change of pace. Once I got to the end of Green Street, I'd be in Arnold Road. That would be busier . . . other people . . . and that bit closer to home . . .

The footsteps splish-sploshed faster.

I sped up until I was nearly jogging.

I heard the hiss of a car's tyres on the wet road behind me. I glanced back. He was closer, much closer, and there was a silver car cruising alongside, keeping pace with him . . .

I dropped my violin case and bag, and ran. Pain shot through my ankle and I half hopped, half staggered, fighting back a wave of nausea. But I had no choice than to carry on: I couldn't stop, no matter how much it hurt. He was too close.

I slushed through puddles and swallowed rain in with air as I tried to run-hop fast enough to stay ahead.

The slap of trainers behind . . . he was gaining on me . . . the hiss of tyres on the road . . .

Then a hand at my neck, one over my mouth, jerking me to a stop.

I tried to scream . . .

Argh! Argghhh! Argghhh!

I shoot upright, sweat running cold down my back. I can hear the screaming. It's not me. *Not me.* My heart hammers against my ribs.

Is it them? . . . Are they here? . . . Who's screaming?

My eyes adjust to the dark. I'm in bed.

In. Bed.

There's a crash, like a door slamming back . . . feet pounding . . . a second crash . . .

My head falls back on to the pillow. In bed. In the new house, and it's Katie who's screaming. Just Katie. And now I can hear Dad's voice soothing her once she starts to quieten down.

More feet on the landing, and my door opens a crack.

'Mum? Is she OK?'

'Yes, she's fine.' Mum crosses over to my bed and sits down. 'She woke up and couldn't work out where she was, that's all. It was bound to happen. Did she wake you or haven't you been able to sleep?'

'She woke me.' I swallow and my throat's dry so I reach for the water by my bed. 'I had another nightmare.'

Mum's hand finds mine in the darkness. 'It's moving, sweetie. It's set it all off again. When you settle in, the dreams will stop. This will be the last time, I'm sure it will. Tim told us that when he arranged this, didn't he? He said this'll be a safe place. Darling, we're a hundred and fifty miles from home with completely new identities. They won't find us here.'

I squeeze her hand. I don't want her to go but I can't tell her that. She's tired. We all are.

'We'll go and look round your new school next week and buy your uniform. Then we can go to Paperchase and get some new pens and folders. That'll be something to look forward to, won't it?'

Or dread.

A new school. At least I hadn't had to face that before. The last two moves weren't long enough to involve school. Transition moves, they were called. A short stay and then change location again. Confuse the enemy. And give the police time to set up our new identities, which is way more

18

complex than I imagined: all the documentation that's needed and the lies they had to coach us in.

'Yes, something to look forward to.' I let go of Mum's hand so she can go to bed. If I'm lucky, I'll sleep through until the sun comes up. I feel safer in daylight, though that makes no sense at all. They can get you anywhere.

Chapter 4

On the day after the move, Mum says we should go out and explore. Katie claps her hands as if we're about to go on an adventure. I'm tired and my arms ache from lifting boxes. I want to lounge around, not go out and be stared at like the new elephant in the zoo. Dad's warned me about that: 'When you first move into a village, everyone talks about you and everyone stares. You'll get used to it.'

But I don't want to get used to it. I want to be an anonymous face in a city crowd, living in a place that feels alive.

However, when Katie grabs my hand and pulls me off the sofa, I can't say no to her. She won't understand and she doesn't notice how people look at her anyway, so I let her haul me up and drag me to the door with Mum.

The street's quiet. Katie walks along the pavement between me and Mum. She holds our hands and swings her arms, tugging ours up and down, up and down. She's wearing her little backpack, and Charlie Cuddles, her toy monkey, sticks out of the back like a baby in a papoose – so he can see properly, she says.

An old woman is weeding her garden a few houses up. She's bent over, digging at the ground with a trowel, but she straightens up as we pass. I can almost hear her back creak.

'Hello! Settling in?' she calls. Her voice is croaky like an old person's, but demanding too. The voice of someone who expects to be answered. It's unsettling – Dad did say people are more inclined to talk to strangers up here, but it still takes me by surprise. Mum too, from the look on her face.

'Have you moved far?' Our geriatric interrogator gets her next question in before Mum can make an escape. The !Caution! alarm sounds inside my head. We have our prepared history ready of course, but when the questions actually come, our story sounds unreal to my ears and I'm scared that shows in my face.

'Gloucester,' Mum replies. Katie opens her mouth to protest, but Mum yanks her hand so hard that she squeals instead. Mum nods to the woman. 'Nice to meet you. Must hurry. Busy day,' and she charges off, towing Katie. I risk a look back once we've passed the next garden and the old woman is staring after us, mouth open wide.

So that went well. We didn't come across as at all suspicious. And snow is coal-black.

Mum sighs as we get to the path leading to the main street. 'It's harder than you think, isn't it?' She shakes her head. 'They talk you through it all, but when you actually have to do it for real, that's quite another matter.'

'She was nosy.'

'Dad says we'll have to get used to that – neighbours wanting to know our business. Apparently even strangers at bus stops will do it.'

'Really? That's just weird.'

Mum laughs, rubbing Katie's hand because my sister is still whimpering faintly and gazing at her in confusion. 'When your father first moved south, he couldn't get used to how unfriendly he found people there. I used to tease him that he was the oddball and that it was all down to a diet of black pudding and tripe when he was a kid. You don't remember his mother of course, but she was the type of woman to force-feed a child offal.'

'Ew!'

Katie's ears prick up. 'Ew!' she says. 'Ew! Ew! Ew! Ew! EW!'

Mum rolls her eyes at me and I mouth, 'Sorry.' But Mum lets Katie *Ew* all the way to the shops because at least now she's forgotten about having her hand yanked.

I scan the main street: two bakers, a butcher, a couple of hairdressers and a beauty salon, three cafés (one also moon-lighting as a restaurant), a couple of general stores, a post office and a pet shop. And that's just the shops on this street. There are more on the road leading up to the church, but I can't tell what they are from here.

The village looks very clean. I notice that immediately. There's no sign of litter and the pavements look almost scrubbed. The main street is like a photograph from a country magazine. There aren't many people about, but the ones I can see also look scrubbed, and freshly pressed too. Wholesome somehow, like the seeded, uber-nutritious bread Mum used to buy before Katie mutinied and decided she didn't like bread with 'bits' in it and we had to go back to the flabby white stuff. Katie screaming at her toast at 7.30 in the morning is much worse for us than a few slices of white bread.

'EW!'

The whole queue in the baker's shop turns to look at us as Katie yells when we walk in. Even the woman serving at the counter looks up. My cheeks flush hot as they stare at us.

'Yargh!' Katie squeals at them. It's a friendly noise, a kind of hello, but I'm not sure they realise that. Mum keeps a firm hold on her hand, but I let her go so they can join the queue.

'Cake!' Katie spots them straight away: slices of gateaux,

23

carrot cake, chocolate fudge, Victoria sponge. Her face shines with excitement, but the queue frowns as one.

'Yes, cake.' Mum points to the shelves. 'And bread.'

'Bread!' Katie points too. Then she squints at the loaves until she finds what she's looking for and her pointing finger tracks her find. 'No bits!'

'Correct. That's white bread.'

'White!' Katie grins. 'No bits.'

The frowns on the faces around us deepen. They don't know what to make of this horrible, spoilt child. I stand behind Mum and Katie, my face sour. Who do they think they are to look down their noses at us?

The woman at the front of the queue picks up her carrier bag from the counter, casts a last scathing look at Katie and leaves. We all shuffle forwards.

'Doughnuts!' Katie says in her too-loud-for-a-shop voice. She's spotted the contents of the glass case under the counter. Her favourite is there, with custard filling and chocolate icing on the top.

There's a definite tut from the queue, and a cool wave of disapproval – I can almost feel it freeze my hot cheeks. And then I get a prickle of hate over my skin. How stupid are these people?

We move forward again and Katie squeals. We've edged closer to the doughnuts and she wants to share her joy about that with the rest of the shop. And now, finally, there's a flicker of doubt on their faces – *Is there something wrong with her?* Well done! Round of applause for you all, and a fat ring doughnut with sugar sprinkles for being the bright sparks . . .

'Eeee . . . eeee . . . eeee . . .' Katie bounces on her heels as we get closer still. Mum smiles, vague and placid. She's better at this than me. I'm still bubbling with anger as the rest of the stupid queue start to get it. They glance down, then turn away. They turn towards anything, look at anything rather than us. I glare at all of them, even though they won't know it because they're not watching us now. I glare at every single one in turn.

I guess the awkward thing about Katie is that she looks completely normal and she's just young enough to pass for being badly behaved at first, especially when she has a tantrum. This is how it usually goes: stares, frowns; sometimes they say things to each other; sometimes they even say things to us in the case of the really rude ones. To be honest, the rude ones are easier to deal with because you can look at them with contempt and say, 'Actually she's autistic,' and then watch them squirm. Mostly they don't say anything though, but stand there and look disgusted. Either way, the result is the same. They duck their eyes down, ashamed of what they were thinking before they knew she has autism, and then they turn away. That's how ninety-nine per cent of people react around Katie.

Then there's the other one per cent. The ones who hate. Who believe they're so much better than her that they have the right to shout insults or throw things. They make me so mad that I can't speak and the breath chokes inside my lungs just thinking about them.

The woman directly in front turns to face us. She's older than Mum with smartly cut grey hair and she winks at Katie. 'I like doughnuts too.'

'Eeee!' Katie says in delight.

I don't know why my sister makes these noises because she can speak perfectly well when she wants. I guess she must like the sound.

Mum's looking at the woman with a half-smiling, half-wary expression. And the woman looks back at her with a question in her eyes — *What's wrong with her?*

Suddenly I hate, hate, *hate* the stranger for that. Even though she's the one being nice when the others aren't. Even though she's right and there is something wrong with Katie. I hate her for being able to understand what Katie can't and never will. I hate her for being normal when Katie isn't. And I hate her for not having to live the way we do now, memory-less and past-less. And of course, that's to do with Katie not being normal too. Because if she had been normal she would never have noticed what she did and we wouldn't —

It all boils up in my throat and I know I'm on the verge of

screaming, so I hurry out of the baker's and across the road to look in the window of the gift shop opposite. I'm still shaking when Mum comes out. Katie's chewing on her doughnut. Waiting is another of those things she can't understand, no matter how hard we try to teach her.

'OK?' Mum asks.

'Yeah, just got . . . you know . . .'

She nods. 'But one good thing about being in a village is that they'll all know who she is soon and they'll stop staring.'

I know she's right, but the hate is still lodged in my throat like unchewed bread.

Later that afternoon, I'm hanging out in my room trying to sort out where to put my stuff when Dad calls up, 'Holly, she's here!'

I want to pretend I haven't heard but Dad will only come up if I do so I abandon the pile of shoes and trudge down the stairs.

'Hi, Holly.' There's a woman with a fakely bright smile sitting in the kitchen. 'Here to see how you're settling in.'

One of the witness protection mob who's been assigned to check up on us here. I prefer our guy from home. OK, I've not even met this woman properly, but I still prefer our guy from home. It's one of those knee-jerk things – as soon as I see her, I don't like her.

I raise an eyebrow at her and sit down at the table without a word. Dad's glaring at me as if he can glower me back into good behaviour.

Mum ignores me and tactfully changes the subject. 'So everything's set up for Katie at St Antrobus?'

'Yes, we've managed to get her records transferred with her previous school blanked out. The Head's been very discreet — as soon as we told her it was a child protection issue and a police matter, she stopped asking questions. I'm happy we've got that angle covered. It's such a small school that she's the only person who'll have access to those records anyway.'

'Oh, well done!' Mum says. 'That's a major weight off my mind.'

'Yes, just a pity we can't do the same for Holly. But too many people have access to a school file in a comprehensive and I think we're safer sticking to the cover story you agreed with your Liaison Officer in London.'

She turns to me again. 'You are quite happy with that story, Holly? Because you'll have to maintain it.' She smiles — patronisingly, I think. 'I don't know if they told you this, but most witness protection placements fail because the people involved find it too difficult to keep to their stories and they begin to share things they shouldn't with friends.'

Really? No way.

Dad glares again.

'Yeah, they mentioned that.'

'And the people who find it hardest are the children. We recommend no use of social media. It's simply too risky with the potential for posting photos and –'

'Yes, like I said, they already went through that with me back in London.'

'Oh.' She deflates a bit. 'Good. Well, if you are having any difficulties and need to talk things through, your parents have my number. You can give me a call. How's that sound?'

'Great. Thanks.'

'She's finding settling in hard,' Mum cut in. 'Not feeling quite herself yet.'

'Oh, of course.' The patronising smile came back. 'It must be very difficult. I would have hated it at her age.'

Yes, you would. You really have no idea how much.

As soon as I can escape, I run off back upstairs and put my earphones in and turn my iPod up high.

Dumb woman. I mean, who wouldn't want to spend the rest of their life spinning a web of lies and looking over their shoulder the whole time?

I don't have to be asleep. The nightmares follow me into the daylight some days. I can sit on my bed and smell the wet earth like I'm lying face down in the forest again, the scent of the trees like it's all around me. They're out there searching for me. The gun's in his hand. And I wonder if it hurts, being shot in the head. Will I know or will it be over too quickly to feel the agony? How will they explain to Katie that I'm dead? How will they get her to understand?

My breath comes in short pants like I've been running. My skin's icy like I'm lying on cold winter ground, even though I'm curled up in a ball, face buried in my pillow. I'm choking on tears and I just want it to stop.

Chapter 5

Wednesday morning, 8.30 a.m., and I'm walking down the road to Daneshill High School. There's tons of people in front of me going the same way in twos, threes and bigger groups. I trail behind on my own. That's fine; walking along here alone is fine, as long as I don't look as if I'm trying to latch on to the others like some desperate case.

Ahead at the school building, all glass and steel front with shabby Portakabins tucked at the rear, the coaches pull up and bodies in uniform stream off. The bus bays turn into a sea of black sweatshirts pooling out over the tarmac.

I don't want this flutter of fear to be here inside me, but it is all the same.

I expected to have time to get ready for this day. Mum took

me into the school on Monday to look around and somehow, an hour later, I was signed up to start immediately. They even sold us a sweatshirt and polo shirt on the spot. No escape – a uniformed Holly, signed, sealed and ready for delivery. It was the Head's fault. Because the exams are so close, she said I should start straight away.

Lots of the girls appear to be wearing skirts. Really short skirts, some just a few centimetres below the hem of their sweatshirts. My last school would have sent me home for dressing like that. Good thing Dad doesn't know – he's already been bitching about how low the exam results are here, even though Mum reminded him we don't have much choice because of having to be near a special school for Katie. He's a total uniform fascist though, as if having a blazer and tie makes you better at exams. Fortunately Mum's a bit more chilled, though she won't allow me to wear make-up for school. She did give me a manicure last night to cheer me up – soaked my hands, pushed my cuticles back and rubbed oil into them, buffed my nails until they shone just as much as if I had clear varnish on them. Gave me a facial too, to make me feel better about her no make-up rule. I told her the other girls would be wearing it, but she wouldn't give way, except for letting me apply a tiny stroke of brown mascara. I hate my eyelashes – way too blonde – and she knows that.

There's a white dot in the black ocean flowing across the

coach park. It draws the eye like a seagull bobbing on the waves, only this white shape is static. I keep my eye on it as I get closer until I'm near enough to recognise the freak boy from moving day by the sweep of hair over his face and the black Converses. He's wearing just his white polo shirt again without a sweatshirt and a teacher has stopped him. Is he crazy? It's freezing this morning. What is wrong with the boy? The teacher stands over him with a pained expression while he fiddles first with his ear and then his eyebrow. So piercings *aren't* allowed. He bends over to pull the hem of his trousers over the top of the Converses and straighten the scrunched-up legs out.

A passing girl slows down and takes a long, leisurely look at his bum. He's facing the wrong way for me to judge if it's worth the effort of her surreptitious ogle, but she clearly thinks it is from the way her head turns so her eyes can linger on him for as long as possible. Either that or she has some weird thing for aggressive Emo freaks with abnormal body-temperature regulation. I laugh as the teacher makes him take a sweatshirt out of his bag and put it on before she releases him. I can't see why she's so keen for him to cover his arms up when some of those girls are almost showing their knickers, but maybe he irritates her and I *can* understand that.

I go to Reception. It takes fifteen minutes for a stressy-looking woman with frizzy hair to come and fetch me. She's wearing a narky expression and the ugliest shoes I've ever seen — black, clumpy things with a thick sole and wide, square toes.

'Follow me. I need to arrange a timetable for you before you can go to classes,' she says, flapping a tatty piece of paper at me. My name and details are scribbled on it. 'I have no information on what courses you've been doing, what your predicted grades are, no details at all from your last school.' She looks expectantly at me, for me to fill in the blanks, but she's crotchety too as if it's my fault. In a way I suppose it is.

I give her the pre-prepared lie. 'I've been educated at home for the last three years. We moved a lot because of Dad's job so it was more practical, but he's settled here now. I've brought all my coursework with me if you'd like to see it.'

She takes me to an office and logs on to a computer. 'I'll print a blank timetable. You can fill your classes in on that because it'll take a while to have your details loaded on to the system.' She looks at my list and then calls someone. They talk for a while about sets and class codes and I wonder why they couldn't have done this before I arrived because we discussed all this on Monday.

A few people my age knock on the door over the next ten minutes but she waves them away and they wander off. The bell rings — five loud, shrill bursts — and the corridors fill with bodies and noise. The teacher, who still hasn't told

34

me her name, scrolls down her computer screen, tutting occasionally and scribbling on her pad of paper.

'OK,' the teacher says, handing me a blank grid with days and lesson numbers printed on it. 'Fill this in while I read out your class details.'

She drones through the days and periods and I copy the classes in. After that, I follow her again, this time to a room on the other side of the school. It's an English lesson and it's already started. I want to cringe away when she opens the door, but I force myself to walk in, head held high.

Everyone stares, even the teacher.

I look at him because it's easier than looking at the other faces. He's around forty with sandy hair and a round face with little round glasses. It's a look that shouldn't work, but it does in a preppy, older guy way.

'Hi, Holly,' he says when the woman introduces him as Mr Jenkins and I realise he's the first person to say hello to me today. 'We're in the middle of something right now, but take a seat. Don't worry about keeping up, just get your bearings. We're moving on to look at another poem next lesson so you can pick up with the rest of the class then.' He looks around the room. There're two seats free, one next to . . . oh no, Emo Boy . . . and another table where no one is sitting. The Emo looks up at me. He deliberately spreads his arms and legs, and pushes his books further across the table so there's

35

no room for me. Something between hurt and hate jabs me. Not that I want to sit with him, but does he really have to make it so obvious he doesn't want me there? How would he like it if someone did that to him on his first day?

Maybe the teacher sees my face fall or maybe he wouldn't want to sit next to the weird boy either because he gestures to the empty table. It's right at the front and I feel exposed, but it's much better than the alternative. I can feel everyone staring at me even though I can't see them and the hair on the back of my neck stands up in paranoid prickles. I feel as if I've just walked on to a set in *Mean Girls*. One mistake and the back-row crew will chew me up.

The girls will be scoring me against themselves and calculating my rank order. I know this because I've been one of those girls. The boys will be deciding how hot I am. So far I might be doing OK on appearances alone, even if I am wearing a too-straight uniform. I'm aiming for the 'natural because I don't need make-up to look good' effect, not the 'my mum won't let me and I have to do as I'm told' one. I may be getting away with it, but how I look is only half the battle. The rest hangs on how I act. If I mess up now, I'm bitch-food forever.

The boys are an added complication that I'm not used to dealing with in school. If the wrong one looks at me in the right way, and one of those girls wants/owns him, then they'll get their claws out. Because of course, it will be my fault and not the boy's.

The English teacher is right. I do need to get my bearings, though maybe not in the way he meant. The class is studying war poems, which could have been difficult except that I did this topic already last year.

This should be so much easier than it feels. These people are bumpkins and I should be the last word in cool to them. But Holly's not from a big cosmopolitan city, is she? Holly's unobtrusive. I'm not one of those back-row girls any more and I have to learn to live with that. I'm near-the-front girl now. Girl without a hot boyfriend. Head-down, work-hard, never-get-noticed girl.

Sometimes the unfairness stops my breath. I didn't ask for any of this.

The teacher finishes up the lesson and asks me if I know where I'm going, while the others pack up.

'No. I have French next but I don't know where that is.'

He raises his voice. 'Anyone here able to take Holly to French?'

I don't dare turn around to see if there are any volunteers, but I breathe out in relief when a girl's voice replies. 'Yes, sir. I'll take her.'

I do turn then to mouth 'Thanks' at her. She's sitting in the middle of the class and she's prettyish with long brown hair.

Not the kind of girl it'll make me look bad to be seen with, but not too noticeable either – that's good.

When did I get so scheming? I don't like myself this way, but it's Darwinism in action – survival of the fittest. Prey has to stay one step ahead of the predators.

The girl comes over as the bell rings. 'Hi, I'm Nicole. Are you ready?'

I don't answer but I smile a little and pick my bag up. I probably look shy, nervous. Normally I would never allow that to show, but that is who I am now so that's what Nicole needs to see. She smiles back, warm but not too confident herself. When we go into the corridor, she says hesitantly, 'It's this way,' and then she's silent as we push along past Year 7s staggering under schoolbags almost bigger than them. I don't know if I find her silence reassuring or nerve-racking.

We skirt round the outside of the building towards some Portakabins and a group of girls wanders past. They're the type Mum would describe as 'slightly common' with a certain tone in her voice. There's nothing about them that you could exactly put your finger on, except for a sort of hard look to their make-up and something in the way they walk that Mum would read as 'not quite our kind of people'. Tasha and I used to roll our eyes at her when she had one of her snobby moments, yet I find myself wanting to avoid these girls. Nicole walks a discrete arc around them. I catch a bit of their conversation – bitching about someone in their Health and Social Care class. I'm not entirely sure what Health and Social Care is, but from how they look and talk I guess it's one of those subjects that would make Dad groan and say, 'You see, *this* is why we sent you to a private school.'

'What's the French teacher like?' I ask and Nicole's face relaxes in relief as I break the ice. I decide she's much shyer than I am . . . than I was, I mean.

'She's OK . . . ish. But you can't talk in her lesson or have a laugh like you can with Mr Jenkins.'

I nod, half wondering from her face when she says the teacher's name whether she might have offered to take me to French to make herself look good in front of him. Leetle bit of a crush perhaps?

We enter a scratty Portakabin with rotten wood on the door frame. 'It's break after this lesson. I'll show you around if you like,' Nicole says tentatively.

'Yeah, great. Thanks.' I smile again. My mouth's beginning to ache with the effort of trying to look genuine when I really don't feel like smiling at all. When I really feel like turning around and walking right out of this school. I don't want to try to like it. It sucks and I . . .

I want to go back home.

But Holly Latham has no home to go back to. There is no other life.

I don't want to be Holly Latham.

Nicole leads me to the French teacher's desk. 'Mme Carrière, this is Holly. She's new. Can she sit with me and Ella?'

Mme Carrière's eyebrows shoot up in an expression of such Gallic surprise that I would normally have giggled. 'New? At this time? In Year 11? *Zut alors!*'

I nod and stare past her to a poster on the wall about Paris, for something to focus on.

'I have not had information on you, Holly.' She shuffles the papers on her desk and the sound they make signals her exasperation. 'What is your predicted grade?'

I can feel the rest of the class listening intently as they get books out of their bags.

'A-star,' I say quietly.

'Oh!' She stops rustling the papers. 'Oh! Hmm, *très bien. Oui!* It's not easy to change schools at this point, but *tant pis.* We shall manage, *non?*'

'*Oui, madame.*'

'Perhaps you should sit with Nicole and Ella. Do you know anyone at Daneshill?'

'*Non, madame.*'

'Yes, with Nicole and Ella then.' She nods to dismiss me and I slide into the chair next to Nicole. Opposite her is a girl with wavy, mouse-coloured hair who must be Ella.

'Year 11, vocab lists from last lesson – read through. *En Vacances, s'il vous plaît!*' Mme Carrière flicks through a range of books on the shelves behind her as she speaks, pulling several out with brisk efficiency and placing them on the table in front of me. '*Voici, Holly, vos cahiers et manuels.*'

I'm glad Nicole warned me that we can't talk in this lesson, and more than that I'm glad that we *aren't* allowed to. Glad of the excuse to be quiet and reassess. Mme Carrière is OK. She's not friendly but she's businesslike. You'll know where you stand with her, and that's a relief to someone trying to work out how to fit in.

The classroom door opens quietly and Emo Boy slopes in. Mme Carrière turns sharply and her mouth is open to scold, but when she sees him her face changes and she pulls back from the telling-off she was about to give him.

'Joe, you're late,' is all she says.

'Sorry,' he mutters. He doesn't offer any explanation, but she seems to accept that.

He walks towards our table. I scan the room quickly, stiffening. Oh no! Only one seat left, opposite me. He takes it. Nicole and Ella don't react so perhaps this is where he usually sits. Which means, yuck, he'll be opposite me in every French lesson. Like I need someone scowling at me three times a week.

He doesn't speak to us, just gets his books out of his bag

without even looking over. I take a peek at his bag – a scruffy rucksack with badges all over it. Badges with band names I've never heard of. I don't need to wonder why he was late because the stench of cigarette smoke coming from him makes my nose wrinkle.

As the lesson gets under way, Mme Carrière moves round the room, asking us in turn for five-sentence summaries of our holiday. 'You need to add some less familiar vocabulary to shine in your oral exam. Throw in a few words or phrases that others won't. Make sure you stand out.'

The first few people she asks stumble their sentences out. I'm confident when it comes to my turn, bolstered by summer holidays in Brittany that Holly shouldn't remember, though the language centre in her brain can't forget them to order. I know my accent's good and Mme Carrière's eyebrows do their Gallic shrug again. Perhaps nobody around here goes on holiday to France to improve their language skills. Too busy milking cows or shearing sheep or having country fêtes with hog roasts, or whatever they do in villages that they think is living.

The Emo goes next and it's the turn of my eyebrows to shoot up. His speech is quick, like a native's, and his accent is faultless. Clever Emo Freak? No, Emo *Geek*!

I adjust his status from being the boy who thinks he's too cool for life as we know it to being the geek no one likes. Maybe he stinks because he's been bullied by smokers blowing it in his face until he gives up his lunch money. The boy who goes home and cuts himself because no one will talk to him. Who writes really bad poetry on a LiveJournal account nobody reads, about how no one understands him because he's so deep.

I'm being really silly, but somehow thinking all this bad stuff about him cheers me up.

Nicole and Ella do their sentences and he writes in his exercise book, head down, fringe over his face. He chews his lips while he works and when his mouth isn't screwed up because he's scowling, it's actually quite a nice shape. Noticeably. Better than most other boys I know. Oh well, everyone has something about them that's attractive-ish, I guess. I feel mean for a second for thinking that nasty stuff a few moments ago, but after all he was the one who gave me evils when we moved in and he was mean in English so I shouldn't really feel that bad. It isn't as if he knows what I'm thinking.

As I watch him covertly, a wave of dislike surges up as I remember how uncomfortable he made me feel outside my house that first day, and again today in English class. The sensation makes me feel better somehow, like the release you get when you're angry and thump the pillow or throw a cushion at the wall.

There are all these simmering feelings that normally hide inside me – the ones I can't talk to friends about because I don't have friends now and, even if I did, I couldn't talk to them about *that* . . . I can't talk to Mum and Dad about them either because they have their own worries to face in all of this mess, as well as dealing with Katie's problems . . . All of the feelings that sometimes overwhelm – in that second, I channel them towards a focus. Him.

Insanely crazy and totally wrong, it helps. For that moment, I have a target. One I can see, that doesn't hide in shadows. One right here, right now. Tangible.

I concentrate all my anger and confusion and fear on to him. On to hating him. My scapegoat. My own personal whipping boy.

He looks up at me. His lip curls slightly, as if I'm too ugly to be near him. His dark eyes are just as confrontational as when I first saw him.

He makes it easy for me to turn him into a villain.

Chapter 6

'How was your first day? Did you make any friends?' Mum puts the salad bowl down in the middle of the table as we sit down to dinner and looks at me expectantly. The scrubbed farmhouse table from our old kitchen looks silly in this more modern kitchen-diner, but the big American oak table we had in the dining room wouldn't have fitted in here. It seated twelve and when Mum and Dad had dinner parties –

Don't!

But it's so hard to stop. Memories creep up on me when I'm not expecting them, and I'm plunged again into an icy-cold pool of the misery of missing home. It steals my breath and I feel the pain sharp and new every time it happens.

I pick up a slice of pizza and pretend to nibble the crust. 'I talked to a few people in my classes.' Nicole had introduced me to some other girls at break. They were a lot like her: quietish, prettyish, niceish. Girls I'd never have noticed before. I couldn't remember which name went with which face, they were so much the same.

I hadn't had any other lessons with Nicole for the rest of the day, but she and Ella met me at lunch and showed me the dining hall. Part of me would rather have been on my own than making the effort to talk to them, remembering my role and trying not to make any slips. But another part would have been crushed to have to sit alone in the cafeteria. It would be OK if I was invisible and I could sit there and watch people. Learn about this strange environment I've been dropped into. Even so, I couldn't face people looking at me so I kept my head down while I ate lunch – some disgusting pasta and sauce served in a cardboard tub. Nicole and Ella probably think I'm shy. Maybe I am now. Maybe that's what Holly Latham is.

Nobody else in my classes spoke to me for the rest of the day. That was fine though. Most people seem too focused on the exams looming to pay attention to a newbie who gives every appearance of not wanting to talk to them either. Is this who Holly is? Holly the *Geek*? No, that's a step too far. I rebel at that thought.

Katie arranges the salad around her plate in a pattern. Only when she's got it all exactly where she wants it will she start eating, and nobody is allowed to arrange it for her or to help. She must do it herself. She puts the cherry tomato halves on the rim of the plate like numbers on a clock face. Cucumber slices go beneath in a ring. Lettuce is piled in the middle, with pepper rings crowning them. Her pizza slices are on another plate because she screams if hot food touches cold food. She eats the salad first, then the pizza. There's something hypnotic about watching her. She's been doing this for three or four years in exactly the same way and the repetitiveness pulls me back to another room, another house, another life.

I'm Lou . . . and I'm happy . . . safe . . . no worries . . . my world is turning as it should . . .

'Are you OK – Holly?' Mum asks sharply. There's that unnatural moment's pause between her breath in to speak and her actually saying my name. It brings me back. My world tilts on its axis again.

'Just tired. Today was kind of stressful.'

Katie nibbles on a cucumber slice now the tomatoes are gone.

Mum makes a sympathetic face. 'Of course. It'll be easier tomorrow, darling. But I'll run you a nice hot bath after dinner and you can have a relaxing soak.'

Mum firmly believes that bubble bath can cure most ills and it's only when I see her pouring the last of her Molton

47

Brown foam under the hot tap that I realise she knows how stressed I was about my first day in the new school. Every Christmas, Dad buys her a hamper with those bath gels, but not the last one. That Christmas was marked by a few hastily wrapped presents and a pub lunch, followed by afternoon TV in a strange house in Devon surrounded by cardboard boxes. We tried to be cheerful, but we're a family who love the old rituals: the patchwork stockings with our names cross-stitched on the top, hung at the foot of the bed; gathering round the tree in the morning with coffee and OJ and croissants to open our presents; the pre-lunch walk to get out of Mum's way while she does the last preparations in peace; Dad's stupid festive CDs playing in the background all day. These are the things that make it Christmas, that make us safe and secure and at home.

Away from the familiar patterns, Christmas Day felt like walking a rope bridge over a waterfall. I finally understood how Katie must feel when we break her routine. I hugged my sister extra hard that day.

'Ready, darling,' Mum calls as I collect my bathrobe.

'I could have done it myself.' I'm guilty that she's wasting her time on me when she has so much to do herself.

She strokes my hair. 'I know, but a little pampering after a hard day never hurt anyone.'

Mum always could read me better than anyone. I smile

a thank you and hook my robe on the bathroom door. She closes it quietly behind me and the scent of ginger and some flower I don't recognise envelops me. I sink into the warm water gratefully and inhale the aroma. Mum's right — a long soak in expensive bubbles does make the world seem a better place for a while.

I breathe in and out, and in and out, letting the scent and the warmth calm me until I feel boneless and floaty. When I close my eyes, the smell transports me back to my old bathroom: the en-suite with its cool, tiled floor, heated chrome towel rail with soft fluffy towels waiting. I pretend I'm there. It's wrong, I know, but I can't resist. Today was my hardest ever day of being Holly. Maybe because it was my first day alone? I don't know. I just know I'm sick of her.

I breathe in. I breathe out.

I'm Lou again now. Holly's put to sleep. When I get out of the bath and pad through on to the white carpet in my bedroom, I'll turn on my netbook and check out my Facebook page. Listen to the latest YouTube tracks that Kirsten's linked to. Flick through Talia's photo uploads. See who's changed their relationship status, and who's written what on their wall, while I dry off and lounge on the bed.

And I can't wait to do it. The bolt of elation at the thought of it is like an electric shock. I splash around with the soap hastily and wash my hair in record time. I hop out of the bath, ignoring that it's grotty lino under my feet, not smooth tiles. I ignore that I have to walk down the hall to my room and that there's hard grey cord carpet under my feet when I get there. I ignore the fact that when I log into my netbook, my Facebook account isn't saved in my Favourites and I have to do a search to find my page.

My fingers tremble as I key in my account name and password.

I ignore the voice that tells me I shouldn't be doing this.

Ignore everything I've been told.

Ignore . . . ignore . . . ignore.

My profile page flashes up.

Four weeks ago, from Tasha:

wherever ur, hope ur ok. stay safe, babe <3

That's the last post on my wall. There's nothing since.

I scroll down and read the earlier posts from the start. 6th December at 19.36 from Tasha.

why u not in school 2day? i txtd u like 15x!!! what's going on with u? call me xox

7th December at 18.56 from Kirsten.

Retro time! Check these out!

7th December at 19.05 from Tasha.

ur scaring me. ru ok? plz call <3x1000

It's hard to read some of them but I do, through the whole lot since the day Holly was born. Next I click on to Tasha's page and read that. Then Kirsten's, Talia's, Lea's . . .

At first, it's all full of where am I and has anyone seen me, and worry and then fear. But then . . . and I swallow hard here . . . then it all gradually goes back to normal. Lea's seeing a new guy. Kirsten's blown away by this track from a band she's just discovered. Talia's slaving away on a portfolio of photographs for her art project. Hardest of all, Tasha's mum is sick and it's serious.

Their lives are going on without me. I feel like a peeping Tom, spying on them. There's no place for me with them now. I don't even exist.

Four weeks since the last message on my page. They've forgotten me. They've moved on.

And then I do it. I force my finger down to tap the touchpad and open up Dan's profile page. I read his wall.

Dan Wharton
In a relationship with Callie Tyler

It's like someone's spun me upside down and round and over and . . . I feel sick . . . I don't know whether I'm standing up, lying down . . .

He has a new girlfriend.

It should be no surprise. He hasn't posted on my wall at all since I've been gone.

But still, to see it there in text on the screen . . .

I know I'm crying. I can feel the tears on my cheeks, but I don't know what to do to stop them. It's like I could cry forever.

Chapter 7

I realise I'm angry when I'm sitting in assembly the next day. I'm not angry just with Dan, or Kirsten, Talia, Lea, Tasha. I'm not even just angry with *Them*, the reason I have to be Holly. I'm angry with myself. If I hadn't stuck my nose into stuff that was none of my business then we wouldn't be here and I wouldn't have lost my friends, my boyfriend and be marooned here in Boringsville. This isn't a red mist of anger. It's more like embers smouldering inside, heating slowly until I feel their burn all the way through me.

This morning I went into registration and everyone looked at me. I didn't recognise anyone from yesterday. One or two might have been in a class I had but the faces merged together into one big mess as I tried to avoid their gaze. A girl with a dyed blonde ponytail looked me up and down and sniggered. I eyeballed her. My stomach wobbled – part stress and part anger at the attitude she was giving me. Who did she think she was? She had a face like a camel.

There was an empty chair by the front and I dropped my bag beside it.

'Are you the new girl?' Ponytail Girl's friend didn't waste any time, sauntering over.

'Yes.'

'Where did you go before?'

'You wouldn't know it. I'm not from around here.'

She shrugged and walked away, back to her friends in the corner. I got my timetable out and looked where I was supposed to be next. The girls glanced over at me a couple of times, but mostly they lost interest. I'd checked that timetable four times already since yesterday, like a nervous tic, but I couldn't just sit and stare at nothing.

The room hummed with conversation. I could have listened in, but I couldn't be bothered. I didn't want to be here at all. Speaking to those people would make it feel more real than I could stand. My mind was with my heart – back home, wanting to pick up the pieces of my life. *Holly* could go to hell.

A teacher came in and walked to the front desk. She did a double take when she saw me sitting there. She was youngish with OK-looking clothes, which seemed to be a rarity among teachers in this place.

'Hi! You must be the new starter. I didn't know you were going to be in my form. Sorry, I've forgotten your name. They did say but . . .'

'Holly.'

She smiled, and pathetically I felt a puff of tension release at the sight of a friendly face. 'Hi then, Holly. Do you know anyone?'

'I don't think so. The girls who showed me around yesterday – Nicole and Ella – I don't think they're in this form?'

She frowned for a second. 'Oh, I know who you mean! No, they're not. I'll introduce you once I've done the register.'

She took the register quickly and then beckoned a couple of girls over and asked them to take me to assembly. They smiled and nodded politely, eyeing me with faint curiosity. The bell rang quickly, one blast, and I got up and followed them to the hall, feeling like a spare part. It appeared we had to sit on the floor, because there were no chairs out. I hadn't sat on a hall floor since primary school.

Another form trooped in and sat behind us and younger kids arrived to sit on the other side of the hall. I recognised the Head standing on the stage from the day I came to look around.

People were talking noisily, but the teachers didn't try to

stop them, nor did the Head. Nicole and Ella came in with a bunch of other girls I vaguely recognised from lunchtime yesterday. They smiled over at me and I was surprised by how grateful my return smile was. The Emo was obviously in their form because he came in after them. A girl was talking to him, but he didn't seem to be listening to her. Ignorant pig. He sat down a couple of rows in front of me and a flash of a skinny but very toned bum caught my eye. I blinked, and remembered the girl from yesterday copping a good look. OK, she had a point, but his personality definitely didn't match the quality of the rear view.

The last few people shuffled in and the Head started the assembly. It was much less formal than I'm used to, with no standing for a hymn or a prayer. Just a long and patronising reading about racism, which she gave in a monotone that could cause an insomniac to fall asleep in seconds.

It's during this lecture that I understand I'm angry. It takes a while for me to recognise the burning feeling inside, which gets stronger and stronger as we sit in silence and I think about what I saw on Facebook last night.

Dan and I were never a forever thing. I'm not ready for one of those. There's exams and uni and a career to build before I think seriously about all that. But Dan was hot and good fun to be with. It wasn't love with a capital L, but that doesn't mean I want to think of him being with another girl.

It gives me a pain like bad tummy ache to think of Callie — who I never liked much — stroking the back of his neck while they kissed, the way I used to. I don't even have Tasha to bitch to about it like I would if we'd had a normal break-up.

Tasha. And the others. They'll be out this weekend, in our old haunts. And I'll be here in Dump Central, thinking of them, wishing I was there, wondering what they're doing. They'll be having fun and not giving me a second thought. Or if they do, it'll be something like, 'I wonder what happened to her. Wasn't it weird how she disappeared like that?' And then they'll shrug and forget me again.

I wish, wish, wish I'd never done it now. I wish I'd stayed silent, never run out of the cottage that night last summer, never listened to Katie when she told me what she saw. I wish Katie hadn't seen the car. I wish she wasn't so stupid and retarded so I could just have told her to —

No!

I close my eyes and drown in shame.

Wrong, wrong, wrong.

I hate myself for a moment.

Because the awful thing is that, no matter how bad this feels for me, it feels worse for Katie. Routine and ritual are her twin gods and we sacrifice them every time she has to move.

I know why she screams now. I've learned the hard way how it must feel to be in her head. I want to scream

57

too at everything I've lost, and the much-too-newness of how my life is now. I wish I could sit here and rock and scream until someone with familiar arms comes and makes it all better.

Two rows down and six to my left, the Emo boy shifts on the hard floor and I glare at the back of his dumb, floppy-haired head. He's chewing on a hangnail as the Head starts reading out notices. I shift my glare to her for a second. I didn't like her to begin with and I like her even less after being bored to death by her for fifteen long minutes. But I dislike Emo even more; when I imagine what it's like to be inside his head, I shudder. I bet it's all about him, the self-centred loser.

I'm angry with Dan, yes. I'm angry with Tasha and Co. too. I'm angry with me, and with Katie when I'm honest. I'm angry with the world's most tedious head teacher for having such a sucky school. I'm angry with the Emo just because. And I'm angry with Holly for having to exist at all.

For having to be dull, mousy, unobtrusive little Holly. Hiding from shadows. Passive. Always running, never fighting back.

So sick of it all. The endlessly long months of it. Months of her. Of the real me being squashed down, like I'm the one who did something wrong.

Well, I didn't.

I didn't do anything wrong at all and I've taken as much as I can of my life being destroyed.

Screw Holly. Screw *Them*. I don't care what happens any more.

Chapter 8

First lesson is maths. I get there quickly and take a seat on the back row, second from the corner. The other students come in gradually, but the teachers often arrive last, I've noticed, as if they don't want to be here either.

Predictably, I'm stared at.

Yes, I'm new and I dared to take a back-row seat. What are you bumpkins going to do about it?

The first few people into the room sit at the front, but eventually a group comes in who head for the back. They don't need to get there early. Their status is established and no one will take their seats.

Except today someone just did.

They stop and look at me, three boys and three girls.

'Don't you know who we are?' their shocked faces ask.

Don't you know I outrank you in every way possible? You're top set in a grotty comp in Nowhere's End. Get over yourselves.

I feel hot all over with the anger still burning inside me.

Is it a stand-off? I'm not sure yet. But I'm not backing down. Because Holly can be this person instead. Holly can be whatever I want her to be.

The girls are pretty. The boys are cute – not smokin' hot in the case of two of them, but the third is gorgeous. He looks right at me and I look back without any discomfort.

Holly is going to be confident and unintimidated now. I choose *this*.

The teacher comes in behind them and the gorgeous one tilts his head on one side. 'You're the new girl.'

It's not a question but I answer anyway. 'Yes.'

He grins. It's mega cute. 'Got a name?'

The girls laugh and roll their eyes in a way that tells me he's not with any of them.

'Holly.'

His grin settles into a smile that melts my insides in a totally different way to the anger I was feeling just a few seconds ago. He nudges the boy closest to him, who shakes his head good-naturedly and takes the seat in front of me with exaggerated resignation. The hot one sits down beside me, and the others sit at the tables to the right of us. I'm too distracted by the dark-haired, blue-eyed gorgeousness next to me to pay much attention to them.

'And do you?' I say, trying to sound cool and unruffled.

His grin dispels any calmness I've managed to gather.

'I was wondering when you'd ask.' He winks at me and my stomach twirls again. 'Yes, I do.'

I wait . . . and wait . . . and then I can't help laughing. 'What is it then?

He laughs too. A proper laugh, head thrown back. 'Fraser.'

'Can we get started now?' the teacher calls, making me jump. I'd forgotten she was there.

Fraser gives me a slow, lingering smile and then faces forward. The teacher starts her introduction, writing the 'aims' of the lesson on the board. Seems pointless to me but they all do that here. Halfway through her scribbling, the door opens and Emo comes in. He walks to the back and takes the empty table to my left. Suddenly I understand why Fraser's friend didn't sit there.

Again, nobody shows any reaction to his lateness, not even the teacher. What is it with him? Is he the village mafia or something?

I notice him glance at me as he sits down. Then his eyes slide over to Fraser and he suppresses a snigger. Idiot. Who does he think he is?

I know exactly who he is – a nobody with no friends.

As the teacher doesn't seem to notice me, Fraser gets up and walks to the front and I get a great view of the back of him. It's just as good as the front. He's tall and toned, as if he does a lot of sport. He picks up an exercise book from a pile on the shelf behind the teacher. She doesn't register this at all, and he brings it back and passes it to me.

'Thanks.'

'No problem.' That smile again.

He's the perfect distraction to stop me from brooding over Dan, but he's not going to have it all his way. He might be uber-cute, but I'm not going to throw myself at him.

Yes, screw you, Dan. You don't know what happened to me and you wasted about five minutes before getting it together with Little Miss Vapid.

I'm not going to let Fraser know the effect he's having. He has to earn me. Tasha's older sister sat us down when we were twelve and told us the harder a boy works to get a girl, the more he appreciates the victory. Her advice has never let either of us down. Lea could never understand why she struggled to keep boys interested for longer than a few weeks when we didn't have any trouble at all. We tried to tell her, but she always turned herself into a doormat straight away. She just couldn't seem to act any other way around a boy she liked.

I guess I didn't do too well with Dan though. I can't believe he forgot me so quickly. I can't believe they all did. It hurts. Even with the distraction of the hottest boy I've seen in Dumpshill Comp sitting right next to me and flashing me a quick smile as he looks up from his maths book.

On my other side, Emo Boy has his head down, leaning it on his hand, as he scribbles furiously. Doesn't he ever speak to anyone?

'So, do you know people here?' Fraser says after he checks I'm ready to turn the page over.

'No. We lived down in the Midlands and we've only been here a few days.'

He smiles. 'Come to the canteen with us at break. I'll introduce you around.'

So this break-time I'm sitting in the canteen surrounded by a way cooler bunch of people than Holly was with yesterday. The Holly of yesterday tells me to be careful. I tell her to shut up. This is *my* future now. I have to have something to make up for everything I've lost.

Chapter 9

'So how was today?' Mum passes me the carrots to grate. Katie holds the grater steady. She likes this job.

'Better.' I run the first carrot up and down the rough grating side. Katie sticks her tongue between her teeth in concentration and hangs on to the grater handle. 'I met some people.'

'That's nice. Just be careful not to give too much away.'

I nod while I grate energetically. 'I'm meeting some of them on the playing fields later,' I say casually.

She isn't fooled. Her head flies up and the baking potatoes she's scrubbing are abandoned. 'That's not like you.' She looks me straight in the eye and I squirm. She's right of course. Tasha and I despised the girls who hung around in the park.

That kind of thing was for girls who wore too much fake tan and false eyelashes heavy enough to start a tsunami in the Pacific if they blinked. We went out and did things; we didn't hang around on park benches hoping we'd be noticed by some saddo with a souped-up Corsa.

'No.' I keep grating the carrots. 'But I don't know how people do things around here so . . .' She purses her lips and I shrug. 'I have to try to fit in, Mum.'

'Maybe not like that though?'

'You don't know what it's like here with no friends.'

She shakes her head at me and turns back to the potatoes. 'Of course I do!'

I'm ashamed then of snapping at her. She gave up her life too. So did Dad. Why is it so easy to forget what they had to sacrifice? Is it because I'm a selfish bitch at heart? That's not who I want to be.

I finish the carrots and take the potatoes off her, telling her I'll make dinner now. Maybe she wants to do her yoga DVD or something.

She nods. 'That's a really good idea. I think I need to de-stress. But *Holly*' – and she emphasises my name – 'you need to be careful. You know that.'

I have a flash of anger again. *Yes, I know that. I know. The thing is, Mum, with the ghosts of Tasha and Co. haunting me, and Dan's abandonment fresh and stinging, I don't really care.*

66

I search my wardrobe for something warm to wear because it's cold outside. A frost is forming – I can see the car windscreens starting to sparkle from my bedroom window. I'm feeling a bit ashamed of grouching at Mum over her advice to be cautious. I can't blame her. When we went into witness protection, they made it clear to us that we had to be so, so careful.

I remember that first day in the hotel room, when I got out of hospital and the police took me to Mum and Dad. The moment the hotel door opened and I was ushered in, Mum ran full pelt across the room and flung her arms round me – carefully in case I was still in pain or dizzy, but she bear-hugged me all the same. Dad was only a second behind her, and Katie danced round us all shouting 'Boo-Boo! Boo-Boo!' at the top of her voice. As soon as I saw them, I started to cry and I couldn't stop. Dad asked if we could be alone for a while and so they left us for half an hour.

'What happened to you?' I asked when I could stop crying and Mum finally let go of me.

Dad was sitting beside me, holding my hand. 'Once we agreed to go along with what the police suggested, we had to get out straight away. Mum brought Katie to the hotel and they sent me to pack some essentials. We're going to sell the house now, but it'll take a while so we'll have to rent until it does sell.'

Selling? So it was permanent then. We were never going back home.

I started to cry again.

We weren't left alone for long though. When they came back, they told me about how a hairdresser would call round tomorrow. I told them no and I wasn't changing my hair. They got cross then until Mum suggested a temporary colour just until we moved and they accepted that. They told me how Katie was getting to keep her name because nobody could get her to understand otherwise. How all the ID needed was being prepared. And most of all, never, never to talk about it. Never to give anything away. That I was Holly now, everywhere. Even at home. Even in the privacy of the family. Lou was gone forever.

They even talked us through an outline of a cover story we might use: Dad quits his job as troubleshooter for a nationwide company to go solo as an accountant, downsizing our house until he gets his business off the ground; Mum looks after Katie. Well, at least that was true. Mum had been doing freelance editing too, but they said she'd have to stop that as her name was too well known.

I meet the group from school on the village playing fields at half seven. It's dark but the pavilion is lit up. I can see Gemma and Lucy, two of the girls who were with Fraser in maths, sitting inside and I walk over, unexpected flutters of nerves in my tummy. They see me and wave. 'Hi, Holly!' The boy sitting beside them turns. It's not Fraser but one of his friends – Stuart. He's holding Lucy's hand.

There's noise coming from further up the field, but it's too dark to see what's going on. Girls are laughing and squealing over the racket of engines revving and spluttering. There's the occasional flash of a headlight.

Lucy laughs as an especially shrill squeal floats towards us. 'I just bet that's my little sister.'

I go in and sit beside Gemma under a security light that's wrapped in a mesh cage. 'What's going on?'

'Some of the boys brought quad bikes up and they're giving rides at the top of the field. I think they're having some kind of competition to see who can make the girls scream the most. Want to go see?' Gemma grins. I don't ask her if Fraser's up there. 'Leave Lucy and Stuart to eat each other's faces, which they're dying to do.'

Lucy giggles and slaps at her, but it's more grateful than annoyed so I get up and follow.

It's inky dark outside the pavilion and the ground is uneven under our feet. Gemma grabs my arm as she stumbles.

'Ow!' she yells, then puts two fingers in her mouth and gives a sharp whistle.

'Oh my God, how do you do that? You have to teach me.'

She laughs. 'My brother taught me. He says I was the

slowest ever to learn. Ah, here he is.'

An engine vrooms towards us and I'm blinded by the lights until it pulls up, so I can't see the rider in the darkness. 'Want a lift, lazybones?' he asks.

'Yes, but can you fit Holly on too?'

I'm being appraised in the headlights, I know it.

'Sure.'

I can hear his smile. I passed the test. Gemma shoves and wiggles me around until I'm somehow wedged on the bike between her and her brother. It's good one of us knows how to get on this thing in the dark because I don't have a clue. Gemma introduces me and her brother gives an approving grunt. Obviously 'Hi' is beyond him. We zoom off up the field and my teeth rattle – this thing is a total boneshaker.

When we get to the top of the field, we hop off. Or rather Gemma hops off. My effort is more an inelegant topple to the side.

Someone's lit a small fire in a pit in the grass and the flames flicker on the faces of the people standing around. I scan quickly for Fraser, but he's not in sight. A couple of the boys look vaguely familiar from school. They're in my year, but I don't know their names.

A girl with strawberry-blonde hair makes her way over to Gemma.

'Oh my freakin' God! That just scared the living crap out

of me. I thought we were going to crash for sure.' She's got a mid-Atlantic twang, which sounds odd out here.

Gemma laughs. 'Hi, Cam. Holly, this is Camilla, but everyone calls her Cam.'

I say hi politely and Camilla looks me up and down. In much the same way, actually, as Mum would have looked over those girls from the Health and Social Care class and come to the conclusion that they weren't the right sort. I bristle immediately. This has never happened to me before.

'So what are you into, besides getting nearly dead on quad bikes?' Cam asks, though I'm not sure she really wants to know.

'Music, mostly. And I used to play a lot of tennis and hockey.'

It could be my accent that reassures her, or what I said, or she's noted the lack of yokelness in what I'm wearing. She smiles condescendingly and Gemma relaxes. I guess she's relieved Camilla has approved me and she's not made a gaffe by turning up with me.

I want to be open-mouthed at the sheer bad-American-high-school-movieness of this. Camilla's Queen Bee, that much is obvious. I guess from her accent that she's lived in the US recently – maybe that gives her some kind of exotic appeal out here.

'So you're at Gemma's school?'

'Yes, just started. You're not?'

I get the condescending smile. 'No, no.' And then with a little laugh, 'I'm at the Roundle School.'

I've heard of it. Good facilities, but not up to much academically. Really nothing for her to turn her nose up at me about. Oh no, I forgot – I'm at Dumpshill Comp now. Well then, she might have a point.

Were Tasha and I this bad at talking to newbies? I don't think so and I certainly hope not.

Five quad bikes roar past and head to the bank of trees on the other side of the fire. The screams from the girls intensify and I roll my eyes at their idea of entertainment – being driven round a field by a conversationless lump who thinks making them scream turns him into a man. So, so sophisticated.

Gemma's brother comes up. 'Want a ride?' He doesn't address the question to anyone in particular, but Camilla assumes it's to her. Why does that not surprise me?

She giggles and simpers and flicks her hair. I think I want to be sick.

'Do you think you can make me scream louder than last time?'

'Get on and find out.'

Wow, he's so . . . no, I'm not sure how to describe him. Bovine? Perhaps it's a good thing he's pretty as he doesn't seem to be packing many brain cells in that skull. But Camilla giggles as if he's a stand-up comic and she grabs his hand.

'Come on then. Let's see what you've got.'

I breathe a sigh of relief when she trots off with him.

'Cam's dad owns Saltcombe Park,' Gemma says pointedly.

I shrug.

'The hotel complex with the golf course and spa. It's a couple of miles down the lane towards Trencham.'

So she's loaded. That explains why she's Queen Bee. 'What's the story with her accent?'

'Her dad ran chains of hotels or something in the US and then decided to move back here. She's so lucky – she lived in LA for a couple of years.'

Gemma's tone of awe is vomit-inducing and I'm disinterested already. LA – yeah, yeah. Tasha's been there on holiday and she said it's way overhyped.

I can't remember when I've been as bored as I am now. Listening to people race round a field on an overgrown buggy. And Gemma's prattling on about wedding dresses now. Is there some reason for this that I missed or is she one of those girls obsessed with getting married as soon as possible? Whatever, it's completely yawnworthy.

'So you know what I think would be totes cool?'

Totes cool? Not saying that would be a good start.

'Like, a big white wedding dress with a silk puffball skirt that finishes just at my ankles . . . and . . . you ready for this . . . white Nike trainers. Yeah?'

I'm speechless.

'But you know you always have to wear heels at your wedding? Well, I thought what about *platform* Nike trainers with a wedge heel? That would be amazing. With maybe some white fishnets.'

Oh, Katie, Katie. I love you, but I may never forgive you for us having to be marooned in this place with these people.

Salvation arrives on the back of a quad bike pulling up beside us. Fraser's face grins in the fire glow and my bones turn liquid.

'Hi, Holly. I was hoping you'd be here.'

Suddenly bouncing round a dark field on a crappy little cart no longer seems quite so stupid.

Chapter 10

I hang on to Fraser's shoulders as we zoom over the grass. I can see faint flashes of the ground ahead in the headlights and I'm not sure how he knows where he's going, how he's steering in this light. I get it now, why the others screamed.

But I won't. I refuse to.

The quad veers to the left sharply and I suck my breath in, but I won't scream. I sense Fraser's impatience through my hands on his jacket.

Yeah, you should know I'm different to the others.

He accelerates, tearing ridiculously close to the other bikes, and one of the drivers yells out at him: 'Jeez, moron!' My stomach lurches as he turns the bike again, and I think it's making the manoeuvre on two wheels, but I still don't make a sound.

I've learned not to scream. I've been taught that lesson by masters.

I feel his frustrated breath hiss out. He charges the bike down the hill away from the others. My teeth go *chugga-chugga* in my head as we bounce over the uneven ground.

Down, down, down the bike plunges. The screams behind us grow fainter. I clamp my lips tight. I've never seen this place in daylight so I've no idea what we're heading towards.

There's a darker shadow looming ahead – a line of deeper black blocking our horizon. As we plummet towards it, I make out a bank of trees. My fingers tighten on Fraser's shoulders, I can't help that, and he's tense too under my hands.

I will not show fear. I will not.

If *they* didn't break me, this boy can't.

He comes off the throttle a little and I think he's going to go for the brakes . . . but no . . . So what's he . . .? Ah! There's a lighter patch in the dark of the treeline – a gap. He's heading for that. He thinks I haven't seen it but I'm not going to fall for that trick. I force my hands to ease their grip on him and I hear his growl of annoyance even over the noise of the bike.

We shoot into the trees and the ground becomes even more uneven for a few bike-lengths until we swerve on to a track, where Fraser pulls up in a hiss-crunch of gravel.

'You don't scare easily,' he says and there's a mix of admiration and anger in his voice.

'Mmm,' I reply. I intend to be as cryptic as possible though he's completely right. If there's one thing about Holly, whoever she is, it's that she may never scare easily again.

'I guess I'll have to keep trying,' he adds.

'Will you? Why?' I throw his attitude right back at him.

He laughs. 'To find something that impresses you.'

I laugh too. 'You might have to try quite hard.' I sense how he deflates and that's not really what I want either. 'But *trying's* the point, yeah?'

He chuckles. 'A challenge? Yeah, I'm up for that.'

I'm a prize to him now, and that is what I wanted. One worth winning. Result.

'Come on, I'll drive you back up there,' he says. 'Maybe a bit slower this time!'

He turns the bike and we head through the trees and back up the field. Once again, the sound of excited screaming rings out. When we get up to the fire, I hop off the bike. Lucy and Stuart have come up to join the others and Stuart shouts over to Fraser, 'Did you get her?'

'No, man, not a squeak.' There's a boast in his voice that wasn't there before. 'I can't believe it. I even went down Strigg Bank and on to the lane and she didn't make a sound.'

Stuart's jaw drops. 'That is hardcore. Respect!' he says to me.

There's something very funny about village boys trying to sound street, but I hold my giggles in. Holly the Urban Ice Queen, that's who I am tonight.

Gemma is still yapping on. 'Yeah, so my dad got me gym membership at Cam's dad's place. And I went for the induction and there was this uber-fit personal trainer there working with some old fat woman, and I was so hoping to get him, but no, I got the spotty ugly one instead. So I was there like every day for a week and then finally one day he was in working with the grandma again and I was sure he was totally checking me out. But then the treadmill went wrong, like it went crazy or something, and I tripped and fell off. Seriously I should sue and I would if it wasn't Cam's dad because it was so their fault and I could have broken my neck or my arms and legs . . . but, oh yeah, the fit guy saw the whole thing and I wanted to *die*. I just got up straight away and *ran* to the changing rooms. I swear to God, I have not been back there since and my dad is going mental about the money, but I can't. I am just too mortified. It's completely screwed with my fitness regime and . . .'

I wonder if she's actually breathing at all. Amazingly the girl she's talking to, who I don't recognise, seems to hang on her every word. But hey, maybe she wants to get married in Nike trainers too.

A siren interrupts us.

'Shit, police! Get out of here.'

'Which way? Where are they?'

'Danny, Danny – take the bike. Move it. Now! Now!'

'Cam! Behind you, come on, run.'

They erupt into a hubbub of shouting and action. At first I don't know which way to go, but then Fraser grabs my hand and hauls me back on to his quad. 'Hang on!' and we're racing over the grass again. I'm not sure where we're going but the bikes scatter in different directions. Headlights flash up the field and they're coming towards us. I'm confused at first by how slowly, but then I realise there's only one car – they're here to break us up, not seriously catch anyone – and now it's funny watching everyone run off so fast.

Once we're off the field and on a back lane, Fraser kills the engine and gets off to push. There are houses with lights on to the side of us and I guess he doesn't want to attract attention.

'Let me drop this off and I'll walk you home,' he says.

Walk me home. That has a nice old-fashioned feel. I like it. Nobody's ever walked me home before.

We push the quad bike forward in silence, him on one side, me on the other, and come out of the lane on to a wider one with smooth tarmac underfoot. The houses here are bigger – detached with garages the size of some of the cottages we've just passed. I can hear raised voices from the open door of one house: 'And just where have you been, young lady? No nonsense! I said you were to be in by nine. I haven't forgotten this is a school night even if you have.'

'Lucy's place,' Fraser whispers, suppressing a laugh. 'Her dad is a control freak.'

I nod and we push the bike on a few more houses until we reach a gated drive leading to a large white house. Fraser stops and swings one of the huge iron gates open.

'Come in, but shush,' he says and we take the bike inside. He leads me to the garage and we park it in there. The four cars are all parked outside on the drive and I wonder what the point of a vast garage is if you're going to do that. All I know is that this is the polar opposite of the place I live in now.

He beckons to me and we leave as quietly as we came. He closes the gate behind him and looks at me expectantly.

'I don't know the way home from here,' I admit. 'Where are the shops? I know how to get back from there.'

He waves further down the lane. 'This way.'

As we walk back, I wonder if I can fob him off when we get to the main street. Can I convince him to let me find my own way from there? For the first time in my life, I'm ashamed to let someone see where I live. It's the most horrible feeling.

I understand the word dread now. I live with it every day in one form or another. It's not the adrenalin-inducing things that scare me, like being raced around on the quad bike. It's these little deaths every day. These, and the waiting for . . .

STOP! Now that is out of bounds . . . I can't think about what's coming this summer because I really will choke up and break out of role. It terrifies me that much.

We come out on to the high street by one of the hairdressers.

'I can find my way from here. You go back home.'

He smiles. This time, my bones are too full of wanting to get rid of him to even think about melting. 'But I want to.'

'Really, you don't have to.'

He frowns slightly. 'Really, I do. Now which way?'

I give up and prepare myself for the worst. 'Down here.'

He doesn't say a word as we walk through the estate to my house and I don't try to make conversation. When we get to my door, I say, 'Thanks,' and don't meet his eyes.

'See you tomorrow in school?'

'Yes, sure.' I risk a look at him but I can't read what's in his face.

I grit my teeth and smile. 'See you tomorrow then.' And I run up the path and close the door before he notices my embarrassment.

Chapter 11

At break-time next day, I am absolutely starving and I race out of the science block as soon as the bell goes. The canteen is at the opposite end of school and there's a piece of cheese on toast with my name on it if I can beat the rush. Nobody got breakfast at home because Katie decided to have a screaming fit at the table and knock everything on to the floor. We were expecting her to erupt – it's her first day at school, and first days and Katie don't mix. The neighbours must have thought we were half killing her from the noise she made.

So with nothing more than a hastily gulped glass of juice in my stomach, it's crucial that I get to that cheese on toast. If I miss a meal I'm always ravenous.

Thankfully there's no queue, but it looks as if PE let the Year 10s out early because the canteen is full of red, sweaty faces filling their mouths as fast as they can.

Urgh, bacon rolls – microwaved, anaemic bacon with a rind of white, greasy fat poking out of a doughy burger bun. Gross. But there on the rack beside the bacon rolls is one last slice of cheese on toast. It's the only thing here that tastes like real food and they mix mustard in with the cheese for some extra kick. My stomach growls in anticipation.

I scoot through the chrome barriers and reach for the slice . . . but my fingers close on air. I look in surprise at the empty rack . . . realise it's empty . . . and then look round . . . to see that stupid Emo holding my, *my*, cheese on toast. My stomach howls in protest, and so do I.

'Oi! That's mine! You pushed in.'

He looks at the empty space behind him and shrugs. 'Can't push in if there's no queue.'

'But I was here first. That's mine.'

'If you were here first, you would have got it. I was here before you.' He scowls and turns to go to the till.

My temper bubbles to a boil, encouraged by my furious stomach, and I grab his arm to pull him back. 'It was mine and you know it. You snatched it on purpose, you freak!'

His face twists in anger. 'Get off me, posh bitch.' He wrenches his arm free and walks to the till.

If I was Lea, I'd have burst into tears. That was her favourite trick. But I have more self-respect, so I snatch up a bacon roll and march to the till myself. He pays for his toast and slouches off, with a last glare back at me.

Moron!

I do a quick scan round the canteen and spot Fraser in the far corner with Stuart. He catches my eye as if he's been waiting to do that and waves to me to join them. I wander over with the disgusting bacon roll, taking my time. Fraser gets up and pulls out a chair for me. 'Hey, I was hoping I'd see you. Are you busy a week on Saturday?'

I sit down beside him and nod at Stuart, who smiles in return and then gives an excuse about having to see a teacher before making his exit. I wonder if that was planned, but there's no clue in Fraser's face.

'Next Saturday? Not sure yet. Why?' I have nothing planned of course, but he doesn't need to know that.

'There's a party at Cam's place. Her parents are away and she has the house to herself. I thought you might like to come. My sister's giving me a lift – it's too far from the village to walk.'

He's asking me out. He's actually asking me out. I feel insanely pleased and I'm embarrassed by it. When did I get this sappy over a boy?

Since I moved here and lost myself?

Whatever. He asked me out and I'm going, and I will have fun and I will feel like me again. Caution can go straight to hell on a quad bike.

'Yeah, sounds OK. Thanks.'

He grins and I like how grateful he looks that I said yes. If that makes me a bitch, so be it. My ego has been in bits for too long – it needs a boost, and a Fraser-shaped boost will do just fine.

Katie's waiting for me when I get home from school, sitting on the doorstep and sucking a lolly.

'How was school?' I ask.

'Poop.'

'Is your teacher nice?'

'Poop.'

I sigh; she's in one of those moods.

'Did you make any friends today?'

'Boo-Boo is a poophead.'

I sit down next to her on the step.

'You learned that word today, didn't you? Who from?'

'Sammy. Sammy told it to me. It's a good word, isn't it, Boo-Boo? I like it. Pooooop!'

I have to laugh. She's smiling and Katie's smile always cheers me up. 'So school wasn't so bad after all? Who's Sammy – a boy or a girl?'

'Poooop! A boy. He's funny. We played on the slide and in the ball pool.'

I put my arm round her shoulders and give her a hug. 'Is Sammy your friend now?'

She nods and sucks furiously on the lolly. 'Yes. Best friend.'

'Hey, do you want me to take you to the swings before tea?'

'Don't you have homework?' Mum says as she passes through the hall with a pile of washing.

'I can find the time to take my sister to the park first.'

Katie's already bouncing on the spot. 'Swings! Swings!'

Mum shakes her head and walks off laughing. 'Take her, please, and give us all some peace.'

I get her coat and we walk through the houses and across the main street. There are a few people I know by sight hanging around outside the post office, but we don't meet anyone I talk to at school. There's a little playground on the playing fields and I take her there. A girl her age is on the climbing frame with what must be her younger sister as they look so alike, and their mum sits on a bench half watching them and reading a book at the same time. Katie runs to the swings and perches on one.

'Pushies, Boo-Boo! Pushies!'

I pull the swing back and shove hard, sending her soaring up in the air. She screams in excitement and I send her higher next time, and higher.

'WHEEEEEEEEEEE!'

I push her and push her until my arms ache and her throat grows hoarse from squealing. The kids on the climbing frame go home and I'm still there making my sister fly.

'More, Boo-Boo, more.'

Just me and her. It feels like none of it ever happened.

Until the car goes past.

It's a white car with a rear spoiler and the exhaust roars as it goes down the lane by the playing fields. It's the sound that attracts us; we see it at the same time. I can tell the exact moment Katie notices the car because her 'Wheeeeeeeeee' changes to a shriek.

I stop pushing.

The swing slows as the car travels out of sight and Katie starts to howl.

My fingers, arms, legs, head all feel like they've turned to ice. I can't move. I think my heart has stopped beating. I can't even move to comfort Katie who's now sitting with her feet on the ground, bawling her eyes out.

I'm back there again, last summer . . . back where it all started . . .

I pushed Katie again and the swing whooshed skywards to the sound of her shouting, 'Higher, higher, Boo-Boo.' I gave a nervous glance at the tree branch the swing was tied to, but it seemed to be holding strong, so I gave her an extra hard shove when she flew back my way.

'Wooooo-hooooo!' she yelled.

I turned my face up to catch the hot August sun in between pushes. The smell of dinner cooking from the white cottage behind us wafted out of the open window and mixed with the scent of drying seaweed on the rocks at the bottom of the cliff. This had been our favourite holiday location since forever. No matter where else we went, no matter how exotic, if we didn't come here at least once a year, to this tiny bay buried deep in Cornwall, we all felt cheated.

Even the name, Treliske Cove, could make me excited on a grey winter's day at home in London. Being here in the afternoon sunshine, with a warm breeze stirring my hair and the seagulls diving from the cliffs to the glinting sea, that was paradise. And tucking up tight under the handmade quilt in the little bed under the eaves in my room in the cottage, all snug and sleepy and smelling of fresh air and sea – that was the very best feeling in the world. Or was that waking in the morning when the sun came up, and snatching up a swimsuit to pad my way down the steep cliff steps to the bay, where I'd swim in the sea and hope to see a dolphin offshore?

Katie finally got tired of swinging and hopped off the old tyre to play on her trike. I took her place and swung lazily, letting my feet trail through the long grass. The cotton curtains fluttered in the open casement window of Katie's room and there was a bird perched on the windowsill of mine, something tiny like a chaffinch. The cottage was painted stone with bright green windows and doors. It looked like the definition of happiness to me.

The chaffinch took to the air and I followed its path over the field of grass mixed with wild flowers to the cottage on the other side of the fence, a twin of ours, but rented out whereas we owned ours. At the moment, it was occupied by another family from London. Mum had spoken to them; I hadn't. She went over to welcome them when they arrived a couple of hours after us. Apparently they owned a place in Hampstead, which meant they were worth serious megabucks. Mum said there was a woman about her age and her daughter, who looked a year or so older than me, but her husband was joining them later – he was dealing with a problem at work. The woman – Natalia, said with a Russian accent that was hardly noticeable until she told Mum her name – looked weary, as if that happened a lot.

The daughter's name was Katya, but Mum said she seemed very quiet. I could see she was working up to sending me round there to be sociable with her so I'd made a hasty exit. I took my violin to the bottom of the orchard to practise so I missed the rest of the gossip. But playing under the old apple trees was another piece in the paradise jigsaw of this place.

As I gazed across the field to their cottage, I could see a face in the window. It was the girl. Pretty, with long, light brown hair and a pale oval face. Her Russian heritage showed, I thought, in the set of her eyes and cheekbones. She looked what Mum would call 'quietly expensive'.

Katie and I had been out here in the sunshine for most of the day; the Russian girl hadn't set a toe outside. How could you come on holiday to a place like this and stay cooped up in the house? I thought about waving to her, but something about her expression stopped me and I looked away.

When I turned back, she was gone. I shrugged and watched Katie playing race tracks on her tricycle along the lines I'd flattened in the long grass for her that morning.

The roasting chicken smell from the kitchen was making my mouth water. 'Katie,' I called, 'last time round now. It's nearly time for dinner.'

'*Rrrroooommmm-rrrooommmm*,' she called as she pedalled past furiously.

I laughed and got up to cut off her path if she tried to go round again, holding her discarded cardigan out as a flag for the finish line. She leaned in on the corners like she'd seen the racing drivers do on TV when she and Dad watched motor sport, making her *rroommm*-ing noises on the straight stretches where she could accelerate, her little legs whirring round until finally she was on the home stretch speeding towards me.

I give the commentary. 'And it's Katie Drummond in pole position . . . can she hold on? She's nearly there . . . it doesn't look like anyone can beat her now . . . and . . . and . . . YES, YES, YES . . . it's Katie Drummond finishing first . . . the WINNER!'

Katie pulled her trike up and clapped and giggled, her face red-flushed and happy. That was how I loved to see my sister best.

She got off the trike and came to get her cardigan.

'Aren't you too warm for that? You don't have to put it on if you are.' I hated the flash of anxiety in her face when I said that, when I made her question what would have been an automatic action, but fortunately something distracted her from my mistake.

Katie frowned and I turned to see a white car drive slowly down the lane. I didn't see anything unusual about that myself – driving slowly was sensible on these twisty lanes, even if it did seem maybe a bit overcautious to be crawling along that slowly. But Katie made a harrumphing noise and frowned harder. Why? The driver didn't look unusual, just an average man you wouldn't have taken a second look at, youngish, driving a car with one of those stupid rear spoilers some guys think look good, but are actually cheap and tacky.

'What's up?' I asked her. Later, I would wish a thousand times over and more that I had left that question unasked.

She pointed to the car. 'He goes past lots.'

Did he? I shrugged. 'Maybe he lives down the lane somewhere.'

Katie shook her head. 'No.'

I didn't question her. Katie knew every car in every house in the locale just from driving around with Dad. She could remember the makes, colours and often the number plates simply from having driven past them while they were parked outside the houses. 'It might just be one you haven't seen –'

'No. It only started the yesterday before yesterday. But he goes past lots. You should count, Boo-Boo. It's lots and lots and lots.'

It was my turn to frown. OK, that did sound a bit weird. 'Like how many lots?'

'Ten times on the yesterday before yesterday, eight times yesterday and today nine times to now . . . there and back is one time.'

Yes, that did seem a lot in such a remote place. In the city, I'd have assumed he was just posing with his naff car, but out here? It didn't make sense.

'OK, you tell me when you see the car again and I'll count too.'

Katie beamed and ran to hug me. 'Boo-Boo counting too. Love you!'

I hugged her back. Sometimes she just wanted someone to join her in her world, I thought, when she couldn't make it across into ours. That was the hardest thing about Katie's autism — the constant suspicion that she didn't want to be marooned in her bubble of handicap and cut off from the rest of us. Some children in her therapy centre did seem to want that, but Katie was different. 'Love you too, Katie-pops.'

Mum stuck her head out of the door to call us in for dinner and I forgot all about the car. Until I was going to bed and I went to draw the curtains. In the fading light, I could just make out the outline of a white car with a rear spoiler driving slowly past again.

Chapter 12

The weekend goes by too quickly and I don't seem to get a break from the pile of revision and catch-up coursework that I've set myself. Being in a new school with different exam syllabuses is tough, especially having to make up for the several months I tried to teach myself from the revision guides while we moved from place to place. Katie grumbles that I haven't spent time playing with her and Mum tries to pacify her about that, but she doesn't let up until Dad takes her for a drive and peace descends on the house for a couple of hours. Mum naps in front of the TV and I sit on my bed revising maths and trying not to look out of the window because the view depresses me. By eight o'clock on Monday morning, I'm tired from too much sitting around and concentrating, and grouchy from lack of down time. The only bonus is at least inside the house I don't have to keep looking over my shoulder to check no one is following me.

School's a drag too, tests and timed coursework assessments all day. I have an important science piece in the afternoon so I grab a sandwich from the canteen, which tastes like margarine on dough with some unidentifiable filling, and sit in the library preparing. When I get home, I'm so tired I crash out on the bed before tea and Mum has to wake me up.

Tuesday isn't much better, except I do get to have a lunch break and I sit with Gemma and Lucy. The boys are off playing football in some team practice thing. Thankfully Gemma's got over droning about wedding dresses and she's in the middle of a bitch-fest about a girl they both know. It's quite entertaining listening to Gemma tear her to shreds, especially as I don't know the girl so I don't have to take sides. Gemma's vicious when she gets her claws out.

I see a little bit more of Fraser as the week goes on, but I don't get much chance to speak to him alone. He stops me in the corridor once to check I'm still OK for the party at the weekend and to sort out pick-up times but that's mostly it. Except he does get my phone number and he texts me later to say he's looking forward to it. I text to say 'me too', but he doesn't reply and neither do I after that. I'm not sure I am looking forward to it actually. It's a funny feeling – more like stress than real excitement, and not enjoyable but something to be endured and got through because I might feel better once I've done it. If I compare that to the last party I went to, and the buzz before that, getting ready with Tasha . . . it's just too depressing in a grey, shitty, hugely depressing week.

And to add to the depressing, some idiot running the school had the idea to put a team-building event slap in the middle of this term when we're getting ready for exams. So on Friday, instead of doing our GCSE work which we're all getting stressy about, we have an activity afternoon with the army. The whole year group is stuck out on the school field in a force-nine gale and lashing rain with a bunch of really fed-up guys in khaki who look as unenthusiastic as we do. Awesome. We've been out there for precisely three minutes and my hair is wrecked already.

They shout numbers at us and then tell us to stand in groups. A few kids try a quick shuffle-round, but the lead army guy notices and yells at them so the rest of us go where we're told. 'He looks a bit like a psycho killer,' I whisper to Gemma who's in my group.

'Scary eyes,' she says with a shudder.

She nudges me as we're all sent to different locations around the field, and points to the group next to us. It's mostly Fraser and his friends – and I wonder how they managed to engineer that – but also a quiet girl, who looks utterly miserable, and the Emo. Gemma sniggers. 'Now this should be funny.'

'Why?'

She grins. 'Watch and see.'

So I do. While our army guy prepares something boring with a pile of ropes and nets, I watch the next group. They have some kind of landmine task, where they have to use planks and tyres to get the team to safety on the other side. Fraser's obviously up for it and so is Stuart. The others look reasonably interested, except for the quiet girl who looks like she's about to cry. But Emo Boy is more sullen than ever. In fact, he's glowering at the army guy.

My attention is pulled away while our guy explains what to do. Excellent – crawling under nets on wet ground!

When I look back, Stuart is fronting up to Emo, staring him in the face. 'It's bad enough we get landed with you, pussy, but if you think you're going to mess this up for us, think again.' Fraser's laughing and I'm not sure what's going on.

Emo doesn't back away though, just curls his lip in that way I know is really annoying when you're on the receiving end of it.

I blink and look again.

Actually, now I'm not on the receiving end of it, it looks . . . no, I can't mean that . . . because what I think I just thought is that it looks . . . *hot*? No, what I mean is it would look hot if someone else other than Emo was doing it. It's that dark-eyed, glowering thing he's got going on. On someone with a better personality it would look hot, but not on him obviously.

'Stu and Fraser are really competitive with stuff like this,' Gemma says in my ear. 'They'll hate being stuck with him.'

'Why? Is he useless?'

She considers it. 'Probably not if he doesn't want to be. He's OK at PE when he can be bothered. Which is only when we have track stuff. Then he runs like someone strapped a rocket to him and lit it.'

I frown. 'He doesn't look like he'd go fast.'

'You'd be surprised! He could be really good but he won't join the teams. Which is why Stu is going to lose it with him. He won't even try in group stuff. Plus Stu can't stand him.'

And that is pretty obvious now. Stu is getting up in Emo's face in a way that's frankly making me uncomfortable. I wish their army guy would intervene because it looks like there might be a fight, but the man's busy with his planks and tyres and doesn't seem to care. I look around but there are no teachers on our side of the field.

'I didn't know you knew him,' I say to her, keeping a nervous eye on them.

'Yeah, since primary.'

Of course they do if they've all lived in Daneshill all their lives. I never thought of that.

Their army guy finally looks up and goes over to them. Emo hasn't said anything back to Stuart. He's just not moving and glaring straight back at him.

'Problem?' the guy says in a bored voice.

'Just sorting who's doing what,' Stuart says, and Fraser and the other boys laugh.

The guy frowns and looks at Emo.

Emo shrugs. 'He can fuck off. I'm not doing any of this shit.'

I hear myself gasp. 'Oooh,' Gemma says and she sounds excited at the prospect of trouble.

Stuart steps forward and would have barged Emo, but the army guy puts a hand out and says, 'No.' Stuart backs off. I would too – he sounds like he means it.

'You don't want to take part? Are you ill or is there some other problem?' the guy says to Emo.

'No, I'm just not doing it.'

'Why?'

'I don't want to.'

'Now look, son, you're going to come across a lot of things in life you don't want to –'

'Fuck you with your psychological bullshit! I'm not interested and I'm not doing it whatever you say so you can fuck right off. You're a coward anyway, pissing about doing this stuff while the rest of your regiment are getting the shit blown out of them in Helmand.'

My jaw drops as Emo spins on his heel and starts to walk off. The army guy looks livid and then his face changes . . . to something I don't quite understand. 'Start planning your route,' he says to the group and he jogs after Emo.

'What the . . .?' I turn to Gemma who looks equally shocked. Emo Geek just a) spoke more than a sentence and b) totally, totally lost it.

'Ooh, I forgot about that – Matt! Of course!'

'Who's Matt?'

'His brother. He's in the army – he's off in Afghanistan at the moment, I think. He is *so* hot. I used to have the biggest crush on him.'

The soldier has caught up with Emo and has a hand on his shoulder. Emo's back is stiff and angry, but as the guy talks to him, he relaxes a little and begins to nod. Our army guy shouts at us then to start the stupid crawling through nets so I miss what happens next because I'm on my face in wet grass. When I get to the other side and tie the dumb ropes while he yells over my head for me to go faster, Emo has disappeared and his group are getting on with their task without him.

'What happened?' I ask Gemma when I get back to her.

'I don't know.'

I watched Emo's group. Was it my imagination or was

100

the soldier giving Stuart an extra hard time? Now what was *that* about?

'Is he close to his brother?' I ask Gemma suddenly. So suddenly that she looks confused.

'Who?'

I can't exactly say Emo . . . 'Um, Joe – is that his name?'

'Oh yes. He always hung out with Matt and his friends more than he did anyone in our year. It's the farmer thing – they all tend to stick together.'

Now I'm confused. Emo lives down my street, doesn't he? He's not a farmer. But I'm not asking Gemma any more questions about him or it'll look weird.

Our army guy yells at us for not paying attention so I forget about Emo and concentrate on not getting into more trouble.

But on the way home later, I spot Emo shuffling down the street ahead of me, head down and listening to music as usual. I slow down and stay well behind, and instead of turning off down my usual path, I carry on and follow him round the corner and down the street into a cul-de-sac. At the end of it, he turns on to a footpath.

Once he's out of sight, I sneak up to the top of the path. It snakes down the hill and out into the fields to rise up the next hill, where there's a large white farmhouse surrounded by metal barns. I decide for some unfathomable reason to wait and watch him. He heads towards the farm and, once he's turned up the next hill, a black-and-white collie comes flying out of the yard, over fields and down the path to meet him. It greets him in a whirl of jumps and excited yips.

So Emo's a farm boy. I never would have guessed that. I turn and walk slowly back up to my house. No, that's totally unexpected.

Chapter 13

I haven't exactly been looking forward to Cam's party all week and by the middle of Saturday afternoon I'm almost dreading it. I'm in that state where I so wish I hadn't said yes that part of me wants to text Fraser and say something's come up. But the other part of me would be frustrated if I did because it might turn out to be good in the end . . . maybe?

Whatever.

I am not happy. Not one bit.

I'm trawling through my wardrobe trying to decide what to wear. I have of course extracted information from Gemma and Lucy on what they're wearing and apparently Cam thought it'd be good if the girls dress up and the boys dress down. There's something about that girl that needles me enough to want to needle her. Maybe it's the way she looked at me at first, or perhaps it's how the others act around her, as if she's better than the rest of us.

I finally decide on a slinky black number that shows my hair off to advantage. I try it on and check myself in the mirror. Not bad. Especially now my hair's back to its proper ash-blonde colour. And I think back to the first time I looked in the mirror after they dyed it brown.

'It looks hideous,' I told the hairdresser they'd sent over to do the job.

She sniffed. 'It looks different. That's the point.'

Mum doesn't look impressed. 'It's only temporary though, darling. It'll wash out. Just put up with it for a few weeks until we've moved on somewhere safer and then you can let it fade.'

'I still think it'd be better to cut it,' the hairdresser told her.

'Hasn't she been through enough?' Mum replied. 'Let her keep something of herself.'

At least she understands. Her shoulder-length glossy dark bob is now a muddy mouse-coloured crop that I know she hates. And I feel unaccountably guilty every time I look at her, as if all this is my fault.

I hang the black dress back in the wardrobe until later. Deciding what to wear calms me down and that means I can de-stress a bit more now by playing dolls with Katie. It's awesome having a little sister sometimes because you get to play with the stuff you're supposed to be too old for now. I find that comforting – like eating egg with toast soldiers to dip, or Mum running me a bath. Now and again, holding on to something from childhood grounds me. Especially since what happened last year. Nobody can make the monsters go away any more, but playing dolls with Katie can help me forget for a while. The world feels simple and safe again.

Fraser's picking me up at eight so I have tea early and go for a bath before I get ready. I need to look good tonight. It's not about hooking Fraser, though that's on my mind. It's about feeling good about myself again. I've begun to recognise how very not good I've felt since we came here. But when part of you, the person you are, is taken away, you don't feel good. You don't feel confident. You're diminished.

Fraser picks me up at eight on the dot. His face when I open the front door is everything I'd hoped for. Just as I'm climbing in the back of his sister's car, I notice Emo walking past on the other side of the road with another boy. It's the first time I've seen him with a friend. He looks at me for a moment and I see surprise on his face, but then he scowls and turns away.

I don't know why I let that deflate me. Fraser looked awestruck, still does, and he's what matters, right? Not some stupid, geeky Emo.

But I don't feel quite so amazing now. The doubt has crept in. I say hi and thanks for the lift to Fraser's sister, but I don't say much other than that on the way over to Camilla's. It doesn't take long before we get to her place: a gateway with thick stone posts on either side leading to a large cobbled courtyard. It's an old house and it's huge, but the hall is crammed full of people. I recognise faces from school but there are lots of others I don't know. Stuart appears and tosses a can to Fraser, who pops the tab immediately. He takes a swig and then proffers it to me. I shake my head. 'I'm not wild about beer.'

'What do you want? There's a free bar in the kitchen.'

That was inevitable. Cam wouldn't throw a party where we couldn't drink – it would totally destroy her image. Whereas my dad would have been hovering by the door practically frisking guests for hidden bottles of vodka.

'Try the punch.' Lucy comes towards us carrying a plastic glass of some red stuff that looks lethal. 'It's wicked.'

Fraser quirks an eyebrow at me.

I laugh. 'Yes, punch then.'

He grins and goes off to get me a glass. The bass from the sound system is so loud it's coming through my feet and the vibration makes my nerves tingle until every part of me feels alive. I can feel a grin spreading over my face that I couldn't stop if I tried. Through the doorway ahead I can see a crush of bodies dancing and that's where I want to be – it's been so long and I *need* to move.

Fraser comes back with a glass. As he hands it to me, he bends to my ear and whispers, 'You look *so* hot.' His breath shivers across my neck. He looks pretty radically hot himself. He's also in black, a designer polo shirt showing off his muscles. What he says dispels most of that lingering downer that's been plaguing me since I got into the car.

I still don't know why Emo hated me on sight that first day though. If I'm honest, that bugs me. And I don't know why that is either.

But forget him. I want to dance.

I knock back the glass of punch – it is lethal, I can tell from the first gulp – and grab Fraser's hand. 'What?' He laughs and resists for a second but then lets me drag him to the room that's been beckoning me for the last five minutes. 'Oh what, you want to dance?'

I grin and nod as I pull him through the door, because the music's too loud for anything else. And then I lose myself in the beat and the movement.

I don't care whether Fraser can dance or not – I notice as an afterthought that he's OK at it but nothing to pay special attention to. I don't care if he's enjoying it or not. This is my Zen place, where the energy touches my consciousness and recharges it.

I dance.

Nothing comes close to this feeling. Nothing else ever touches me this way. Only music takes me here.

I don't know how long it is before Fraser presses another drink into my hand and I glug that down gratefully. He retreats to the side of the room and watches me. I can't stop – it's been months and months and this feels so good.

Freedom. In every cell.

What stops me in the end is when someone changes the playlist and puts some dumb-ass boy band track on. I head towards the open French doors for air. Fraser follows and we meet on the terrace. He's holding a bottle of wine and swigging from it. When he passes it to me, I take a drink. It tastes vile, but I drink more anyway just because.

He's saying something, but my ears are still blocked from the music and I can't hear him. It doesn't matter. I can tell from his face that he wants us to go down the steps into the garden. I nod and walk off, leaving him to follow and taking another swig of the wine, which now tastes of 'to hell with everything sensible'. That's a good taste, whatever the wine is like.

When we get to the bottom of the steps, he grabs me and pulls me close to him. I stare up into his face, part challenge and part encouragement.

What do I feel now? Not sure . . .

He bends his head. I focus on how good-looking he is. His lips touch mine.

I feel . . . nothing.

Nothing? How come?

Maybe it's the wine.

His fingertips are stroking up and down my arms. But they could be anybody's. Not the hottest boy in the year's. Nothing special. No electric charge across my skin.

Maybe the punch was too lethal.

But I can walk straight. I don't feel drunk. Just distant from this, from him. What's wrong? He's gorgeous, isn't he?

He kisses me properly and I go through the motions puppet-like. I doubt he can tell. I think I fake it well enough.

This is too, too weird. It wasn't this way with Dan or any other boy I've kissed. How can I be left cold by a guy this good-looking? It doesn't make sense. Maybe I'm in a funny mood, maybe it's the punch. But I'm not messing this up in case I change my mind later. With luck he thinks I'm just holding him off a little so he doesn't get carried away. When he pulls back to look at my face, he doesn't have a clue that I was less into it than him.

'You're beautiful,' he says and kisses me again. But his words do more to me than his mouth does.

Now, with manufactured pop belching out of the speakers and his lips moving over mine, I know I'll be glad when the evening is over and we go home. I need to figure out what's going on because I don't get it at all.

I make excuses to get him back inside – I need more punch, I'm thirsty. I drag him over to talk to his mates, then I run off with Gemma for a while and let her drone on about some guy she fancies in the year above. I fake excitement and squeal along with her. Fraser follows and his hands are all over me, but my skin is still numb to his touch. So weird. I let him all but grope me for a while, just so I can get a handle on how strange it is.

There's a vase in an alcove opposite us high up in the wall. It has a Chinese pattern and looks expensive, and it *is* beautiful. But it's of no use. A decoration with no substance. That's what it feels like with Fraser. He's pretty, but . . . there's nothing more . . .

I wish I could talk to Tasha right now. Maybe she could help me understand it. Hot is hot, right? Except now it seems like it's not.

When he takes me home later and kisses me goodnight, I'm glad to wave goodbye to him and close the door behind me so I can stop pretending.

Chapter 14

So it seems Fraser and I are an item. How did that happen? A week ago I might have wanted it. Now? I'd have to say not really.

Maybe it'll get better. Maybe I'll feel different next time he touches me. Maybe I'm simply weirded out from all the freakiness of the past months.

Maybe not.

He texts me on Sunday, not loads but enough to show he's definitely interested. On Monday at school, he makes for me on the way to registration and slips his arm round me in the corridor. And suddenly everyone knows about us. Everyone is speaking like we're together.

So I guess we are together. It could be worse. He's good

for my image. He knows people. He'll help me fit in.

Only Holly isn't supposed to be dating the school stud. She's supposed to keep her head down. For the first time in the last few weeks, I wonder if I've been stupid. What have I got out of the tangential leap I made after the Facebook episode? I talk to some people I don't really care for and I've somehow acquired a boyfriend that I'm not really into, bizarre though that is.

I mean, what am I doing? All the lengths I went to, to make myself into someone else. I even gave up playing my violin.

Why did I give it up? I can't fully remember my reasoning now, or rather I can't get it to make sense any more. Was it the association with everything that happened? Or did I just overreact to the identity change? It wasn't as if they told me I had to radically alter *everything* about myself. That was all me.

But when someone holds a gun to your head to blow your brains out, when you've seen what they did to a friend, to Katya, you never want them to find you as long as you live. You'll do anything to stop that. How did I manage to forget that in the last few weeks?

I remember when the police came to speak to me in the hospital when I was recovering after I got away from the men they sent to kill me. Two women came to talk to me – I never did recall their names.

'Where's Mum and Dad?' I'd kept asking the nurses that

question, but they wouldn't tell me. Perhaps these women would. 'And why is there a policeman outside my door all the time?'

They looked at each other. 'Don't you remember what happened?' the first one said.

'The doctor never said anything about amnesia,' the second said to her with a frown.

'Of course I remember what happened. I want to see my mum and dad. Where are they?'

'The officer is there for your protection.'

'Where's my mum and dad?' I was starting to panic that they weren't going to answer this.

'You'll see them soon. As soon as you can be discharged. They did come to see you while you were unconscious. But if you remember what happened, Louisa, you'll understand why it's not safe for them to come here right now.'

I burst into tears. My head still hurt, with a sharp throbbing pain despite the painkillers, and I wanted my mum so badly.

One of the women tried to put her arm round me. I pushed her away. I didn't want her. If I couldn't have Mum, I wanted a nurse there, not those two with their hard faces and lack of sympathy. Even the woman's arm around me felt bony and irritated, as if she was only doing it because she had to.

'Louisa, we need you to try to calm down. I know it's been very difficult and you've had a frightening experience, but we're here to try to explain how we can keep you safe from now onwards.'

'Can I see one of the nurses, please?' I said through the tears.

'I'd prefer it if you didn't. We do need to explain procedures to you and we can't do that with a third party here. It's just too dangerous.'

The second woman passed me a tissue. 'You and your family are now in the witness protection programme, Louisa. We were concerned that the people who came after you in relation to Katya Chernokov's kidnapping would come after your family as a revenge attack or to try to stop you from testifying against them.'

'Why didn't anyone think of that before it happened? And what do you mean, testifying? I can't testify when you haven't caught them.'

'No, of course not.' The first woman sounded irritated. 'But you did indicate your willingness to testify if they were caught.'

Yes, I had. I'd seen Katya and what they'd done to her. I'd said yes to testifying after that. I guess that was why they'd let me see her, so I'd agree. I couldn't say no after seeing her in that state.

I took a deep breath and tried to regain control. 'So when can I see Mum and Dad? And what do you mean about witness protection?'

'We'll take you to your parents as soon as you can be discharged from hospital. Perhaps tomorrow or the day after. Your doctor says you're doing well.'

My panic subsides. Not long. I can see them soon.

'They're in a hotel in a location only your Witness Protection Liaison Officer knows. He'll take you to them and from there you'll go to another location. He'll explain it all to you as soon as you come out of hospital. Any questions?'

Any questions? How about a million?

Perhaps I was right in the beginning about who Holly should be – quiet, unobtrusive, invisible. Really I just wanted to be me. But who is me when my friends and my home are gone, and even Mum and Dad have to be who they're not? The only one who can still be herself is Katie and suddenly I have an overwhelming desire to be with her. I avoid the others in school for the rest of the day, making excuses about coursework, and I slope off to the library. The truth is I can't stand to have to act. Of course, I could *not* put on an act, but I can't remember how to do that, except when I'm with Katie.

I race home at the end of the day and my sister is waiting for me. I grab her and hug her, squeezing hard until she squeals.

'Come on, Popsicle, we're going to the park.'

I can see the signs of spring bursting through in the gardens as we walk up to the playing fields: daffodils with yellow trumpet heads nodding at us in the stiff April breeze, buds starting to form on shrubs and trees, and the afternoon sun is that bit warmer than it was last week. I'm with Katie, the day is over and my mood lifts. Maybe life isn't so bad.

The playground is empty this time so Katie has it all to herself. 'What first? Climbing frame, slide or swings?' She's not a fan of roundabouts generally. I can see her eyes drawn to the swings, but she surprises me by going for the climbing frame first. I help her out when she gets to the monkey bars – she likes some support when she's reaching from bar to bar because she's scared of falling off. Funny, because she's got no fear on the swings at all.

It's on her third time down the slide that I hear a voice call, 'Hey, Holly!' When I turn, there's a bunch of people from school walking across the basketball court behind us – Fraser's friends, though he's not with them. He's back up the field talking to someone, a girl I can't recognise from this distance. Lucy is wrapped round Stuart as usual and Gemma's showing renewed interest in an ex of hers that she ditched because he can't kiss well enough. But maybe she's changing her mind. Being without a boyfriend when Lucy is perma-bonded to Stuart is bugging her.

They all wave but don't come over, except Cam who detaches herself from the group and wanders towards the netting. 'Who's this?' She nods at Katie who's zooming down the slide with a squeal that makes everyone look at her.

I grit my teeth.

'My little sister.'

'Aw, how cute,' Cam says in a patronising voice, like Katie is a puppy or something.

Katie bounds up. 'HELLO!'

Cam takes a step back from the netting. The group are staring. 'Er, hello. What's your name?'

I clench my fingers round my thumbs as Katie stares at Cam, and stares. And stares some more. 'I don't like you,' she announces after careful consideration. If it wasn't so awkward, I'd laugh. Her timing is just so crazy funny.

Cam takes another step back and looks at me, prickling with hostility. 'What's her problem?' Yep, everyone is definitely riveted to us now and Fraser is heading over. The girl he was with has disappeared.

Katie glowers as a couple of others wander over to join Cam. She feels crowded, I can tell, and I put my arm round her.

One of the boys, a friend of Cam's I recognise from the party, leans on the netting. 'You should teach her some manners. That was well rude. You shouldn't let her get away with that.'

'Yeah, tell her off,' Lucy's younger sister adds.

They stare at me, waiting, and I can feel my cheeks

getting hotter and hotter, and then Fraser arrives. 'What's going on?'

'Holly's sister was just completely rude to me and she's just let her get away with it,' Cam says indignantly. 'I didn't do a thing and it's so out of order.' Her eyes start to fill up and I could slap her face for that, the faker. She's not that upset at all, just going for the sympathy vote because she doesn't like me.

Fraser frowns at me but says nothing . . . yet. I sense there's a 'yet'.

'Katie's autistic.' I hate saying that in front of my sister. She knows of course, but to say it in front of her feels wrong, like I'm saying *she's* wrong for being that way.

'Oh,' Cam says, looking at Katie like she's something in a Victorian freak show. The others change the way they look at her too, including Fraser.

I swallow hard. 'She doesn't understand why she shouldn't say things like that.' I could have told her off to mollify them, but I would never do that to Katie. She gets so upset if you're cross with her and she doesn't understand why.

Cam shrugs. She clearly doesn't believe me. 'Yeah, well, whatever, I have to go now. Bye.' She turns and walks off. The others mutter a goodbye and follow her off up the field. I wonder where they're going. Once again, I haven't been invited to hang out with them after school.

Fraser turns and watches them. 'I should go too . . . er . . .'

'Yeah, see you at school.' I get it in quickly and breezily before he can come up with some pathetic excuse why he doesn't want to be with me now.

If we are together, this is the weirdest together I've ever known.

'Text you later.' He flashes me his melting grin, but it doesn't turn me to goo this time.

I smile and turn away and walk Katie over to the swings. After I make sure she's settled in the middle of the seat, I look back. Fraser's jogging up the field after Cam and Crew who've disappeared from sight down one of the back lanes.

Am I ever going to fit in here?

Then again, I don't want to fit in with people who look at my sister the way they did. I watch Katie's face as I make the swing fly – she's so innocent of all the complications that make the rest of us shitty people sometimes. How can anyone look down on her for that? Sometimes I don't understand people at all.

When I'm lying in bed later that night, I think about how Cam and the others looked at Katie again, and then I remember how Katya looked at her the first time we met her. Because it's different. So very different.

Katya. Who's ruined my life.

But I can't hate her for that, because hers has been ruined worse.

I'd got up early to go for a swim on the beach, but just as I was about to leave the cottage, Katie appeared on the stairs fully dressed and grinning. 'Me too, Boo-Boo.'

I shushed her with a finger on my lips. 'Don't wake Mum and Dad. They're having a lie-in. OK, but you have to promise to sit nicely on the beach while I swim and then I'll take you for a paddle.' She wasn't a good enough swimmer to go more than knee-deep in the sea yet.

She made a silent squeal of joy at me and ran to get her costume.

Ten minutes later, we picked our way down the steep cliff path, my hand holding tightly to hers in case she stumbled. The sound of sea swooshing on sand as we descended gave me such a rush – there was something magical about it, especially in the early morning light. In the same way that there was magic in the air at Christmas when the streets were lit up with stars, and shop windows were full of glitter and tinsel. The way that makes your blood fizz with excitement at how amazing it is to be alive in that moment.

I got Katie to sit on a rock where I could see her and I slipped into the cold sea, shivering and teeth chattering at first until I'd splashed around enough for my muscles to work and heat the rest of me. After the initial bracing cold, it was like a fire slowly warming me through. So good.

When I got out, I wrapped a towel round my shoulders and stripped Katie's jeans and sweatshirt off so she was just in her cossie, then I took her to paddle.

She flinched at first at the chilly water on her toes.

'Ha ha, Popsicle – is that freezing? Deep breath before the wave comes again. Ready? Wheee . . .'

'Wheeeee!'

'OK, next time we're going to run in a bit.' I grasp her hand. 'Now!'

Once she was in, she forgot the cold and splashed about, scrunching her toes in the sand. I bent to scoop water over her with my hands and she giggled happily and kicked some back at me. Then I chased her down the beach, in and out of the shallows.

When I realised we'd been there nearly an hour, just messing about, I decided we'd better go back and get breakfast. My tummy had begun to complain. I called Katie to come back and pulled my jeans and hoody on. When I looked up from lacing my trainers, there was a girl standing at the bottom of the steps watching us. I hadn't realised from seeing her in the little cottage window that she would be so tall, model tall and slim, with sleek hair around her shoulders and those exotic cheekbones and eyes.

We walked over to her. 'Hey, you're from next door, right? I'm Lou.'

'Yes. Hello. I'm Katya.' Her voice was accented a little, but her English was flawless. 'I met your mother. She was very nice to mine. Very welcoming. This is your sister?'

'Yes – Katie.'

Katya smiled at her. 'Hello, Katie, you are very pretty.'

Katie beamed. 'Thank you.' And she turned to me. 'I like her, Boo-Boo. She's nice.'

Katya laughed. Even her laugh had a Russian accent, which made me giggle inwardly, but it really, truly did. 'Boo-Boo?'

'Yeah, she couldn't say my name when she was a baby. It was the closest she could get and it's sort of stuck. Now she won't stop. It's Louisa really, but everyone calls me Lou.'

She nodded. 'The girls at my school call me Kat. I like that.'

'It suits you with those eyes.' I smiled to show her it was a compliment.

'Yes, they said that. Is the water cold?' She had a towel in her hand.

'Very, but it's worth it.'

'I am looking forward to it. In Russia, swimming outdoors in winter is a national hobby. This will be nothing compared to the crazy people who break the ice and jump in.'

'Wow! That sounds mental. How long did you live in Russia for?'

'Until I was thirteen and then Papa moved us to London. It is good there, but I miss Russia also.'

I didn't know what to say to that really — her eyes looked so sad when she talked about home — so I smiled. Katie tugged my hand. 'I'm hungry!'

Katya smiled and cupped Katie's face with her hands, long slim fingers with immaculately polished pink nails. 'Then you must have your breakfast, Katyenka. And I have been keeping you from it. That is very bad of me. Do you know we have the same name, you and I? Katie in Russian is Katya.'

Katie giggled adoringly and Katya gained a new admirer.

The Russian girl moved aside to let us pass. 'Enjoy your swim,' I said as we started up the steps.

She smiled and nodded. 'Enjoy your breakfast!'

We left each other without offers to meet later. I sensed a reserve behind her initial friendliness and didn't want to push further. When we got to the top of the cliff, she was wading out into the sea, apparently immune to the coldness of the water as it didn't seem to cause her to pause when the waves washed into her. She had a strange aura of sadness wrapped round her like a cloak. She cast if off briefly to talk to my sister, but now she'd shrouded herself in it again.

Why was such a beautiful girl so unhappy and so alone? Her solitude was almost tangible. She was on holiday, yet she was holed up in that cottage and scarcely came out. They'd been there three days and this was the first time I'd seen her outdoors.

And she had the saddest eyes I'd ever seen.

Chapter 15

Fraser does text me after we get back from the park. To ask me out. He wants to take me ice skating at the weekend. I've been to ice rinks before and I'm good enough not to make a total fool of myself so I say yes. Maybe he's one of those boys who don't like to mix time with his friends with time with the girlfriend. Is that why he blows hot and cold?

I feel like saying no and telling him to forget it permanently after the way he looked at Katie, but I hardly know anyone in Daneshill who isn't associated with him and I don't feel brave enough at the moment to have no one to talk to in school.

I can live with them leaving me out of stuff away from school because I've got my family and it's not like being left out by my old friends. I don't feel anything for these guys. There's no connection.

I want to open my Facebook account so badly. Just to see their photos again – Tasha and Co. of course, not Dan. But it won't make it any better. We're never, ever going back.

They told me that. This is a forever thing.

Three days after the policewomen visited me in hospital, the doctor pronounced me well enough to be sent home. My head wound was healing and the headaches had stopped. They were still sedating me at night for the nightmares but no one seemed surprised at that. I was collected by a detective and she took me to a police station just outside London where a man came to meet me and told me he was the Witness Protection Liaison Officer. 'Just call me Tim,' he said, the original name he introduced himself with being something long and unpronounceable that sounded Polish, but he said it so fast I wasn't sure. Mum and I nicknamed him Tim W-P eventually, like it stood for a double-barrelled surname or something. He had a nice smile and a face I wanted to trust, and for the first time since I walked home from my music lesson over a week ago, I felt safe.

'How's your head?'

'OK now, I think.'

'You're a very lucky girl. And a very brave one. I hear you put up quite a fight.'

'I didn't have much choice. Is there any chance of them being caught?'

'We're trying. But you've got to understand, these men are working for a powerful group in the criminal world with a lot of connections. That's why we've advised your parents that the safest option for all of you is to go into witness protection. They'll stop at nothing to remove a witness who could link them in any way to the Chernokov kidnapping.'

'Where are Mum and Dad?' In retrospect, I wonder why this didn't freak me out. But after witnessing Katya's kidnapping and then escaping from an attempted murder, I didn't feel very freaked by the idea that the police wanted to keep us *safe*.

'In a hotel in Norfolk waiting for you. As soon as you can join them, we'll move you to a holiday cottage in Devon. It's all arranged. You'll stay there until we can set up your new identities, which will probably be January now that Christmas is so close, so your story will be that you're having an extended family break over the holiday season.'

'And when the new identities are ready? What does that really mean?'

'Then you'll be moved again. Gloucester, we think. We use these short transition moves in the beginning to prevent you being tracked, and the one after Christmas will be for a couple of months so that you have the chance to get to know a town well enough so that when we do move you on, you can sound as if you came from there. You have to be convincing enough to fool anybody who knows the place.'

'Oh.' It was all getting a bit much to follow. I needed space to think.

'As to what the new identity means, well, basically you cease to exist as Louisa Drummond. We give you a new name and passport, set up doctored records for you when and where you need them and give you a new life in another place. You won't have any contact with anybody you know from your life now. After the trial, we'll consider letting you exchange letters with relatives, but they'll have to come through us. Until then we recommend total non-contact, with the exception of one letter to very close relatives to let them know you're safe and not to worry.'

I cease to exist . . .

'What will my name be?'

'You can choose. Your parents picked the surname Latham already, so choose something to go with that. I need to go and arrange the cars and the concealed escort so maybe you can choose a name while I'm away doing that. We're going to move you in a couple of hours, once it gets dark.'

'Will I have to change my appearance?'

'Not drastically. We usually recommend a change in hairstyle, but to be honest, given the situation with your little sister, our approach is going to be to put you in a location where they will simply never track you down.'

Katie . . . I hadn't given a thought to her. She must be terrified. This would be a living hell for her.

'Is she OK?'

'A bit unsettled and upset, your mum said, but I bet she'll cheer up once she has you back. It sounds like she's missing you.'

They took me to a room when he went and they gave me a book to choose my new name, along with a cup of hot chocolate. And then they left me there alone.

When I remember Katya holding my sister's face and smiling at her, calling her Katyenka, I also remember why it has to be this way. Why I can never back out, no matter how much I want to.

I have to try to make my life here now. Maybe if I could have said goodbye it would have been easier.

Something kind of strange happened later that night after I got back from the park. Dad was out late working, and Mum wanted the oven cleaner from the garage. She had her head in the oven, attacking it with wire wool, so I was sent out to get it. Typically for this stupid house there's no back door to the garage so you have to go in through the main up-and-over thing, which I hate. It's heavy and shakes when you lift it and it always feels as if it's about to come off. The wind was gusting up into a gale and whipped the front door closed behind me. I fought with the garage door to get it open and then ran inside to pick up the bottle Mum wanted. Then I had to try to get the stupid thing shut again. I wrestled with it for a moment, dropping the oven cleaner on the ground as the wind slammed the door back up out of my hands. Swearing, I took the bottle indoors before I went back to try and wrench the door down.

But the wind was too strong and it battered the door up out of my grasp again, slamming it against the top of the mechanism with an echoing crack that made me think it was going to come off its hinges. It shook violently and I took a step back, sucking my fingers. It felt as if my fingernails had been wrenched off. 'Stupid, *stupid* thing!' Now what did I do?

Someone walked round me, who reached up and grabbed the door. I took another step back as I recognised him — Emo. He was with an older boy, who stood behind, waiting for him and looking at me with interest.

Emo pulled the door down with annoying ease and settled it back into place. He gave me a brief nod and walked off back to his friend without a word, and they went off together down the street.

I couldn't decide how to feel. Part of me was mad that I'd needed his help, especially when he was so . . . GRRR! But

130

then part of me was pleased I wasn't still there trying to get the stupid door to close either. Like I said, kind of strange.

That boy is so, so weird.

Chapter 16

The next day after school, Mum sends me to the baker's to pick up some French bread to go with dinner. On the way back, there's a knock on the glass as I pass the coffee shop. I jump a mile until I see Lucy inside. She waves at me. Gemma's sitting beside her and smiles, though I think she looks unenthusiastic about it, and Cam is with them, with her back to me.

Lucy beckons me in, waving her coffee cup as if she wants me to join them. I manage to slow my breathing as I go in, but my heart's still thumping from the shock. So many little shocks make me jittery still. Maybe they always will.

'Hi, Holly,' she says as I go over to their table. 'Want a latte or a cappuccino or something? My big sis is working here this afternoon so we get free drinks while her boss is out.'

'Oh, thanks. Cappuccino then, please.'

'So what are you up to?'

I wave the loaf in its paper bag as I sit down, noticing Camilla is stirring her latte too loudly not to be making a point that's she unhappy about me being here. Gemma looks a bit sour too, probably to keep in with Cam. She was perfectly fine with me in school earlier. 'Went to the shop for my mum. How about you?'

'Just met Cam for coffee and then I'm going home for dinner. I'm grounded tonight because Dad thinks I'm not working hard enough.' She makes a glum face at me. 'If I worked any harder I think my head would explode.'

I remember what Fraser said about her dad being strict and nod sympathetically. 'How about you, Gemma?'

She shrugs non-committally as Cam stirs the spoon so it clanks against the coffee glass. 'I don't know really. Not sorted it yet. We'll probably go out later. Hang out around the village or something.' She hesitates when Camilla glares at her. 'Are you doing anything?'

Judging by Cam's face, she'll suffer for that later. Has that girl really got enough power to stop everyone wanting to be around me after school? No, she can't have. Power like that over Gemma perhaps, because Gemma seems to idolise her, but not the rest. Surely? They have minds of their own. They must do.

'I don't know,' I reply, keeping a careful eye on Camilla. 'Revising, I guess.'

'Yeah.' Gemma grins and looks relieved. 'I've got a load of homework I have to do before I go out. My mum's getting really naggy about checking my planner and making sure I've done it all.'

Camilla snorts and finishes her coffee. 'I'm going across to the playing fields later. Revision can wait.' There's a challenge in her voice to me, daring me to invite myself where I haven't been invited. *Nobody wants you there*, she says with her eyes.

'I should make it there eventually,' Gemma says, casting nervous looks between us while Lucy fidgets uncomfortably.

'So how do I find you on Facebook? I keep meaning to add you,' Lucy asks. I guess it's to make me feel better because you can't miss the negative vibes coming off Cam. Is her change in attitude just about Katie? How pathetic. But . . . *oh!* I focus on what Lucy actually said and my skin turns cold.

Facebook?

Um . . . how do I get out of this one?

'Oh, er, I'm not on Facebook.'

It's impossible. To suddenly activate an account for Holly Latham with no friends, no past. No messages on her page. No posting history. It couldn't be done. Way too suspicious. And that was one of the things I'd been warned against by Tim W-P.

'Oh! Have you got Twitter then?'

'No.' They stare at me and I feel myself flush. 'I'm not really into all that stuff.'

They're still staring at me, like I'm a bearded woman in a freak show.

'I prefer to text or do my social life face to face.'

'Jeez,' Camilla drawls. 'How twentieth century.'

I sniff. 'You think?'

She curls her lip in return. 'It's kinda weird.'

'Yeah, well, whatever. People should just do what they think and act how they feel. Live how they want and not do what everyone else expects. That's what I think.'

Camilla gives me a sickly-sweet smile. 'Of course you do.'

My heart is pounding in my chest with the effort of lying and it's making it harder to breathe. I get up. 'I should get back with the bread. Thanks for the coffee, Lucy. And you two have a good time tonight if you do go out.'

'Any time,' Lucy says, and Gemma gives me a placatory smile. But Cam glowers.

Why is she suddenly being like this? It can't just be Katie. There must be something else going on.

I shrug at her and smile at the others, then leave.

It takes until I'm home for my heart to calm down. Why wasn't I better prepared for that question? Stupid, stupid, *stupid*.

But no matter how witness protection prepares you, the first time something happens you never do know how to deal with it. I guess that's where the danger lies. Why so many people mess this kind of deal up, or at least that's what they told us. Too many people get careless and compromise their identity.

I don't think they realise how hard it is. They might be professionals, but they don't have to live it. I remember that first day we were in the hotel in Norfolk and we had to be our new selves . . .

We were getting ready to go out. There was a supermarket within easy driving distance, we'd been told. The new driving licences weren't ready yet, but if Mum or Dad got stopped by the police they were to tell them to contact a certain number and that would deal with the problem. We put coats and gloves on, all being very careful to use the correct names and ignore Katie's utterly bewildered face. 'Boo?' she said.

'No, angel – Holly,' Dad corrected.

She frowned. 'Boo!'

'I did tell you,' Mum said to him, wrapping a scarf round Katie's neck. 'You're wasting your time. She won't understand.'

We got into the car and Dad drove us to the supermarket. I sat in the back with Katie. 'Where's *our* car?' she grumbled.

I don't know, Katie. 'This is our car for now. We're having a change.'

Predictably, she screwed her face up.

Mum skewed round in the seat to glare at me and distract her before she cried. I bit my lip and looked out of the window at the strange streets flashing by.

When we walked round the supermarket, nothing was where we expected it to be. It took ten minutes to find the eggs and in the end Mum had to ask an assistant where they were. Katie's face crumpled when the sweets weren't where they should be. And I knew exactly how she felt. Every time we turned down an aisle and it didn't have the produce that our usual shop at home did, I felt like crying. It was stupid — when we went away on holiday I didn't feel this way. When I looked at Mum, there were tears glistening in her eyes. Dad strode ahead, filling the trolley stoically. 'It's so stupid,' Mum whispered, 'to get upset over a strange supermarket, but . . .' She didn't need to finish.

Dad took us in the café for coffee and cakes, the way we always did at home if Katie had been good and not whined. The white cups were the same as the ones in our supermarket at home. Such a stupid little thing but . . . Mum and I gripped our hands round them gratefully. I saw her do it and I knew she'd seen me too when she gave me a tight smile and then looked away out of the window, blinking hard.

Chapter 17

Fraser recruits his dad to act as chauffeur and drive us to the ice rink, which is on the outskirts of the city, about half an hour away. I suffer his father's stony face all the way. He doesn't approve of me, I can tell, from the moment he picks me up outside my house. I'm not quite their kind of people.

I feel cold inside with a shame that I shouldn't have to feel because it's not my fault we live here. A tiny, quiet voice tells me I shouldn't feel ashamed anyway and I'm being a massive snob for caring what he thinks about my house at all.

Outside the rink, the buzz of *city* hits me. And it's awesome. I close my eyes and let the traffic noise and the voices batter my ears.

So good.

Like home.

I've missed this so badly.

The foyer of the rink is busy and we have to queue for skates. Fraser slips his arm round my shoulders and then as we wait and wait, he slides it down my back so his hand rests on my bum. It feels like an invasion of my space. I tolerate it to examine the strangeness of this. Uber-hot boy getting touchy with me . . . and nothing . . . I'm just not interested.

I wish I could speak to Tasha's sister about this. She'd know the answer. Or maybe Mum would? But that would be verrry strange, talking to her about boys like that.

We collect the skates and make our way to the rinkside to change. 'So when you said you could skate a bit, how much is a bit?' Fraser asks, looking suddenly worried that I might eclipse him on the ice.

'I can not fall over too much. Don't worry, I'm not going to start racing you round the rink. How good are you?'

He laughs. 'I'm not bad. I used to play ice hockey before it started messing with my cricket because I was picking up too many injuries.'

He holds my hand while I edge on to the ice. 'Hold on to the side until you find your balance again,' he tells me and pushes off to glide along, before he whirls round in a loop to come back to me.

139

A few staggering steps and I let go of the rail and try to skate. His hand hovers under my elbow in case I fall, but I don't, and after another few attempts I find my ice legs and take off properly. When he sees I'm stable, he relaxes and takes my hand. 'Hey, you're not bad at all,' and he sounds proud. I'm not as good as him so that's OK, but I'm not going to make him look bad either.

Was it like this with me and Dan? All about appearances and power play?

I know it was, deep down, and I'm not sure I'm happy with that. It seems so . . . oh, I don't know. Tasha and I used to think we were so great for keeping a boy dangling. We loved the game.

When you're not operating at the top end of the league though, it's a lot less fun. A little voice in my head suggests it might have been less fun too for the ones that Tasha and I played with.

I never meant to hurt anyone. It was just a game. Being tough. Being in control. The buzz of having a new power and using it. The power of being a girl that boys wanted.

Fraser laughs as a fat girl loses her balance and crashes over. 'How did she not crack the ice?' he says with a snigger. I laugh with him but I don't find it very funny.

We skate around for a while and it's kind of fun. Or is it? It's like I feel it should be but it just isn't making the grade.

Once I'd have flirted like crazy with Fraser because he's cute, but I'm just not getting any buzz from it. I keep remembering how he looked at Katie and I can't bring myself to smile at him in *that* way.

When he suggests taking a break and getting a drink in the café, I agree with relief. Forcing out laughs as if I'm having a good time is a lot easier when I'm sitting in a café with a shot of caffeine than it is wobbling around on blades. He cocks an eyebrow when he asks me if I want food and I order a triple choc-chip muffin.

'I thought girls didn't eat that stuff, always on diets.'

I shrug. 'I don't need to be that careful.'

He grins . . . actually, no, it's more a leer. 'Yeah, well, whatever you're doing, you look good on it.'

I shrug again, and sip my coffee. If it was Dan here, I'd be tempted to break off a piece of my muffin and feed it to him with my fingers. As it's Fraser, I cut it in quarters and push one piece in his direction.

'Thanks.' He eats like a typical boy – it's gone in two bites. He's picked a seat in a quiet corner overlooking the rink. We're on a squashy sofa and he moves closer, letting his knee rest against mine. 'You know most of our year think you're the hottest girl in the school.'

'No, I didn't know.' Can't say I've seen any signs either. They've not been falling over themselves to talk to me.

'Well, they do. And you know what I think?'

'No.' He's started rubbing his knee against mine.

'I think they're right.'

'Oh.' I think that was supposed to have some kind of profound effect on me. I wish it did. I wish I could get enthusiastic about him. It would solve all my fitting in problems, but I don't think it's going to happen.

But I should check with Mum — as she's the only one I've got to talk to — before I decide so, for now, I'll go along with him.

'That's good.' I make the effort. I give him my best 'come and get me' smile.

It works and he pounces, lips locked on mine.

It's not slobbery. He doesn't kiss like a washing machine in fast spin or anything gross like that. It just isn't *anything*. But I sigh and make a little moan like I'm enjoying it. And his hands get more enthusiastic about roaming over me. It's OK — they haven't hit anywhere out of bounds yet, so I let him get on with it. I wind my fingers into the back of his hair and run them over his neck a few times.

Then, when I really can't think of anything more inventive and convincing, I pull away. 'Want to skate more?' I smile brightly, and check his eyes to see if he's noticed it's not working for me.

If he has, he's not letting on.

It's when we're skating round the rink again that I realise we never know what to say to each other. We don't talk. I'm amazed it took me so long to notice.

When I get home, Mum's baking. She does that from time to time, calls these her domestic goddess moments where she likes to dress up in a chef's apron and cook complicated recipes with at least twenty ingredients. And if it takes less than two hours to prepare and cook, she's not satisfied. Most days she won't spend more than twenty minutes on a meal, but on a goddess day, she goes mad.

Dad's taken Katie out for a walk so I have Mum to myself. I make us a cup of tea each and then sit at the table while she chops some ingredient I don't recognise into tiny pieces.

'Can I ask you something?'

She looks up at me and pauses. 'Yes?'

'It's OK, you don't have to stop. I just . . . well, I wanted some advice. Not about something specific, just general.'

'Fire away.'

'I was reading this magazine someone at school lent me and on the problem page was a letter from a girl who's going out with this boy —'

Mum turns and looks at me. 'Oh, come on, Holly, I wasn't born yesterday!'

I sigh. 'Oh, all right then. I'm sort of going out with someone at the moment and it's kind of weird.'

She brings her tea over and sits at the table with me. 'How so?'

'He's really good-looking. And popular. And I should find him attractive. I thought I would.'

'But you don't?'

'It's strange. When he . . . er . . . um . . .'

Mum rolls her eyes.

'OK, when he kisses me, I don't . . . feel anything, I guess. Is that not weird?'

'Not at all.' Mum sips her tea, trying and failing to hide a smile.

'But I don't get it. He's hot. Why don't I fancy him? This has never happened to me before. I thought he was cute before he kissed me. He has an uber-gorgeous smile, so why?'

'There's no chemistry between you. That's the way it is sometimes.'

'What do you mean?'

She does laugh at me now and I wince. 'You've heard people say they've met someone and just clicked with them, yes? Well, it happens the other way too. When it comes to the crunch, there's nothing there. No attraction. If you listen to the scientists, they'll talk about pheromones and the scent of attraction acting on you without you even knowing, or acting to put you off someone you aren't genetically compatible with. But whatever the reason, the result is the same. You can

144

meet an attractive guy and he does nothing for you at all.'

'So it's not weird?'

She reaches over and strokes my cheek. 'No, baby, it's not weird at all. So who is he and why haven't I met him?'

'A boy at school. He's the one I went skating with today, and he took me to the party last week.'

Mum eyeballs me. 'You said you were going with some girls from school.'

'Yeah, I know. Sorry. The girls were at the party.' I screw my face up, thinking, and she gives me a questioning look. 'I don't get these people, Mum. I mean, Fraser's taken me out a couple of times, but they all hang out together after school and they obviously don't want me around then. He doesn't either. What's with that?'

Mum sips her tea thoughtfully. 'Villages can be strange places. I've noticed that too. They want to know everything about you so they're friendly to the point of annoying at first. Then, when they've found out what they want, they back off and exclude you as if they don't want an outsider to get too close. Some of the women in the avenue have been like that with me. They see me outside tidying up the garden or with Katie, and they come straight over to talk. It's like they avoid me when they think they know everything about us.'

At least it's not just me, I guess. Though I'm beginning to

145

wonder if I'll ever make real friends here, or if it will always be this way — having to have boyfriend-talk with my mum because I don't have anyone else.

Chapter 18

Fraser didn't text on Sunday and I was starting to wonder if he really had noticed my lack of enthusiasm, but there he was hanging around the lockers on Monday morning. His smile broke out as soon as he saw me, leaving me even more confused about his take on 'us'.

But it's April, and as I sit there in registration filling in my planner, I realise that I've got more to worry about than Fraser and friends/not-friends. The exams start in one month . . . ONE month . . .

It's Head Down Time. Maybe it should have been Head Down Time all along. How could I be so stupid? I had a plan. Stay under the radar, work hard, pass exams, get that *other* date . . . the trial always hanging over my head . . . over and done with, and then maybe I could have my life back just a little bit. What's left of it.

I was not supposed to go off on some crazy tangent and start trying to be Little Miss Prom Queen.

I groan and let my head fall on to the desk, not caring what the people around me think. I used to have a plan for my life; I knew exactly where I was going, and the kind of people who'd be around me on the journey. But it's like living in Hampton Court maze now. I can't find my way; I can't see where I'm going. The whole thing is just a mess.

I've been off wandering down a route I should never have taken, like I threw down my map to the maze and decided to walk in quite the opposite direction. Yes, I was upset about the Facebook stuff, but where has this path got me? Hanging out with a bunch of people I don't really like and no happier than I was before.

How do I get out of this? How do I get back to where I should've been?

The bell goes and I make my way into the corridor to push through the crush to my English lesson.

Who is Holly? I wish someone would tell me because I certainly don't know any more.

Mr Jenkins tells us not to sit down when we get into the classroom. We're working in groups of four, so we're to get together and sit at a table – he's arranged them in blocks already.

I look around. There's nobody in English I talk to that much. A few vague hangers-on of Fraser's crowd who I don't really know. Then there's Nicole of course, who I haven't spoken to since the first few days. Who should really tell me to go to hell since I dropped her for the popular crew without a second thought.

Who is Holly?

Crunch time.

And I don't know.

Who do I want her to be?

And I still don't know.

Mr Jenkins makes the decision for me. Tired of waiting for us to stop dithering and get into fours, he quickly numbers us and groups us. I find myself on a table at the front with Nicole, another quiet girl called Maria and — oh, joy — Emo Freak, who looks as pleased about it as I am.

The task is waiting for us on a piece of paper, along with a sheet of flipchart and a marker pen: How does Wilfred Owen's *Dulce et Decorum Est* affect us and how does his use of language control our response to the poem?

We have to brainstorm and include the full range of opinions in the group. First, we have to elect a chair. Nobody volunteers. I can see Nicole looking at me, expecting me to step up, but I'm not volunteering for anything.

We sit in silence. Emo reads the poem and doesn't make

eye contact, and soon we're all copying him. Mr Jenkins comes round to check. 'Have you picked a chair yet?' No one answers him. He shakes his head. 'I don't know! Maria, how about having a go?'

Maria looks like a rabbit facing the headlights of a jeep doing 70 mph towards her, but she nods. Emo's scribbling away in a tatty notebook, oblivious. I make my face deliberately blank and Nicole sighs in relief that it's not her who's been put in charge.

Maria clears her throat. 'Um, so overall impressions first? Is that all right? Nicole?'

'Oh, er, me? Um, well, it's quite obvious that we're supposed to be repelled by the soldier's death and feel that war . . . is . . . er . . . wrong. Um, I know that sounds a bit lame, but . . . oh . . . um . . . maybe someone else can say it better.' Nicole colours up.

Maria bites her lip. 'It *is* quite hard to explain it. Um, Joe, what do you think?'

He glances up. 'Still working it out.' And he ducks his head down again.

I can't help myself. He just bugs me so much. 'This is supposed to be a group effort.'

He raises his head again and looks at me. If I thought he'd looked hostile before, it's nothing compared to how he's looking at me now. 'And when I've finished thinking about it, I'll say.'

I now understand the term 'withering glance'. I do actually feel withered.

'What do you think?' Maria says to me, casting anxious glances between me and the freak.

Here's something I can get my teeth into. 'I think the poet wants us to feel like we're there with him seeing it, so he tries to make us feel how exhausted and drained and sore they are. Then he breaks it up with the suddenness of the attack, and the language goes all staccato, and contrasts with a few lines later where they've got their masks on and it slows down, like you're watching the dying soldier in slow motion, and that's linked to the dream-like state . . . because he's remembering this so it's like he's put it into slo-mo himself –'

Emo cuts in suddenly. 'He pulls every tool of language he has out of his kit to make you feel how sickening, how despicable, how *wrong* it is for the soldier to die like that. And to make the men who were selling those deaths with the label of glorious as haunted as he is by the results of what they're doing . . .' He stops, mid-rant, and he looks so shocked that I wonder if he knew until this moment that he's spoken aloud.

Nicole and Maria stare at us.

'If he can make them see then maybe he can make it stop,' he finishes shakily.

I'm not so sure. 'No, because that would mean the war stopped and that would be in the hands of the politicians, and he's not addressing the politics of it here. I think he wants them to stop going into war innocently and blindly, to know what they're doing and not be misled.'

Emo curls his lip. 'He's in the trenches getting the shit blown out of him and his men. He just wants it to stop.'

'Do you have to be so aggressive?'

'Yeah, I do.'

We glare at each other – stand-off.

'Um, wow,' says Maria, 'can you just wait while I get some of that written down?'

'If nobody will fight then there can be no war,' Emo growls at me. Those eyes of his are so dark it's hard to read them exactly right but there's no mistaking the animosity in his voice.

'Oh, I'm sure that would have stopped Hitler. If men hadn't fought in the Second World War then the Nazis would have been able to exterminate whole races and minorities.'

'Don't you know anything about history? If there'd been no First World War, there'd have been no Second! Hitler was glorified as a war hero from the First – that's how come he was so popular and the Germans were still pissed off from losing –'

'And that's not at all a simplistic analysis –'

'OK, everyone, stop!' Mr Jenkins calls. 'Let's see what you've got. Chairmen to read out a summary, please.'

I can't concentrate on what is being said after that. I'm still blazing with fury at Geek Freak for speaking to me that way. And how dumb is he? Like it's all that easy – just stop war by not fighting and all the bad stuff will go away. Naïve idiot. And rude too. And aggressive. And . . . I *really* hate that boy!

Chapter 19

I deviate home via the shops on Tuesday after school, but my heart sinks when I see Fraser and friends sitting on the wall by the bus stop. I don't really want to run into them now. I've spent two days avoiding Fraser while I try to get my head round what I'm going to do with myself. When he sent me a text last night about meeting up at school today, I ignored it.

Cam's with them, still in her uniform. She's taken her tie off and has it tied round her waist like a sash, as if she thinks that's some kind of fashion statement. Actually she just looks really stupid. Her shirt is unbuttoned halfway. I can see the boys trying to look down her blouse, even though there's nothing to see. Even Stuart who has his arm round Lucy. Poor

Lucy — of all of them, she's not too bad. She deserves better than Stuart.

Fraser watches me approach. He doesn't look particularly pleased to see me. 'Hi,' he says as I walk up to them. I'd rather walk past but of course I can't.

'Hi.' I don't know what else to say.

Cam puts a hand on her hip and looks me in the eye. 'So where's your spaz sister?'

There's a collective gasp as if they can't believe she's said it. I'm ahead of them with that. I can believe — I've heard it before, other times, other places.

'She's at home, and she's fine, thanks.'

Fraser doesn't say a word. So that's how it is. Oh well, I can look after myself. Time they knew that.

'How's the slut look working out for you, Camilla? Managed to get any of these guys interested yet, or are you just working on pissing off their girlfriends enough so that they dump them and you can get your claws in that way?'

Another collective gasp, louder than the first. Fraser's face is blank.

Camilla shifts her stance to square on, both hands on hips. 'I don't know how you've got the face to even speak to us. You turn up acting like you're better than everyone else, but what are you really? A nobody. Fraser's told me where you live.'

Oh, has he? Well, I guess that's that then.

She carries on. 'Why do you think you're better than any of these guys? Huh? You think you're pretty. You're nothing special. You think you're smart, right? You can't even keep your man interested.'

They're all looking at me – Lucy, Stuart, Gemma, Fraser and the others – and their faces show they agree with her. Is that what they really think?

'What I just don't get,' Cam says, laughing, 'is why *you* think *you're* so amazing. It's like it's written all over you that you think you're awesome. But you're weird, you live in some shitty little house and you've got no friends. Isn't that right?'

I turn to Fraser. 'And this is what you think, is it?'

He shrugs and stares past me.

'Right. OK.' I turn away and walk off, forgetting the shop. I just want to get home.

But before I do . . . I'm going to settle the score a little. I turn back. 'You know, you should ask yourself, Camilla, how many of this lot would still be friends with you if you had no money. If your dad went bust. Ask yourself that.' I laugh at her. 'I know what the answer would be. Do you?'

And I go down the lane at the back of the shops, forcing myself to walk at a normal pace and not break into a run to get away from them.

Fortunately Katie is helping Mum make cookies when I

get home and I escape upstairs relatively easily when I tell them I need a shower after PE. In truth I want to wash Cam's words off my skin where I feel like they've stuck.

I let hot water cascade over me and I hear her in my head over and over again. 'You turn up acting like you're better than everyone else . . . It's like it's written all over you that you think you're awesome . . .'

A traitorous little voice inside says she's right. I did . . . do . . . think that.

Is that why they don't really like me?

Am I that stuck up?

The voice says I have been.

I try to tell it that maybe I just needed some defences. Maybe I was just trying to take care of myself. Maybe I was confused about who I am now.

The voice tells me something back. It tells me that's not completely true.

And then I scream at it to shut up.

I get out of the shower and wrap myself in my robe and lie on my bed staring at the ceiling with its hairline cracks and stupid swirly pattern in the paint. I never had problems making friends before. People actively wanted to hang out with me. I was one of the popular crew. I was fun to be around. What happened?

I swallow as an unwelcome truth forces its way into my

head, though really I must have known it already because I said some of it to Camilla before.

I'm not the same person I was back home. More than that, I'm not in the same environment. Here I'm the girl in the shitty little house with the spaz sister and the dad who doesn't have a proper job, and I'm weird, and I don't have Facebook, and . . .

I never realised how much of people's opinion of me was wrapped up in who and what was around me, and not who *I* am.

I'm in shock . . .

Chapter 20

I'm still thinking about it when I go to bed later. Turning it round and round in my head. Thinking of my old life and whether there were any clues I should have picked up that could have told me people's opinions of me weren't always what they seemed. And I couldn't see it. I really couldn't. I could have gone on for maybe years and never realised.

Thinking about home makes me think about Tasha, and the memory right at the front of my mind is that first day I saw her again after the summer, right before we were due to go back to school. 'So what gives?' Tasha said, throwing herself on to my bed with a bounce. 'What have you been up to while I've been away?'

She'd rushed round the same day that they got back from

their month touring the US. No jet lag for Tasha, which was typical of her.

My heart thumped erratically and my mouth went dry. 'Oh, the usual. Had a week in France, which was cool, being down in Provence for the first time. And it's so different there to everywhere I've been before. And then we were in Cornwall for a few weeks.'

'And how was that?' She wiggled her eyebrows at me. 'Anything interesting happen?'

She meant boys. I knew she meant boys. But nausea rose up inside and a cold sweat broke out all over me. The words wouldn't come out. I just couldn't say, 'Oh, nothing, just the usual. Nothing to report.'

No words would come at all.

Something must have shown in my face because she got up in a hurry and put her arms round me. 'Hey, babe, what's up?' She examined my face anxiously.

I swallowed. Pulled myself together. Fought the nausea down. 'Nothing. Sorry, hon. Just felt a bit sick for a moment. Must be something I ate.'

'Do you want me to get you some water?'

'Oh, please. Thanks, hon, and then you can sit down here and tell me all about America, which is going to be way more interesting than anything I did this summer.'

She smiled. 'Sure,' and ran off downstairs to get me the

water. I leaned against the wall while she was gone and tried to get my heartbeat back to normal and block the hideous memories trying to invade my here and now.

I swallow and hug my arms round myself as I lie in bed, trying to get to sleep and unable to. The house is quiet. Everyone else has been asleep for ages. The display on my alarm clock says it's two in the morning.

I wish Tasha was here to talk to now. I wish I could have talked to her back then. Then maybe I wouldn't feel so alone. Every time I think of that day at the end of the holidays, I wish, wish, *wish* I could go back in time and change it and find the words to tell her.

I turn over and bury my head in the pillow. You can't turn back time and I'm here alone and stuck with it.

Most of the time I'm caught between trying to brave it out and feeling sick about the trial coming up, and being on a constant state of alert in case I'm being followed. I can't get down the village high street without checking behind me three times. But who can I tell that to?

I dread going to school the next day and by eight o'clock, when I'm halfway through a bowl of cornflakes, I decide it's just too much.

'Mum, I don't feel too well. I think I should go back to bed.'

I never try to skip school so she immediately puts the

kettle down and comes to feel my forehead. 'What's wrong, darling?' she says and Dad appears from behind the screen of his laptop where he's checking the news articles.

'I feel headachy and sick. I don't think I can go in today.' I push my cereal away and get up from the table. 'I'm going to try to sleep it off, and then if I feel better I'll get up and do some revision.'

'Do you want me to bring you anything?' Mum calls after me, voice worried.

'No . . . feel too sick,' I mumble on my way up the stairs as she comes into the hall after me.

'Call me when you wake up and I'll bring you a drink.'

'Thanks,' I croak and disappear into my bedroom.

Actually I do have a headache, from not sleeping most of the night. And I do feel sick, at the thought of going into school. So when I lie down on the bed, knowing I don't have to face that for another day at least, my eyes grow heavy and I do drift off to sleep. At first I wake every few minutes, as I remember something that penetrates my subconscious whenever I try to relax, like Fraser's face when I ask him if he agrees with Cam, like hers when she tells me what she thinks of me . . . But eventually I fall into a deep and mercifully dreamless sleep.

It's eleven o'clock when I wake again and I can hear someone moving about downstairs. I turn over and bury my head in the pillow, not wanting to face anyone yet. I can't put on a mask at the moment and if Mum or Dad asks me what's wrong, I think I might break down and cry.

I feel such a fool. Such a freak. I don't know how to get back to being a proper person again.

All the people in this place hate me and it seems like that's all my fault.

I need to feel normal again.

After a while, an idea comes to me. It's so wrong it makes me shiver. But it's so what I need.

I go downstairs and smile at Dad, bolstered by what I'm about to do. He's working on the computer. He smiles back. 'Want a cup of tea or a cold drink?'

'I'll get it. You're busy. I'm feeling much better now. Is it OK if I take the laptop upstairs to revise?'

'Sure, it's in the living room.'

Back upstairs, I sit on the bed and open the browser. It opens slowly and I fidget with impatience before I can type the URL in the address bar. Again, it seems to take forever to load.

Finally the Facebook front page opens and I log into my account. I go to My Friends and click on Tasha's photo, then on the message icon. The text box flashes up and I stare at it for a second, but I know just what I want to say and then my fingers are flying on the keys.

Hi Tasha,

This is gonna be a shock, I guess, to hear from me after so long. I want to say sorry that I didn't get to say goodbye and I want you to know that it had to be that way. I can't tell you why but please trust me – I would never have left without seeing you if I'd had a choice.

I hope you're OK. I saw your mum was ill from your home page. Is she better now? I hope so. I'm all right. It's pretty lonely where I'm living now and I don't like it much but this is how it has to be so I have to get used to it. I miss you SO much. Please don't tell anyone I've been in touch. It's really important that you don't. I just had to speak to you.

Lou xxx

I hit the button to send it and then lean back on the pillows in relief. Which is the wrong thing to feel because I should be panic-stricken at what I just did. It was exactly what I was told I must never, never do. But I need Tasha. I can't do this all on my own. It's too hard.

She won't reply straight away because she'll be at school, but it's done. It'll all be OK now. I get on with some revision until Dad calls me down for lunch at one. He heats me some tinned chicken soup, an old childhood favourite when I'm under the weather.

'How're you feeling?' he says as he watches me spoon up the soup.

'Much better. Where's Mum?'

'She was helping out at Katie's school this morning because they're going on a woodland walk. She said she would go to the supermarket on the way back so I expect she'll be home soon. What are you going to do this afternoon? More revision?'

'Yeah, I've done quite a lot so far but there's always more to do.'

'Never mind, a couple more months and you can have a long break from it. Why don't you pop out for a walk before you start again? Get some oxygen to your brain.'

I look out of the window and the sun is shining. 'Good idea, I think I will.'

I grab a coat and pull on some shoes, then I step outside and the sun shines gently down on my face. I stand on the doorstep for a moment to check for any suspicious signs before setting off down the hill. There's a brook at the bottom with wild flowers growing and I want to see what's come up there since I last looked.

The daffodils are still out, and little white star-shaped flowers have opened by some yellow primroses. As I lean over the white rail fence to see them better, I notice a Land Rover coming towards me down the lane opposite the brook. It takes me a moment to get my bearings, but then I realise that must be the lane to Emo's farm. That piques my curiosity and I pay more attention to the Land Rover as it turns down the track by the side of the brook and then comes over the little bridge to join the road next to me.

There's a man and a woman sitting in the front. They don't look happy. Emo's parents? No wonder he's so miserable all the time.

As the Land Rover passes me, I see him sitting in the back, earphones in and head down, looking at his knees. He looks pale and strained and as unhappy as the two people in the front.

Why isn't he in school?

The car drives off and takes a right turn at the end of the street, heading towards the main road.

I shake my head and walk back up the hill towards home. Emo's weirdness is none of my business.

I get a few more hours of revision done until around four, when I check my Facebook account. Nothing yet.

Every five minutes, I check again. By four thirty, I'm checking every two minutes. Then finally just before five, a message pops up:

Babe!

Where are you! OMG I missed you so much too! I've been so worried. Are you OK? Truly? You sound so unhappy. I just want to come over there and give you a great big hug.

But WHAT is going on? Please, please answer! Don't disappear again.

Love Tasha xxx

PS Mum is better. She had to have an operation, but she's totally OK now and I'm fine too, but REPLY AS SOON AS YOU GET THIS!!!

My eyes fill up with tears and there's a massive lump in my throat. It's going to be OK. It's all OK again.

Chapter 21

Tasha,

It's so good to hear from you. I was sort of down when I sent you the first message, but just hearing from you has cheered me right up. It's so tough where I'm living now because I don't know anybody. I had to go to a new school and I don't like it and the people there are horrible. I miss home and all of you so badly.

I'm not supposed to get in touch with anyone I used to know but I felt so miserable earlier that I had to. That's why you mustn't tell anyone I messaged you. No one can know. You've got to trust me, Tash, because it could be really dangerous

if anyone found out. I know that sounds like I'm
in some kind of massive trouble, but I'm not really.
But I could be if people know where I am. I hope I
can tell you one day what's going on, but for now
all I can say is I'm with Mum and Dad and Katie and
we're all safe.

Please tell me what you're up to and stuff. I feel
so left out of everything and so alone that knowing
what you're doing would help tons.

Love ya, hon!

Lou xxx

It's so easy to ignore all the advice and mail her again. And
so easy not to care that I've just put all of us at risk. But this
is Tasha and she'll never tell anyone.

That night I sleep easily and I don't care about getting up and
going to school the next day. It's fine. I'm armoured by my past
again, even if they don't know it. A part of *me* is back. I don't
care when nobody talks to me at school, when Gemma sniggers
and nudges her ex, who isn't her ex any more, when I walk past
them in the corridor. They don't matter. None of this matters.

School goes quickly and I focus on work, and it's easy to
do that now. All my feelings of loneliness and isolation are
gone. I walk home quickly at the end of the day and there's a
note on the table from Mum:

Holly,

We've just popped out to take Katie to the dentist. School phoned earlier — she has toothache. Raid the fridge if you want. We'll be back soon.

Mum x

Katie pretty much has to be held down at the dentist so I guess Dad's not having fun right now. I open the fridge and find some bread to toast. After I wolf down a few slices, I decide to go for a walk. I wander through the estate and down to the brook. There's no one about so I cross the bridge and slip down the bank to sit among the willow tree roots and watch the water flow by.

After a while, I hear a sharp bark from the lane above and there's a black-and-white collie watching me from the bank. I flinch a little — he doesn't look too friendly. But then I see Emo behind him, snapping his fingers beside his leg and the collie zooms back to heel.

We look at each other.

'I heard what happened,' he says in the unfriendliest tone possible. 'Sorry. But you should know — all that lot are dickheads.'

'Oh.' Well, he's certainly managed to surprise me there. 'Um, thanks, I think.'

He walks down the bank towards me, the collie hugging

his leg in ultra-obedience. 'They like messing with people and making them feel shit. That's what they get off on.'

I smile a little and I'm startled to find I mean it. 'Yeah, they certainly manage that.'

He shrugs. 'Don't let them bug you. Nobody really likes them. They don't even like each other. They're like starving rats in a trap – they'll turn on each other if there's no one else to savage.'

I stare at him, not expecting the eloquence, if that's what it is. His words sound too rough to be described as eloquence precisely.

'Basically, you see, they suck.'

That forces a laugh out of me. 'Thank you. Really.'

He pauses as if about to say more and then nods. As he turns to walk back up the bank with the collie, I realise what it is that looks odd about him. It's his eyes. They're too bright and sore-looking and I feel stupid for not knowing straight away that he's been crying.

'Joe!'

He turns his head back.

'That really was nice of you. I appreciate it.'

His solemn mouth quirks into a slight smile and he shrugs again, embarrassed, and turns back up the bank to disappear back down the lane to the farm.

That boy is an enigma. Why is he out walking the dog and

crying at the same time? And where did he go yesterday that made him look so unhappy? At first I would have put the crying down to some pathetic Emo thing, but I've seen too much of him to think that's the reason. There's something more to this.

Chapter 22

The first person I see at school on Wednesday is Fraser. He's on his own and he stops when he sees me. There's one of those uncomfortable silences where we don't know what to say and stare at each other instead. I remember what Joe said and I don't feel too sorry for him. I wonder if I should, given we maybe didn't work out because I just wasn't enthusiastic enough. Is that why he never wanted to see me outside school, or is he a loser, like Joe says? And then I remember what Cam said too, about how he'd told her where I lived . . .

But does it matter now? What is there for us to say to each other? We're two people who thought we'd connect and found we couldn't. Hardly front-page news. No major drama there. So I pull my gaze away from his and walk quietly away down the corridor.

I have geography first lesson and it passes uneventfully. I'm tired after another night of disturbed sleep. The dreams were especially bad last night and I kept seeing the gun coming towards me whenever I closed my eyes. At break I decide to go to the library for some quiet, but on my way there, a throng of lower-school kids rushes past me, babbling excitedly, followed by some others my age.

Even I recognise the signs of a fight, and while I definitely don't want to see any punches thrown or blood shed, I'm curious just to see who's involved so I follow too.

There's the usual crowd round the bodies in the middle. I stand on the steps outside the library so I can see better. There's a blond head, looking suspiciously like Stuart, locked in battle with a dark one . . . with familiar black floppy hair. A jock's body battling a skinnier Emo type . . .

Joe?

Really?

I blink and look again.

No, that's definitely Joe and Stuart.

There's a shout from the corner, 'Break it up!' and two teachers run towards the crowd. A bit of pushing and shoving and they break through to the middle. 'Lads! Lads! Break it up now!' Stuart loosens his hold, but Joe catches him a hard punch up on the jaw. I wince and turn away so I miss the rest, but when the crowd disperses past me I realise it must be over and I turn back again. Stuart's standing off to one side looking sullen, but Joe's being restrained by the bigger of the two teachers who looks like he's having trouble holding on to him. The other teacher steps in to block his route to Stuart. 'Hopley, calm down! Pull yourself together!' When Joe doesn't respond, the teacher leans into his face and yells, 'Pack it in!'

That seems to get through to him and he stops struggling. The teacher holding him turns him away from Stuart and leads him off down the side of the library, passing me on the steps. He glances at me as he goes past, but he looks numb and shocked as if he's stunned at what he's just done. The remaining teacher frowns at Stuart and gestures towards a door in the opposite direction.

Emo – no, I feel mean for calling him that now – Joe does seem especially wound up and I wonder what's caused it. It bothers me for the rest of the morning and as I walk to the canteen after the twelve o'clock bell goes, I see his skinny black trousers and Converses heading up the field. As I watch, he climbs over the hedge at the far end and vanishes into a field beyond.

Here's my chance to find out what's bugging him. Maybe Holly, whichever version of her I choose, would never go after him. But Lou would.

I break into a trot and jog up the field, scrambling over the hedge when I get that far. He's standing halfway down the field under an oak tree and he's smoking a cigarette. I walk towards him, getting my breath back. By the time I reach him, I'm calm and unruffled, as if I haven't just run up a field in pursuit of him.

'Hey,' I say, trying not to wrinkle my nose at the smell of the smoke from his cigarette. 'You OK?'

His left eye looks a little bruised and he's got a small cut by his mouth, but otherwise he doesn't look too beaten up. 'Yeah. Fine.' He blows out a cloud of smoke slowly.

'Why?'

He stops pretending to be uninterested in my presence. 'Eh?'

'Why? What was that all about?'

'Noth–'

'And don't say nothing.'

He puts his hand up to scratch his face and I think he's hiding a smile. 'Nothing important. I'd just had enough of him. He picked the wrong time to try winding me up.'

'Why is it the wrong time?'

'You ask a lot of questions, you know that?'

'Are you in trouble now?'

'Yeah, they're trying to decide whether to exclude me or stick me in the Time Out room for a day. Personally I'd rather they excluded me.'

I didn't expect him to come out with that. 'Why?'

'Places I'd rather be than here.'

That's a puzzle, but I sense he's given away all he's going to when he takes a last drag of his cigarette and then crushes the stub under his heel. 'So why are you up here?'

Good question. Why am I? 'Checking you're OK.' There's nothing like frankness to disarm an enemy, if he still is an enemy – I'm not sure yet.

'Why would you want to do that?'

'Well, despite your amazing charm and friendliness at every point until yesterday, I wanted to see you suffer so I was hoping you were up here beating your head to a bloody pulp against a tree or something.'

He laughs. He's got a nice laugh. It sounds surprised at being let out but happy to be freed too. 'Do you want me to start now?'

I shake my head. 'No, I might get splashed by the blood. Do you think you could try some mental self-torture instead?'

'Look,' he says, rolling his eyes, 'just because I dress like this, it doesn't mean I do all that emotional shit. I'm off a farm – we don't do affected on farms.'

Well, what do you know? Emo's quite funny in his way. I giggle.

He hides another smile by ducking his head to look at the ground-up cigarette butt. 'So, you still bothered about all that stuff the other day?'

'No, they're not worth it. You were right. And after what they said about my sister, I know they're scum.' I can't help my voice rising in anger at that last part. I am still mad about what Cam said, and about how the rest silently supported her.

'Said what about your sister?' He looks puzzled. I guess he didn't hear that part.

'Camilla called her a spaz and none of the others said anything to her about that, but they were quick enough to criticise Katie when they thought she'd been rude to Cam and —'

'Woah! I'm not following. Where does your sister come into it? I didn't even know you had a sister.'

'Yeah, she's eight. She's autistic. I take her to the playground lots — she loves swings — and they were there this one time. Cam came over and said something to her and then Katie told her she didn't like her. She doesn't understand that's not right. And Cam and her friends got on to me for not telling her off, even though I told them she has autism.'

'And then Crudmilla called her a spaz?'

I have to snigger at Crudmilla. 'Yes.'

He shakes his head at me. 'She's such a bitch. You know she's after your boyfriend.'

'He's not my boyfriend.' Joe raises an eyebrow at me. 'Well, not any more.'

'You're well rid,' he says, kicking against the tree trunk with his toe. 'I've known him since reception class and he's always been the same.'

'I think I liked the idea of him better than I liked *him* –' I stop, confused by why I started down that track, but Joe grins and nods as if he understands exactly what I mean.

'I've got to go – they only gave me a ten-minute break and I'm late already.' He leans up off the tree.

'Oh, I'm sorry.' I genuinely didn't want him to get in trouble because of me.

'Not your fault. I always intended to be late.' He winks at me and starts to walk off back towards school, then he turns. 'You say your sister likes swings?' I nod. 'Bring her over to mine after school if you want. My dad made us a great swing when we were little. It still works.'

'Oh . . . oh . . . thanks . . .'

'I live on the farm down the footpath at the back of Rowan Close. Crow Trees Farm.' And he walks off again, scrambling easily over the hedge and back into the school grounds.

I shake my head vigorously. Did that just happen? The more I find out about Joe, the more confused I become . . .

Chapter 23

Katie hops up and down on one leg. 'Swing? A new swing?'

'Yes, Pops, we're going to try out a new swing.'

'Now?'

'As soon as you change your shoes. Put your old trainers on and get your coat.' I've never been on a farm but I suspect it might be muddy.

I hold Katie's hand as we walk through the cul-de-sac that leads to Joe's footpath.

'Ooh, cows!'

She points at a field of small cows, which might be full-grown adult ones – I'm not sure. Katie's entranced and pulls free of my hand to trot over to the fence.

'Moo!'

A couple of the cows turn to look at her, big dark eyes with long, long lashes regarding her gently. One wanders over and she holds her hand out. I hold my breath. What if it bites her? But she wants to make friends . . .

The cow must be a baby one because when it gets closer I can see it really is small. It sticks out its tongue and licks her. Katie giggles and looks round at me. I give her a big grin and a thumbs up. She moos gently at the cow again, and it raises its head and stares at her. She stares back at it and it looks like they're talking silently to each other. Katie bends and plucks some grass and feeds it to the cow. The others start to wander over and I step back, but she isn't afraid. She reaches over the fence and strokes several noses in turn.

When she looks back at me again, I hold my hand out. 'Come on, Pops, time to go.' Her face is shining with excitement but she comes readily and waves goodbye to the cows.

As we turn back on to the footpath, I see Joe leaning against the fence some way down the path. He starts towards us, collie at his heels.

'Hey,' he says to me, and then, 'Hi, Katie, I'm Joe.'

Katie observes him with her special 'Katie weighing you up' serious face. 'Hello. What's your dog's name?'

'Kip.'

She crouches down. 'Hello, Kip.'

Joe clicks his fingers and the collie darts forward,

released, and licks Katie's face. She puts her arms round its neck and hugs.

'Katie, be careful! Don't squash it!'

'Him,' Joe says. 'And she's OK. She's not squeezing too hard.'

Katie looks up at him. 'This is a good dog.'

He grins at her. 'I think so too. Did you like the heifers?' We must both look blank because he laughs. 'Townies! The cows . . . heifers are young cows.'

'They were good too,' Katie pronounces. She makes me laugh – she says stuff like that with such authority.

It makes Joe chuckle as well. 'So you've come to have a go on the swing?' he asks her.

Katie leaps up, nodding, and Joe jerks his head, beckoning us to follow. The dog trots behind with Katie, who's talking a stream of some nonsense to it as we walk.

'How did you know we were here?' I ask.

'Saw you from my bedroom window. I had a shower after milking and I was getting dressed again.'

I feel slightly odd at the thought of him dripping wet and in a towel. Not turned on or anything – just hard to imagine. But then so is the thought of him milking!

'How many cows have you got?'

'A hundred and twenty that we milk, and then there's the heifers and calves as well.' He sniggers when I gasp. 'You do know we don't milk them by hand, right? Like, we use BIG machines.'

'Of course I know that.' I stick my nose in the air. Actually I had no idea and I know he knows that from the way he laughs at me.

We continue down the track towards the house. The windows are black painted wood frames with small panes, and the front door is painted to match. There are hanging baskets too, but apart from those and the flower beds under the window, there's nothing decorative around. It's a working farm and it looks sturdily practical. Just before we get into the yard, Joe veers off round the side of a barn and leads us into a big field with lots of trees. There's a swing at the far end, facing out towards a range of hills in the distance. Katie shouts when she sees the swing and runs forward, the collie trotting after her. We follow more slowly and I realise we're walking across an orchard. There's blossom beginning to bud on one tree and the rest will probably break out soon. It must look beautiful here then, with the daffodils growing in clumps between the trees.

Katie settles herself on an old but cared-for wooden seat that's tied to the thick branch above by strong rope.

'Push me!'

The dog flops down in the grass well out of the way of the swing as if he's used to its reach from long practice. When

I look more closely at him, I can see the smattering of grey hairs on his muzzle betraying his age. Joe strolls over and pulls the swing back.

'Hang on,' he says as he releases it and sends her whooshing up.

He won't send her as high as I will and soon she yells for me so I take over. I see him wince as I shoot her up higher and higher. 'She'll be fine,' I tell him and he nods uncertainly. 'Didn't you go higher than this?'

'Yeah, but . . .' He frowns and laughs at himself. 'I was going to say "But she's a girl," then I decided you might not like that.'

'And you thought right.' I grin and kick out at his ankle, knowing I won't make contact. He dances away and sticks his tongue out at me. A frisson of something passes through me – the contrast of Emo with cheeky boy. It's somehow appealing in a very, very odd way.

If Tasha could see me now, she'd hoot with laughter. I'm standing in a rustic orchard with a weird Emo boy, pushing my sister on a home-made swing with an old dog watching us, and I feel closer to happy than I've felt in ages.

Woah!

That's strange but true.

How come?

Maybe it's his vibe – I don't feel like putting on an act

around him. I don't feel it'd impress him at all. Or is it that being out here reminds me of the Cornish cottage before it became a bad memory? Whatever it is, I feel . . . relaxed, yes, that's it.

No tension, no anxiety, no pretence or artifice. Like I do with Katie when we're alone, but more so because I feel *safe* down here in this field. Like nothing bad ever comes here.

How can you go from disliking someone so much to feeling like this? Lou never would have, I don't think. But then she never had reason to. Everything was so simple and clear-cut before that summer. And everything's so different now. Holly's still learning, I guess, and maybe she's that bit smarter than Lou ever was.

I let Katie swing free and turn to catch him watching me again. There's a slight curve to his mouth that wants to be a smile if he'd let it. 'Why were you so . . . so . . . ?'

'So what?'

'When I moved here, you were so . . .' I can't find the word. Hostile? Hating?

He sighs. 'Yeah, I know. I dunno really.'

I'm not buying that. He's too smart. 'That's a cop-out.'

He laughs, that surprisingly deep chuckle again. It's infectious and I almost join in. 'Yeah, it is. You won't like the truth though.' He looks at me with solemn eyes. I have an idea that there's more going on behind those eyes than anyone imagines.

'Probably not but I don't think it'll be such a big surprise. I know you didn't like me on sight. You gave me the filthiest look ever the moment you saw me. And then at school that first day, you made it totally clear you didn't want me to sit with you.'

He shrugs, looking a touch ashamed. 'It's no excuse, but I was having a really bad day. A bad week actually.'

'Oh, why?'

'Got some bad news.' He shakes his head as if to dispel a memory. 'And then I walked up the road and there you were, standing on the pavement looking as if the rest of the world was a bad smell under your nose.'

'I was?' That wasn't quite how I remembered it.

'Yeah, and I thought, 'Stuck-up bitch.' Then you looked at me, like I was dirt on your shoe.'

This definitely wasn't how I remembered it. 'I did not!'

'You mean you weren't thinking what a dump the place is and how crap we all are?'

I feel myself flush up from the base of my neck right across my cheeks. Because it's true. I never realised that it showed to others though. But now Joe's said it, and Cam said something like it too . . .

He raises his eyebrow questioningly at my silence.

'I don't know.' My eyes get stingy and to my horror I feel like I'm about to cry. I don't do that, especially not in public with strange boys.

He shakes his head vigorously and I think I must be giving myself away. 'Doesn't matter, does it? If you think it, why hide it?'

Because my whole life is based on people having the right perceptions of me. For my image to fit. For the right people to like me. That's how it was before too.

Is it any wonder I don't know who Holly is when I'm not even sure I know who Lou was . . .

My eyes fill up and I spin on my heel. 'I've got to take my sister home,' I say, fighting to make my voice sound normal. 'Katie, come on, please. Now!'

She doesn't want to come and yelps to tell me that, but I'm walking away and perhaps her tummy is rumbling for her tea because she follows me when she sees I'm not changing my mind. I'm relieved when Joe doesn't come after us.

I walk back up the hill. Katie catches up and then scampers ahead towards home while I blink and blink to keep the tears in.

I just looked *me* in the face and I don't like what I saw.

Chapter 24

I lie in bed later that night thinking about what Joe said and wondering why I care what some skinny Emo boy thinks. And I tell myself I shouldn't.

I get the laptop out and flick to my Facebook profile to read the last message Tasha sent me again:

Lou – HUGS!
Can't you even tell me where you are? Like are you still in the country? If not, I hope you're somewhere amazing like Switzerland living by a lake near a ski resort or something.

Hardly.

OK, OK, I won't nag you but this is so weird. It just freaks me out that I don't even know where you are or anything. It's totally crazy. You know I would never tell if you asked me not to. You know that, right? But it's up to you and I said I wouldn't nag so . . .

What am I up to? The usual. Way too much pressure over exams and I feel like my head is going to blow. I've got a new boyfriend. Do you remember Simon Harefield? It's his older brother, Gideon. I don't think you've met him. I hadn't until a party a few weeks ago and he was down from uni and tagged along. He's twenty-one and Mum and Dad are not to know or they'll kill me. Totally, totally gorgeous though. I'll attach a photo! Tell me what you think.

Got to go now, babes. Mail me soon. Love ya. xxx

I haven't answered her yet. What do I do about her asking where I am? That was the strictest instruction of all from Tim W-P – never get in touch with anyone and tell them where I am. Never. Ever.

But they don't know Tasha. She's a hundred per cent safe.

Still, it's not just my safety I'm gambling with.

But I know what I do want to ask her right now so I start typing:

Hi Tasha,

I know it's weird but I really, really can't tell you where I am.

Yup, that pic's gorgeous, and an older man – wow! Lucky biatch! The girls at school must be so jealous.

Tash, I want to ask you something and I want you to be honest with me. Do I come over as a shallow, snobby, princessy type? Is that what people think of me? Do you? And I really, really mean it – I need you to be honest.

That's what people here think I'm like and if it's true, then it's not how I want to be so I want you to tell me straight.

Katie would send her love if she could, but she doesn't know I'm writing to you.

Miss you always xxx

I power off the laptop and close my eyes. After a second, I reach to turn off the light. For a few moments in Joe's orchard, I'd felt at peace, but that never lasts, does it? Now I'm back to that constant, nagging ache of worry always prowling in the corners of my mind, waiting to pounce. I wonder if I'll ever truly be happy or feel safe again.

This is why I hate thinking about who Lou was, even

though I can't stay away from it, like a scab you have to pick at. Because thinking of who I was inevitably brings all the other memories flooding back, of Katya, of the night they tried to kill me. Which still makes me choke and struggle for breath even though it was so many months ago and we're so far away. The fear never, never goes. Just lies waiting to rise up and catch me again.

Chapter 25

The footsteps splish-sploshed faster behind me and I sped up, running faster. Car tyres hissed . . . I glanced back — he was closer, a silver car cruising beside him.

I dropped everything and ran, fighting the pain in my ankle. Splashing through puddles, swallowing rain in with air.

The slap of trainers gaining on me . . . the hiss of tyres on the road . . .

Then a hand at my neck, one over my mouth, jerking me to a stop.

I tried to scream . . .

But his hand was too tight on my mouth. He lifted me off my feet as if I was no weight at all and bundled me into the back of the car. I reached immediately for the opposite door handle, but it wouldn't open and I only had a second before he was in beside me, pinning me down.

I screamed out, but he'd slammed the door shut and the driver was already accelerating away. He shoved my face hard into the seat so I couldn't breathe. I thrashed and fought until he caught my arms securely behind my back. When I tried to buck against him, he forced my arms upwards and the pain made me scream into the seat cushions.

'Shut her up!' a voice snapped from the front. 'I'm trying to drive.'

'Bullet?' the voice above me asked.

'Jesus, man, how many more times? Not yet! Where we planned. Can you not just keep her quiet until then?'

Oh God, oh God, oh God . . . they were going to kill me. This was it. I couldn't fight off the bulk of the man holding me down. Whenever they got where they were going, my life was over.

I couldn't grasp what that even meant.

Except it meant fight to be free.

I went limp under him, pretending I'd passed out. He didn't relax his grip on me even slightly. Did he know I was faking? Was he good enough at his job to tell?

The car seats smelled of synthetic fabric and cigarettes. Another voice, deeper and more authoritative than the other two, spoke from the front passenger seat. I didn't recognise it. 'Keep calm, please, both of you. Everything is going to plan. We will be at our destination in twenty minutes. We can deal with our little problem there and still be home for a late supper, eh?'

Oh, nice. His words stopped my panic as if I'd been dunked in cold water. After he killed me, he'd be back in time for tea. I was so pleased for him.

Now I was angry. Call me insane, but it was the complete *rudeness* of what he said. That my life was worth less than getting his meal on time. Against all logic and normal behaviour, that made me really mad.

And mad made me determined. And focused. I was going to ruin his supper if it was the last thing I did.

I wake shivering. I hate the dreams, but they won't stop. I sometimes get a few nights' break, but then they're back. And they're not like normal dreams full of crazy, random stuff. These are exact recalls of what happened. I never knew dreams could be like that.

My pyjamas are clammy and I get up and change them before going back to bed with the light on. I read for a while. I'll have eye bags like suitcases in the morning.

I must drift off eventually because the alarm wakes me at half seven. I hit snooze at first and then drag myself to the shower.

I can't manage more than a slice of toast for breakfast and I nibble it slowly. I'm swallowing the last of my coffee when the doorbell rings. Dad's in the bathroom and Mum's trying to persuade Katie to eat cereal so she looks up at me. 'Can you get it, please?'

I walk down the hall, but the view through the glass door tells me who it is before I open it. The build and the shock of dark hair are familiar. After yesterday, I don't want to see him. I can feel myself flushing red already.

'Hi,' he says when I open the door. Nothing more – he just looks at me solemnly.

'What do you want?' I didn't mean to sound unfriendly, but my discomfort level is mountain-high right now.

'Seeing if you'd left yet, as I was going right past.'

'No, I haven't.'

'I can see that.'

We stare at each other. His face is as solemn as anything, but as I search over it, I find laughter lurking in his eyes. It makes my lips twitch too and I want to laugh at the absurdity of us.

'So, you ready?'

'One minute?'

He nods and I scoot off to get my coat and schoolbag and say goodbye to Katie.

We walk down the hill some way before Joe speaks. 'I told

195

you you wouldn't like it. Are you still mad at me?'

'I'm not mad at you.'

'Could have fooled me.'

I deliberately don't look at him. 'I'm not, but I might be mad at me. I haven't decided yet.'

'I didn't think you were just being snobby with me. I guessed you thought I was a dick because of how I dress. Some girls do.'

I do look at him then. 'Emo's not my favourite look, it's true. But no.'

'I'm not Emo.'

'You so are.'

He growls at me through bared teeth, which startles a giggle from me.

'Anyway it wasn't your Emo-ness. It was that you looked at me like you hated me.'

I'm not absolutely convinced but I think he goes a bit red. 'Yeah, like I said – bad day. I didn't mean it.'

'But you were like that in school too, much later on.'

'Yeah, cos I did think you were being snotty with me by then.'

I sigh in exasperation at how we can so misread messages. 'I was just having trouble settling in and I didn't know anyone. If I looked snotty I was probably feeling uncomfortable.'

'Oh. I never thought of that. Makes sense.' He bit his lip. 'I feel stupid now.'

'Don't. You're a boy. You can't help it.'

He does the infectious chuckle and shoves me gently off the kerb into the empty road.

'So what changed your mind? Why did you talk to me that day?'

'I dunno really. You looked really miserable in school when they started bitching about you. I felt sorry for you.'

I don't like that, someone feeling sorry for me. I should be tougher and cooler than that. But I don't think he's the type to gloat so maybe it's not so bad. 'Why were you having a bad day that time I first saw you?'

He shakes his head like before. 'Don't want to talk about it.'

I remember how red his eyes were that time he came over by the brook and perhaps it's better not to push him. It might be something awful, and we're nearly at the school gates. There are certainly too many people around for a private conversation. I remember something suddenly. 'Hey, you're not suspended.'

'No. They just rang my dad in the end and gave me a warning.'

'Oh, good.'

'I'm going up the field for a smoke at break.'

He doesn't invite me to go too but I can't see any other reason for telling me. 'Same place as before? I'll meet you up there.'

'If you want.' He locates a Coke can on the pavement and begins kicking it along. I bite my tongue – he really can be totally charmless when he wants to be. *Why* he wants that is a different puzzle I've yet to solve, or even find a clue to.

We get to the gate. 'See you later then,' he says and he slopes off round the side of the building. I feel as if I've been dismissed.

The morning is the usual round of being pointedly ignored by Camilla's Cronies. Thank God she doesn't come to school here or it'd be even worse. I can't quite explain the difference between being genuinely ignored because people don't realise you're there and being deliberately ignored, but there definitely is one and you can feel it on the skin on the back of your neck.

At break, I scramble over the hedge to find Joe already under the oak tree, smoking. 'That's bad for you, you know.'

'Yeah.'

'When did you start?'

'Couple of years ago. Bad habit I picked up from my brother.'

And then he clams up, turning subtly away from me to look out over the farmland beyond us.

I contemplate saying something, but I'm quite engrossed in watching his reaction and seeing where this is going.

Nowhere is the answer. He carries on smoking as if I'm not there, just staring at the bare fields.

'How come you never hang out with anyone in school?'

The answer isn't what I'm expecting. 'I used to, but they've all left now.'

'Do you still see them?'

'Yeah, when they have time. They're all working though. All my mates here were off farms too and they're either at college over in Colwich – you know, the agricultural college? – or they're working full time on the farm. And the lads at college all have part-time farm jobs so they're too knackered to do much else when they're done for the day.'

'Is that what you're going to do – agricultural college, or work on the farm?'

He gets rid of his cigarette. 'Bell's going in a minute. You ready?'

So that's another thing he doesn't like talking about.

Later, we eat lunch together in the canteen. Silently because he wolfs his food down without speaking. I pick my way through an unappetising jacket potato loaded with plastic cheese, surrounded by salad that looks as if it's crawling with caterpillars. We are observed, both by Camilla's Cronies and practically every other group or clique in the year group. He's oblivious, or pretends to be. I feel each and every gaze of surprise between my shoulder blades.

Do I care? No, I don't think I do.

I've got that feeling of peace again. Weird.

Chapter 26

Tasha has replied:

Babes, why do you sound so down? No, you're not shallow, or snobby, or princessy. If the people you're hanging out with make you feel like that, they must be total losers.

I should feel better, but I remember how Tash and I would sometimes sit in the dining hall when we were in a bitchy mood and pull apart every girl who wasn't in our crowd for how they looked and dressed.

I feel a little bit sick.

If they make you feel that way then they're not good enough for you. You're not like that at all – you just know how much you're worth!

I wince and look away. It's funny how my value has decreased since we lost money and status. Not that the people around here know that of course – they just judge what they see now. So I guess this *is* what I'm worth now – just me, without any back-up behind me.

I lie back on the bed and think about the whole thing. It's a big shock, I guess, to realise that. Even if a magic wand was waved and all the external bad stuff went away and we could go home, I *know* now. And that knowledge is another thing that takes me further away from being Lou.

Something Katya said springs into my mind. She knew.

'I think that a lot of the people at school who talk to me do so because Papa has money. I don't think I have any real friends there, not like you do.'

At the time I didn't really understand what she meant so I gave an awkward half-smile and said, 'Really? No, I bet most of them really like you. What's not to like?'

She smiled back and shook her head. I thought she was probably being a bit paranoid so I dropped the subject. A shame though if she was right and she didn't have real friends. I couldn't imagine how horrible that would be.

We'd been sitting on the bench overlooking the cove. It was late afternoon and Katie was playing behind us on her bike. Mum had made strawberry shortcake and taken some round to Katya's mum and it sounded like she'd all but thrown Katya out here to socialise. Katya had brought some of the cake for us on paper plates.

'I am sorry – we do not have real ones. We forgot to bring some with us.'

'Your mum probably thought there'd be some in the cottage.'

'Yes, I expect so.' But she was lying. I could see it in the way she wouldn't meet my eyes. What was the big deal? It was only plates.

'So is your dad coming down later?'

'I am not sure. He was going to, but then something important came up at work, so we came on alone.' She was lying again, or not telling the whole truth at the very least.

'So what do you like doing out of school?' I decided to change the subject, because her face had grown even paler. Even if she was lying, she clearly didn't want to.

Her eyes lit up. 'I like to paint, and to draw, but most of all to paint.'

'Is that what you've been doing all day?' Her hands looked very clean, but there was a smear of blue by her elbow that was half hidden by her sleeve.

'Yes. I forget myself when I paint. I think you might understand that? I've heard you when you play your violin in the garden. You forget where you are too?' I nod and she goes on, 'So I sat by the little window in the bedroom today and looked out at the sea, and I painted what was inside me.'

'Can I see it?'

She looked reluctant but got up. 'Come up. It's still drying.'

I followed her into the cottage and she led me upstairs. Although the place was the twin of ours, it had a very different feel inside — less lived-in. You could tell it was rented and not loved.

Her room was plain and bare. She hadn't brought much with her except for an easel in the corner and several blank canvases. Paints were spread over the dressing table. I went round the easel, expecting to see something scenic with rocks and clouds and sea.

What I did see stopped my words in my mouth. The canvas was a wild daubing of angry red and purple and black. I could make out shadowy ghost figures in the background, twisted and knotted into tortured shapes. In the centre was some kind of black void that seemed to be sucking the figures towards it.

She painted what was inside, she said. I looked at her, with her sad eyes and passive face. How could all this be inside that sleek-haired head?

'What do you think?' she asked me, calm and serene outwardly at least.

'It's not what I expected . . . I wouldn't like that to be inside me.'

She walked past me to look out of the window at blue sea and beautiful coastline. 'No.' She turned back to me. 'Let's go into the sun. Leave the shadows in here.'

I know now, Katya. I know how it feels to have that inside. Please God, wherever you are now, I hope you're not trapped with those shadows. I hope you're dreaming of the sun shining off the sea. Of swimming in the early morning. Of the sweet, soft crunch of strawberry shortcake on a summer afternoon. Of anything but *that*.

Chapter 27

Katie's sitting on Joe's swing pushing herself back and forth, with his old dog lying panting in the grass, and I'm perched on a low tree branch nearby. The sky's overcast and we've got thick sweaters on — Joe's is black obviously — but the rain is holding off.

He laughs. 'She never gets tired, does she? You'd think she'd want a change and go up to the playground to the slide or something. But she doesn't.'

'It's part of her condition — habits . . . rituals. Anyway I'm glad she doesn't.'

'Why?'

'It's peaceful here. The playground isn't.'

He gives me a curious look. 'You mean because there's no

danger of running into Crudmilla and Co. here.'

'No, not really. It *is* peaceful here. Like the light's different, or the air or something. It doesn't feel like it does back in the village.' *No cars or strangers for me to watch for.*

'Oh.'

'Do you believe places can have spirits? I'm not sure I do but if they can, then this place has a peaceful spirit.'

He sniffs. 'Probably the fertiliser.'

I try not to laugh but I can't help it, so I shove him off the tree branch and he drops to the ground where he makes a swipe for my feet to pull me off too. I kick out and he stops . . . then tips me back off the branch a few seconds later.

I hang backwards, caught by my knees, with his hands hanging on to mine to stop me falling. 'Now, that wasn't being a good girl, was it?' he says, with the chuckle that makes me join in.

'OK, OK, no.'

'Say sorry.' He relaxes his arms and I slide a few centimetres back, and let out a shriek.

'OK, sorry, sorry!' But I'm laughing as he pulls me back up to a sitting position.

I laugh even more a few seconds later as Katie appears silently by his side and sinks her teeth into his hand. He yelps and scoots under the branch behind me.

'Katie, no, it was only a game. You're not to bite.' But I can hardly speak for laughing.

'She bloody bit me,' he whispers. Katie's glaring at him, looking a bit satanic.

'Go back and play on the swing, Katie-pops.'

She throws him a last drop-dead look and stalks back to the swing. Kip gets up and gives her hand a quick lick, then flops down again. Joe hefts himself back up on the branch, openly laughing now Katie isn't looking.

'You're in her bad books now.'

'Ah, I'll fix that. She can bottle-feed the lamb.'

'You've got a lamb?'

He taps me on the head to say 'stupid'. 'We've got about ten. Except this one's mum won't feed him and he won't take to any of the other ewes so he's on the bottle.'

'Ooh, can we see him now?' Any shred of sophistication I may think I have vanishes – I've never seen a baby lamb close up before. He shakes his head at me in amusement and leaps down to the ground again.

'Wait there a bit and I'll get the feed.'

Ten minutes later we're in the corner of a barn and Katie's sitting on a hay bale feeding a teeny tiny lamb with a baby's bottle. Joe and I lean on the railing of the pen.

'So,' he says, chewing on a hay stalk, which I suspect he's doing entirely for comic effect because nobody is that yokel for real, 'are you ever going to tell me why you lot all turned up here, and where you came from?'

It was bound to happen. It's the most natural set of questions in the world and I have my answers all prepared, and yet I still panic inside when he asks.

'Gloucester was the last place we lived. We move about a lot because of Dad's job, which is why I was out of school for a while – it wasn't worth going as we moved so often so I studied from home for the last two years. Anyway he decided to go freelance so we could settle somewhere and we pitched up here. Dad's from the north originally, though he moved about a lot as a kid too, and he wanted to come back to his roots. Why here? Because there's a good school for Katie. She needs proper support. Dad fancied having a house project to do up so he downsized us for a while. We'll move somewhere bigger when he's done all the work on the house and had a chance to look around for somewhere he really wants.'

'Wow, did you write that down as a script and learn it?'

I freeze. He can't know – he's just joking. But I messed up there. Stupid of me – I can't afford to do that with him. He's too sharp. I need to regain control of the situation.

'Yeah, ha ha. It feels like it. You're about the fiftieth person to ask me that. Maybe I *should* write it down and print it off. Then I can just hand it to people and save the questions.'

He turns to look me straight in the eye, spinning the straw

in his mouth, which looks ridiculous. 'Maybe you should. Or maybe you could give me the real version.'

When I look closer, I can see irritation in his dark eyes. They're difficult to read, that dark, dark brown, But he's cross, it's clear. How does he know? Because I bungled the story, or from something else he's picked up? I ask in the end because I can't afford to make more mistakes.

'Apart from the speaking like it's scripted? And good catch – you nearly saved it. But it was you.'

'What?' I cast a distracted glance at Katie with the lamb to make sure she's not listening. She isn't.

'You made me think it's not true. You don't fit.'

Oh, thanks . . .

'What I mean is, you don't behave like someone who's used to moving around or you'd have settled in quicker. You wouldn't have arrived like you were Paris Hilton dropped in the Bronx. You'd have known that'd turn people against you. You'd be more . . . bland.'

Several things strike me at once:

1. He is uncannily astute for a boy.
2. He must have spent a lot of time thinking about this. A lot.
3. He doesn't think I'm bland. Is that an insult or a compliment?
4. He's got really long eyelashes.

'Bland?'

He nods. 'People who fit in everywhere are always bland. I suppose you have to be to get on with so many different types of people.'

I decide 'not bland' is a compliment coming from him.

'So why do you lie about it, and are you going to tell me the truth?'

'I can't.'

His eyes look more disappointed than cross now, or am I imagining that? 'Why not?'

I take a deep breath, trying to find something that will satisfy him. 'It's not just my story to tell, so I can't.'

He bites his lip and nods his head thoughtfully. 'Fair enough.'

I can't believe that's the end of it but it seems to stop him. Katie's finished feeding the lamb and hands him the empty bottle. She's following the little thing around now, stroking it like a dog. He smiles as he watches her.

'What about you?' I flick his arm lightly with my finger.

'What about me?'

'You're not exactly out there with the personal information yourself. I asked you what you were going to do when you leave school and you ducked out of answering. Don't think I didn't notice.'

His smile shifts to a more rueful one. 'I'd never think you don't notice things. I reckon you probably notice too much to be comfortable.'

Hmm, that makes two of us then. 'So what are you going to do?'

'They need me on the farm.'

Flat-voiced, no enthusiasm. Hmm again. 'Is that what you want?'

'Doesn't matter what I want. They need me.'

I straighten up. This doesn't sound right. 'OK, what would you do if they *didn't* need you?' I don't know why I persist when I won't answer anything myself, but it takes the focus off me.

He almost laughs, but not in a pleasant way. 'I'd go to sixth form, then uni, then I'd travel.'

'Studying what?' I keep my eyes averted, watching Katie, so I don't put him off answering.

'Languages. Or maybe English. Or a combi course.'

'Where?'

There's a derisive snort in reply. 'Oxford.'

'Why does it have to be you who works on the farm? What about your brother? Gemma told me he's in the army. But farming's got to be better than killing people, surely!'

He whirls round and I immediately know I've made a terrible mistake. 'You can fuck right off!' he yells in my face as he leaps up and storms past me out of the barn. Kip scrambles up and runs after him.

I'm so taken aback that I don't move at first then . . .

'Joe!'

I rush after him but I can see his back disappearing round the side of the barn opposite. A man emerges from it and stares curiously at me before following Joe. I don't bother going any further. I know it won't do any good.

'Katie.' My voice is shaking. 'It's time to go.' I take her hand and lead her slowly home.

I keep hoping Joe'll come after us, but he doesn't.

Chapter 28

I seem to be developing a frightening knack for losing friends. But I'm not losing this one. I refuse to.

I text Joe after tea: **Sorry. Me and my big mouth** ☹

He doesn't answer for ages. I'm getting into bed, glum and miserable and I haven't even checked my Facebook page, when the text tone goes. I scramble for my phone.

Was helping with lambing. Not ignoring you. It's OK – not your fault.

Sure?

Yes. Good night.

I close my eyes. There's no knowing whether he's being

curt because he's annoyed or it's that peculiar bluntness he has at times. I suppose I'll just have to take it at face value.

I don't want to lose him. He's the only proper friend I have here.

Proper?

Then I realise what I mean: he's the only person I've met since I've been here that I really, really *like*. With all his weird, quirky habits. And even with all the bits about him I don't know. I just like him. Strange how that happens sometimes. And even stranger how it happened even though I detested him at first. I guess maybe first impressions are a sucky way to judge people. I should remember this in future, I think.

Back home there were all those people I didn't really like, but it mattered what they thought. I twisted myself into what they wanted me to be; I knew what they expected of me and I delivered, just to be in the popular crew. Thinking about what Joe said, maybe I *was* bland back then. Before I came here and lost that ability, being so far out of my normal pool that I couldn't cut it — a saltwater fish in a freshwater pond, choking.

I cringe into a ball on the bed when I think about how stupid I used to be. How I thought I could control what happened to me. Follow my pre-planned ideal path as it was all set out in my head. Make it happen because that's how I'd decided it should be. Stupid little girl, Lou. Stupid, stupid.

Holly's smarter. Holly knows life doesn't work that way. That chaos can come and steal your dreams from you. Steal your life from you.

Katya . . .

Holly thinks maybe it's time to stop debating what I was. That girl is dead. They killed Lou at the cottage in Cornwall that night. They killed her again when they took her to the forest to put a bullet through her head.

I don't want to see if there are any messages from Tasha. I just want to go to sleep and not dream.

Chapter 29

It's crazy warm for late April and Joe and I are doing French revision, lying on our tummies in a field he says will be tall hay in a few months. At the moment it's bright green grass. An occasional car drives past on the top road but otherwise it's quiet, though I can see the village centre is busy with the farmers' market. Joe says his mum is down there selling a glut of end-of-winter potatoes from the market garden she has at the back of the farmhouse. His dad is off doing something with the cows. He always seems to be doing something with cows. I never knew cows were so much trouble. I thought they just wandered around fields eating grass. When I say that to Joe, he rolls around on the ground, laughing.

I'm forgiven. We don't mention his brother. I still want to

know why he got so upset but I can wait. I'll find out sooner or later.

I'm learning to be much more patient these days.

Mum's taken Katie to the market so I can have revision time, and Joe and I alternate between reading through lists of vocab, testing each other, and practising conversation. He's tough to work with, making me go over anything I get wrong again and again. I'm relieved when we've finished the travel topic and I can have a break while we read up on the next one.

The sun's warm on my back and I roll over to let it warm my face. 'Don't go to sleep,' he warns. He told me earlier I looked tired and I am. I don't remember dreaming last night but I felt drained when I woke.

'I'm not,' I say huffily. 'I'm having a timed break. Like you're supposed to so your brain operates more efficiently.'

He snorts. 'Good way of describing a nap.'

I hear a rustle as he turns the page of his book and he goes quiet again.

I'll start again in a few minutes. I'm just going to relax here for a while and chill. Soak in the peace and . . .

. . .

I'm floating, weightless . . . feels good . . .

Warm . . .

Not sure where I am but . . . don't care . . .

. . .

. . .

Getting colder . . . and it's dark . . . if I opened my eyes, it'd be dark . . .

Smell of pine needles . . . earth . . .

They're here, with me.

Their breath sounds in the stillness, harsh from running.

I stay perfectly still, fear crawling over my skin like cockroaches.

Air on my face . . . is it wind or their breath? Terror's rising, pounding blood through my veins . . .

The pine needles, sharp and astringent, like Christmas gone horribly, horribly wrong.

I'm in the forest . . . they're here . . . the bullet in the gun is for me . . . they're coming . . .

I wake with a jerk and Joe's crouched over me. 'Are you OK?' He looks worried.

I sit up. My hands are shaking. 'Yes.'

'Don't lie to me.' He puts his hands on my shoulders. 'What was that? A bad dream?'

I nod.

'You have a lot of those?'

I nod again, slower.

He sits beside me, looping his arm round my shoulders. 'Is it because of coming here?'

'Not really. I had them before.' I hesitate. I shouldn't say it but it's so hard never to have anyone who understands. 'Why we came here is part of the reason I have them though.'

He opens his mouth to ask . . . but then closes it again. Maybe he knows I can't tell him.

Is it OK, Joe? Is it OK if I don't tell you? Will you still be there for me? I need someone, you see.

Chapter 30

Hi Tasha,

How's it going with the new guy . . .

Oops, I have to look back to remember his name . . .
delete . . .

with Gideon? I'm starting to settle in a bit here now.
School still sucks massively, but the exams are so
close that everyone is completely focused on them. I
guess it's the same for you. But I finally made at least
one friend and there's a couple of girls in my classes
that I sort of talk to now.

I've given up being ashamed of how I blanked Nicole and Ella after I hooked up with Fraser and instead I'm making the effort to put things right. I don't hang out with them outside lessons, but we say hello etc. in the corridors and sit in a group in class. They never say anything to me about Fraser and the others. In fact we only ever really talk about schoolwork, but that's OK. It feels friendlier than just sitting alone when Joe's not there.

Katie's really enjoying her new school and she seems to have made loads of friends. LOL! She's the one with autism who's supposed to find socialising hard and she's got more than me. Typical, eh?

What are the others up to? Give me news! I need some girly gossip from civilisation!

Love Lou xxx

The funny thing is I don't really mean the last part. I would have a few weeks ago but now it's just a joke. I don't miss my old friends with that awful aching that pulls at my insides and makes me want to scream. I'd like to see them of course, but it doesn't hurt so badly now.

The lack of decent shopping around here still drives me totally crazy though. Once my exams are over, I'm dragging Mum somewhere huge to do serious retail. Bumpkin-ness is not going to take me over. I will resist.

My text tone goes.

What are you doing?

Joe makes me laugh how he never uses text speak. Always proper sentences and grammar.

Not much. Why?

Want to come round? I've just finished milking and Mum's baked. The kitchen is full of cake. She's taken some round to my Aunty Jenny's, but I'm allowed to decimate the rest.

Decimate. He used decimate in a text. Oh, Joe! Spending the rest of your life on a farm is so not the right thing for you.

Cake? I'll be there in 5!

I don't quite fly there, but almost. Just the mention of home-made cake makes my tummy rumble and I know his mother's will be good because it's a farm. All those farm women can bake, right?

I've never been in the house before, but I know where the back door is and Joe's hanging out of it. 'Hurry up, I'm brewing!' he calls. I go into a large kitchen that looks

222

much as I expected – a big range cooker, pine kitchen units, large table in the middle and a tiled floor. Except there's a difference between this one and the ones in the magazines Mum used to buy in her escape-to-the-country moments. And that difference is mud and mess.

The dresser is crammed with stuff, what looks like bills and farm paperwork, balls of twine, and keys, and heavy work gloves.

'Sugar?'

'No thanks.'

Joe slops some milk into a mug of tea and shoves it at me across the table along with a plate. I pick my way across the pile of muddy boots and wellies near the door, trying not to step on the clumps of mud that've dropped off them on to the floor. *Those tiles are in need of a good mopping*, I hear Mum's voice exclaim in my head; there are paw prints all over them.

'Pick a cake and cut,' he says, waving an enormous knife at me. It looks like the kind of thing you could behead someone with. There are three cakes lined up in front of me. One is definitely chocolate, the next looks like lemon and the last is a carrot cake with frosting. They look delicious.

'Where's the knife drawer?'

He gestures behind him in surprise. I take the giant cleaver thing off him and swap it for a bread knife.

'Ohhh!' he says when I come back to the table. 'That's why I always make a mess when I cut things.'

It's incredible how some boys can be so uber-intelligent, or able to fix cars, or do . . . boy . . . stuff. And yet be so domestically *dumb* all at the same time. I decide on the carrot cake and cut a slice.

'Which one do you want?'

'The same.'

I put a slice on his plate and he grins at me before taking a bite that practically demolishes the piece in one go. I take a small bite and chew it pointedly. It's wasted when he fails to notice. However, I was right about one thing – the cake is awesome.

We're on our second pieces when he comes out with: 'So I thought we'd trade.'

I swallow. 'Trade what?'

'Information.' He grins. 'You and me. We'll swap.'

'Oh, look, I told you –'

'Nah, keep your knickers on, I didn't –'

'What? Er, *what?*'

'Oh, sorry . . . just something my dad says . . .' He chuckles and flushes at the same time. 'I didn't mean you to tell me something you really can't. Just something you can but you haven't yet. And I'll tell you. Fair?'

Possibly. 'You'll tell me what?'

He puts his cake down. 'I'll tell you about Matt.'

His brother. A proper trade then. But can I?

'You first then.' He waits expectantly.

'I don't know . . . no, I . . . OK, I can tell you this bit, I guess.' His eyes remain on me, dark and watchful like the collie's by his feet. 'Most of what I said wasn't true. I'm not from Gloucester and we never moved around. Actually until now I've lived in the same house all my life. You were right about that. But I can't tell you where I'm from or why we're here now. Sorry.'

He smiles. 'That's all right. Anything else?'

'I missed my friends really badly when I came here, and I missed home. That's probably why I was so grouchy, and snotty – if I was snotty.'

'You were a bit.' He nudges me gently with his foot under the table. 'You're all right now though.'

'What about you?'

He sighs and lays his hands on the table, clasping them. 'I owe you, I suppose, for being so touchy with you and biting your head off when you mentioned my brother. You weren't to know why.'

'Gemma told me you two are really close.'

'Yeah, we are. I went mental with him when he joined up. Not because of the farm because Dad can just about manage with me to help, and Matt said he'd come back to take over when he'd done a few years' service. But because he left me here. He's my best mate and him going away did my head in.'

'How old is he?'

'Nineteen. He joined up straight from school.' Joe's holding his knuckles so tightly they've gone white and I'm starting to get a bad feeling. 'You know I said I'd had a bad day when I first saw you? Well, we'd just got bad news that morning – Matt got injured in a roadside bomb in Helmand last year and –'

I gasp and my hand flies to my mouth.

'He was critical for days and he lost both his legs, one above the knee and one below. They flew him home but he's still in hospital in Birmingham. He was supposed to be coming home for the first time that day I saw you, but the hospital called to say he wasn't well enough. I was gutted.'

'Oh my God, Joe, I am so sorry . . .'

What do I say? What can you say? He's not crying, but he looks like he's screaming inside and I know how that feels. When you can't let it out, because if you did it would never stop.

He shakes his head. 'You didn't know.'

'He's going to be OK though . . . oh God, no, stupid, stupid thing to say . . . I mean, he's going to . . .'

'Live? Yeah, though he picked up a secondary infection so it was hairy for a while, but yeah, he's going to make it.'

But without his legs. Nineteen, and the rest of his life . . .

226

'What happens now? How long will he be in hospital?'

'He's doing well. He always was stubborn. We're hoping they'll let him out for a visit soon. But then he has to move on to the rehab place before he can come home for good.'

'So he's . . . in a wheelchair . . .?' I say it hesitantly because how *do* you ask that?

'At the moment, but they're building him up so they can give him prosthetic legs and he'll be able to walk on those after they've finished with him. Then he can come home for good.' He closes his eyes for a minute and I think he's crying, but when he opens them again, he's not. He's still holding it inside. 'Don't know what he's going to do when he gets here though.'

No. Of course. Coming home and unable to do things around the farm. I can see how that could be awful. I get up and walk round the table – I'm really not sure Joe will want this but it has to be done.

I bend down and hug him.

He's stiff with shock at first, then he relaxes into my shoulder and I hold him for a moment. Then I let go.

'Thanks,' he says dully.

'Do people know?'

'Not yet, only family. Mum and Dad don't want people going on at them about him all the time.'

Only family. So why did he tell me?

Maybe he needs someone too.

How would I feel if it was Katie? That's what I keep thinking as I walk home. If someone hurt Katie that badly. If Katie had to live her life with limbs missing.

I judged Joe for being miserable and antisocial. When his most important person had had his life ripped apart.

You think you know people and then you find you don't know them at all.

He said they go to the hospital at least once a week. Apparently Matt's in some military wing. Joe wants to go more often but the farm gets in the way.

Always the stupid farm.

As I walk through our front door, I understand something. Matt was supposed to come back after the army, to work on the farm. Joe would have been free to go then. He could have gone to uni. He can't now.

I think over what he said about it and I know that has to be a blow. I wonder if he's ever blamed Matt for it – even if only in the privacy of his own head? I know how thoughts like that can eat you up. They can make you hate yourself.

I know that, don't I, Katya?

I'm still reeling from his news when I open up my laptop and see there's a message from Tasha. I can't be bothered with it right now. Instead I lie on the bed and stare at the ceiling, wondering what Joe's doing right at this moment. Hoping he's OK.

228

I felt something when I hugged him. I don't know exactly what it was. Weird.

I try to find a word for the feeling. All I can come up with is 'right'.

Chapter 31

The scent of the pine needles was crisp and sharp through the darkness. My bones were cold, my muscles frozen into immobility. I couldn't feel my fingers or toes. But I could feel the memory of the man leaning on me from minutes earlier, crushing my body into the car seat.

Wet soil underneath me, and the Christmas tree aroma all around.

I lay motionless on the ground.

I still couldn't seem to breathe right; as if he was still leaning on my ribs, all the air squashed out of me. My heart should be pounding in fear but it wasn't. It beat steadily in icy temper.

They would not win.

No matter how impossible it seemed to overcome them, to get away, they would not win.

My life would not pour out here, accompanied by the smell of Christmas and the sound of harsh voices. It would not end this way. I would not let it. I psyched myself up to run again.

I wake sweating and I realise I'm in bed. Then I throw off the covers to cool myself down and force myself to relax. I'm almost used to it now. The dreams come all the time. Even during the day, if I close my eyes for a few minutes. Will they stop after the trial? I don't know. Maybe they'll never stop.

Maybe I'll be eighty-three and still dreaming of the night three men tried to put a bullet in my brain.

Will I still dream of Katya lying pale and unmoving on the summer grass?

I wish there was a pill I could take to stop the dreams. To make the bad stuff go away. But Mum won't let me take sleeping pills. She says all they'll do is knock me out so deep I won't know if I've dreamed. Right now, in bed, clammy with sweat and sick with fear, being knocked out deep sounds pretty good.

As the bell goes at school the next day, I can't believe it's already the end of the spring term. The geography teacher is giving out packets of past papers for us to practise over the holidays. I've got six similar packets for other subjects in my bag and a couple already on the tiny desk in my bedroom at home.

Home.

To use that word for the house we live in still feels strange and wrong.

Joe's waiting for me by the gate, looking even more down than the rest of us. I'm still pleased to see him. Stupidly I always feel safer walking home with him. Very stupid – as if he could do anything against Them.

'What's up?'

'Matt. He just texted me. I was hoping they'd let him out over Easter but it might only be for a day. He might get to stay with us overnight, but even that's not certain at the moment.'

'Oh, that sucks then. Sorry.' I think about giving him a quick hug, but as I go to put my arms round him I see Fraser watching sidelong. He's seen me notice him. I don't want him thinking I hugged Joe to try to make him jealous so I draw back. 'But they might change their minds again.'

'Yeah, and a day's better than nothing.' We start the walk home. 'You should come round and meet him.'

'Oh, you think? Won't I be in the way? I mean, of family and stuff.'

He shakes his head. 'Mum's changed her mind about not

telling people now he's due to come home. She wants a party for him. She says if it's all quiet and normal day-to-day things, he'll be noticing that we're off doing farm work and he can't do that now. If there's loads going on and it's all focused on him, he won't get the chance to. Dad doesn't agree with her – he says Matt's got to get used to how things are. Mum said yes, but it's too soon and to give him time, not the first day he comes home.'

'What do you think?'

'I think he'll feel shit whatever we do. It's not like you can avoid noticing missing legs. She's right about needing stuff to distract him, but I'm worried if there's loads of people there that they'll look at him funny or say things about him being injured and make him focus on it that way. So maybe Dad is right.'

'Why did you ask me around then?'

'Because you know how not to stare and say stupid things.' He bites his lip a little as he says that, as if he's unsure whether I'll be annoyed. Or maybe even upset.

I'm not. I know exactly what he means, and I'm not. 'People who do that can make you really mad, you know. Are you prepared for that?'

He sighs. 'It'll be harder outside the village, I suppose. Here it'll just be annoying amounts of people wanting to be sympathetic. Or if Matt's really unlucky, and they're really stupid, pitying him, because he'll hate that.'

I grab his arm and hug it briefly. It's thin but surprisingly hard and muscled in a wiry kind of way. 'For what it's worth, I think you'll cope better with it than I do when people treat Katie like that.'

He looks at me and I can see the shadows of worry in his dark, dark eyes. 'No, I won't. If it was me they were being stupid about then yeah, maybe. But not when it's Matt.'

Chapter 32

Whoever invented the concept of exams should have medieval torture techniques practised on them for the rest of eternity.

I google medieval torture techniques to choose one, and then change my mind.

'Oh my God, that is so sick!'

Joe looks up from frowning at his maths textbook. 'What is?'

'I just googled medieval torture. I can't believe people did that stuff to each other. What is wrong with humanity? Why? Just why?'

It reminds me of what they did to Katya. No reason for it but to make another human being suffer. Sick and evil.

He grabs the laptop from me. 'Urgh! OK, that's just wrong in the wrongest way possible. Hit close!'

I don't have his concentration span for revision today. It's exactly fifteen weeks to the beginning of the trial and that fact keeps going round and round in my head. I catch my heart starting to beat faster without my permission, and adrenalin surging through me in response, and the panic trying to build already. And I can't let it. I have to hold it together.

Today is no different to yesterday or tomorrow, I tell myself. It's just a date. It doesn't mean anything and flapping about it now isn't going to help.

Joe watches me steadily. 'What's up?'

'Noth—'

'And don't say nothing.'

I laugh despite the little panic flutters in my stomach. 'OK, something then, but I'm not allowed to say what.'

He comes and flops next to me, leaning on one elbow. 'You're worried.'

'Yes.'

'But not about the exams.'

'No. Well, yes, but no.'

He chuckles. 'Very articulate, but I get you. Is it something you should be worried about? As in really worried because it's something bad.'

I nod slowly. 'It's . . . pretty frightening.'

'Is it something you can get out of?'

I think of Katya the last time I saw her. 'No.'

He looks at me for a moment longer and then pulls me into an unexpected hug. 'I wish you could tell me because I can't help otherwise.'

I'm startled into immobility. I don't hug him back, I just let him keep hugging me for a second longer. And another second.

He smells good. Not of overpowering deodorant or aftershave like some boys, but a natural skin smell that's spicy and has a kick like ginger. I breathe him in like a natural high.

But then I pull away because that's too, too weird. I'm sniffing Joe. That's so not right.

'Thanks,' I say and he's looking at me as if he's puzzled too. I wonder for a moment if he was breathing me in too, but that's even freakier so I smile vaguely and pick up my book again.

I feel him watch me for a little while longer, then he scoots off on to the floor to get on with his work.

I manage to hold my concentration just long enough for him to get lost in what he's working on again, then I can't keep my mind from drifting back to Katya. I keep seeing her face that last time, as she lay there, so pale and still, so many tubes . . .

She was so gentle. But you can be as good as you like in

this world — it doesn't stop the bad things happening to you. They come for you anyway.

After Katie pointed out the white car passing the cottage, I looked for it whenever I passed a window or we were playing around outside. But for the next few days there was no sign of it and I thought it must be someone who'd been renting a nearby cottage and had gone home again.

I called for Katya to go swimming one morning and we picked our way down the cliff path to the cove together. 'Where's my little namesake?' she said.

'In bed, still asleep. She had a difficult night. It happens sometimes.'

'Is that part of her condition?' Katya asked hesitantly. 'Your mother told us that she has a medical problem . . . I am sorry, I cannot remember the name.'

'Autism, and yes, it is. Or it seems to be. Some of her friends with autism have sleep problems too.'

Katya touched my arm. 'It sounds very confusing for her. And she is such a sweet child.'

We arrived on the beach and began pulling off hoodies and jeans. 'She is. She's a poppet, but it must be horrible for her. Sometimes I wish I knew what it felt like to be inside her head, and then other times I'm so glad I don't.'

Katya nodded. I didn't know what it was about her,

but she oozed this air of quiet, calm compassion.

We slipped into the sea, gasping at the cold at first, though that was me more than her. She pointed to a rock ahead and looked at me questioningly. I nodded and we swam out together towards it. Not a race, just a focus for some exercise. As we swam I wondered if Katya was popular at school. Her quiet manner could mean she was overlooked. Or dismissed as boring.

I thought of her painting. No, there was nothing boring about Katya. The surface waters might be still but currents ran beneath.

She touched the rock before I did, swimming with grace and ease, and she waited for me to catch up so we could swim back together. There was no splashing each other and playing in the water when we reached the shore again. I couldn't imagine Katya doing anything like that. Instead we floated for a while and then I suggested swimming out parallel to the shore to a cave just out of sight around the bay. The sea was quiet today so there should be no danger from the rocks.

We set out and again she reached the cave before me. I had to shout to her or she would have passed it because it was hidden from view by a rocky outcrop. When the tide was out, you could walk around to the cave on a narrow strip of sand that edged round the bay and out to the outer coastline, but as the tide was in we swam straight into the cave itself and hauled ourselves out of the water to sit on a large flat rock.

'This is like being a mermaid,' Katya said, gazing around, entranced. 'So beautiful.' She turned the smile on me. 'Thank you so much, Lou, for showing me this place.'

I smiled back. 'Mum showed me it when I was Katie's age. She used to come here on holiday when she was small. It was her parents' cottage. Dad bought it from them as an anniversary present for her one year.'

'That is an amazing present! I hope I'll be lucky and find a husband thoughtful enough to buy me a present like that.'

I noticed she didn't say rich enough. Her dad was probably rich enough to buy the whole of Treliske on a whim.

'Do you think your dad will manage to get down here or is he still tied up at work?'

Her face clouded and I wished I hadn't asked. 'No, I think he is still very busy.'

Well, that killed the conversation. I didn't know what to say to her and we stared at the sea for what seemed like ages before she spoke again.

'Papa is often very busy. He has business interests all over the world.' She shrugged. 'I don't really understand it. He does not talk about his work much except that it is very stressful and sometimes difficult.' She shook her head and changed the subject. 'You live in Muswell Hill, yes?'

'Yes.'

'I thought it might be nice if we kept in touch once we go home?' She played with the strap on her swimming costume as she spoke, flicking it nervously against her shoulder.

I smiled as wide as I could. 'I'd like that. You're right – it would be very nice.'

I was rewarded by a relieved smile in return. 'Oh, I am so pleased you think so too!'

There was another awkward silence when we just smiled at each other, probably looking quite foolish. But at that moment I guess we bonded.

I realised I envied Katya her calm composure, that inner stillness she carried with her, even when she seemed worried. I wasn't quite sure how to describe that envy . . . except . . . I looked up to her, I supposed.

Chapter 33

I recognise Joe's knock now, so when it sounds at half four in the afternoon, I go to open the front door totally puzzled. 'Why aren't you milking?'

It's the first Tuesday afternoon of the Easter break. He's excused farm work for most of the day to revise, but he still has to be there for milking. In fact he only left here a couple of hours ago, after revising all morning and staying for a toasted sandwich for lunch.

'I got another text from Matt.' He's grinning from ear to ear. 'They're letting him come home for the whole of the Easter weekend.'

'That's brilliant!' I hug him briefly and there's that strange buzz of excitement again as I do.

'We can collect him on Thursday afternoon and he doesn't have to be back until Tuesday morning – he's off to rehab then. Oh, but I can't come round tonight because I've got to help Dad move Matt's bed downstairs into the dining room after milking.' Joe can't stop grinning. He looks so happy he could lift off into orbit. 'I had to come and tell someone to make it feel real. Gotta go now.'

He jogs off to the corner, then he stops and waves, before running back to the farm.

I go back inside laughing. I'm so happy for him that his brother's coming home. I couldn't not be happy seeing his face all lit up like that. I've never seen him look so . . . joyous.

I watch TV with Katie for half an hour and then go to help Mum cook while Katie plays with her dolls. Dad's due back from seeing a client at half five and we're sitting down to dinner as a family.

'How's the revision going?' Mum asks while I wash salad.

'Oh, OK. It's better having someone to work with. Not as boring, plus Joe helps me out if I get stuck.'

'He's clever then?'

'He is at maths and English. I'm a bit better than him at French, but probably only because we've been on holiday so often. He was going to come around later, but he's got to help his dad with something at home now.'

Mum opens the fridge and roots around at the back for

the crème fraîche. 'I'm glad you've made a friend. I know it hasn't been easy for you and he seems nice.'

'He is.'

Mum looks at me. 'Terrible hair though, darling. Can't you persuade him to cut it?'

'Mum! That's Emo hair. It's part of his identity.' I grin at her.

'And I've always felt someone should tell those boys that silly skinny jeans do absolutely nothing for them. But that's what girlfriends are for. To sort out their fashion mistakes.'

'We're not going out. We're just friends.'

'Oh.' She smiles vaguely. 'Of course. I didn't mean to imply you were.'

I eyeball her so she knows I know she's not got away with it.

I check my Facebook page before I start revising again and there's a message from Tasha, full of gossip from home. Strangely I feel less interested in what the others are doing than I thought I'd be. I mean, it's still nice to know, but it's as if part of me has really accepted now that I'm never going back and it matters less than it did before. Tasha never fails to make me laugh though. She is just one mad ball of energy. It's like she's sitting on my bed beside me, waving her skinny arms about, her short, choppy, elfin hair sticking out around her head like a jagged blonde halo while she chatters her message.

And I do miss *her* like I've been freshly wrenched away all over again.

I could message her back, but I need someone solid here now so I pick up my phone and text Joe to ask if he's still busy or could he come round.

He shows up about fifteen minutes later, peeking round my bedroom door after Mum lets him in.

'What's up?'

'Why should anything be up?' I know I'm being perverse because he's right, something is up, but I feel stupid admitting it.

'You sounded fed up on the phone.'

'*Pfff*, how can you sound fed up in a text?'

He comes in and sits on the bed. 'You can and you did. So what's up?'

I sigh and flop on to my back. 'I'm just being dumb.'

'Yes, you are but what's up?'

I slap out at him, laughing. 'How do you know I'm being dumb when you don't know what's wrong?'

He shrugs, completely poker-faced. 'It's not like your tractor's broken down beyond repair or –'

'I don't have a tractor!'

'Exactly! So it's not a catastrophe, is it?'

And suddenly I can't stop laughing. 'OK,' I splutter when I can speak again, 'my tractor didn't die and my cows didn't escape so it's not the end of the world as we know it.'

'That's better,' he agrees. 'So what is up?'

It's hard to explain without telling him I've contacted someone from home, and then how it all has to be secret, so how do I tell him what's bothering me without including any of that? 'I just got fed up and missed home and my old friends,' I say in the end. 'So I wanted to see my new one.'

To my surprise, he flushes scarlet. I think he knows it too because he gets up and looks out of the window for a few moments before coming and sitting down again. 'Thought I heard something weird.'

But he doesn't say what and I don't ask as he's still red. I know there was nothing there. It's OK. It freaks me out too, this whatever it is between me and him. Like with Katya, there's some kind of bond there that makes no sense. We've nothing in common. He's a sometimes morose Emo with an oddball sense of humour, living in Hicksville on a farm with a family obsessed with looking after cows. I'm . . . or I was . . . a city girl and my idea of style is definitely not dyeing my hair black (although I think his is natural, not dyed) and flopping it over my face and wearing too-tight clothes in different shades of miserable.

But he sits beside me and doesn't say anything. He takes

246

off a leather band on his wrist and hands it to me. It's studded with black metal skulls. *Icky*.

'Keep it,' he says and I'm glad I didn't say the 'icky' aloud. 'It's good stress relief. When you get fed up, you sit and run it through your fingers. It calms you down.'

Running skulls through my fingers . . . yeah, right. But I take the band and I try running it through my hand.

'Close your eyes,' he says.

I do as he says and I pass the cuff through my fingers. After a moment or so, I'm shocked to find I do feel a bit better. There's something tactile about the warm leather and cool metal in combination. You forget they are skulls when you're feeling them and you focus on the smooth chill and warm rough instead.

When I open my eyes to glare at him, he's leaning back on the bed grinning at me.

The cuff is still warm from his wrist, the heat held in the leather. It occurs to me I'm stroking his wrist by proxy, and I sit up and fasten the cuff back on him.

'I meant you to keep it,' he protests.

There's warmth on the leather on his wrist from my fingers now – now he's feeling my fingers on his skin by proxy.

'Yeah, but if I need it again, I'll call you and you can bring it round,' I tell him.

And he flushes scarlet again.

He goes not long after because it's getting late and he has to be up for morning milking.

It's strange when you tell a person something that you hold within you and don't share with others . . . it's like something of you is inside them, and they're in you too.

Joe told me about his brother; I told him about how there are things I couldn't tell.

So when he leaves, his wrist is still within my fingers, my fingers still comforted by his skin.

Chapter 34

Joe's gone most of Thursday while they drive to Birmingham to pick Matt up. He said he'd come round later, but I told him not to worry if he was busy. I knew he wanted to be with his brother. He'd been waiting for this moment for weeks.

I message Tasha back finally, then I lie on my bed – between bouts of vocab learning and breaks to play with Katie – and think. Am I happier now? Yes, I guess so. It's snuck up on me gradually. Even with the trial looming, perpetually looking over my shoulder and the exams, yes, I'm happier. I miss having a best friend like Tasha that I can do girly stuff with. I can't remember the last time I sat and mucked about putting make-up on and trying new looks, swapping clothes . . . all that stuff me and Tasha used to do together on wet Saturday afternoons. I still feel anxious most of the time, but it's a quieter anxious than before, not that chewing-away-at-my heart feeling of when we first arrived.

I have Joe to hang out with and he's somehow wormed his way into being pretty important in the me-being-happier deal. I don't quite know how that came to be. I could just pass it off that I was desperate for a friend, any friend. Hey, I put up with Crudmilla and Cronies for long enough. But I don't think it is that really. We just fit right together, though we shouldn't at all.

And then I laugh. I know what we are. We're strawberries with black pepper. My mother discovered that combination in one of her crazy cookbook-reading blitzes and it's been a family favourite ever since. People who haven't tried it think you're mad. In theory it makes no sense as a combination. But when you try it, it works. You can't explain why – it just does.

Me and Joe. Strawberries and black pepper.

Katie and I go round to the farm for brunch the day after Matt gets home. I wasn't sure at first when Joe invited Katie too, but when I thought about it I knew she'd love it, getting to go out with me. Or she would once I convinced her that it isn't some freaky, scary change to her routine. But it'd be OK. She's been to the farm before, even if she hasn't been in the house, and she knows Joe. Actually she adores Joe. She *hugs* Joe and Katie only does that to her special people.

I'm proved right when we get to the farm door and Joe opens it.

'Hi, come in. Hey, Katie.'

'Wheeeeeeee!' She grabs him and hugs him tight. She's started making that noise when she sees him. When I asked her why, she said, 'It's his.' Her noise for him, I assume she means, or her personal own name for him as she never calls him Joe.

He hugs her back and then untangles himself from her grip and steers her into the kitchen.

She goes stiff instantly at the sight of people she doesn't know in a room that she's never been in before. 'Waaah,' she says uncertainly.

Joe's mum waves, but keeps her distance. 'Hi, Katie. Would you like some juice?'

Katie eyes her from the safety of leaning back against Joe. 'It's nice juice,' he whispers in her ear.

It hurts to see the confusion on her face as she tries to process who the other people in the room are and what's going on.

Joe's mum's a tall woman with the kind of sturdy build I expect a farmer's wife to have. I can't see any of Joe in her. She's tanned with short blonde hair. Joe's dad looks more like him with his paler skin and dark hair, and the slighter build.

There's no chubbiness around his tummy like my dad has. He looks more reserved than his wife. Neither of Joe's parents have his dark eyes.

Matt's sitting at the table, the metal frame of his wheelchair visible. He does have Joe's eyes. He's broader in the shoulders with close-cropped hair, but he's got Joe's face shape too — wide cheekbones and narrow jaw, and his straight eyebrows. The same nose, the same shaped mouth.

I swallow. He looks like an older version of Joe sitting there without legs. That makes me feel a little sick, as if it *is* Joe.

I snap out of it as Joe introduces Katie to Matt and shepherds her to a chair.

I smile in turn at his mum, his dad, his brother and say polite hellos.

'Sit down, Holly. Tea or coffee? And would you like juice too?'

It's all so very farmhouse. There's bread under the grill as if they don't bother with unnecessaries like a toaster. His mum is scrambling eggs on the hob, and I can see the oven's on too, while she effortlessly coordinates getting real coffee and what looks like freshly squeezed orange juice to the table. My mum would be in awe of the complete domestic goddess-ness of her.

Matt watches me and Katie silently. Joe and his dad have a brief exchange about cows — they've been watching one for

252

some disease I've never heard of. I'm too unnerved by Matt's steady stare to listen properly. Katie stares back at him. She frowns and leans over the table to get a better look. I go cold, because I realise what's about to happen and —

'Where are your legs?' she asks.

Matt laughs and winks at her. 'They fell off.'

I can't believe it and I look around at the others. His dad's pouring more coffee, seemingly oblivious, while his mum's tipping the eggs into a warm dish, and Joe's gazing at his brother with an expression I can only describe as colossal pride.

Katie frowns harder. 'Legs don't just fall off.'

He gives a gentler chuckle, sounding so like Joe that it startles me. 'No, they didn't, you're right. Some bad men made them fall off.'

Katie nods. 'Bad men. I don't like bad men. Bad men hurt Katya, and they tried to hurt Boo-Boo too —'

Oh my God! 'Katie!'

She pouts because I've shouted. Matt and Joe both turn to look at me for a moment, puzzled. Fortunately the food is ready and they get busy mounding their plates with thick slices of toast and creamy scrambled egg so no comment is passed on what Katie said. I'm amazed that Joe's brother could laugh that way and it makes me nervous of him, or in awe, or something. He seems so much more grown-up and resilient than I could ever imagine myself being.

What had I expected? Some sorrowful, sickly guy lying in a bed while the family flock round him in his feeble state, like Beth from *Little Women*?

Yes, I think I did.

Joe nudges me. 'Look at Katie.'

I smile. My sister's cutting her toast into bite-sized squares and then dividing the egg into exactly equal portions on to each piece of toast. She puts the first bite in her mouth and . . . 'Yum!' she says loudly.

Matt chuckles again. 'You like that?'

'Yes!'

He winks at her again. 'Me too.' They grin at each other.

'So how's the revision going?' Joe's mum asks.

It's a classic question and I have a stock answer. 'OK, but I'll be glad when it's over. I just want to get on with the exams.'

'Yes,' his dad says, 'then you can enjoy the rest of the summer.'

Yes. After the exams comes the summer . . . August . . . the trial . . .

When I remember that, I hope the exams never come, that these weeks go on forever, and I don't want the revision to ever stop.

'You like school?' Matt asks. I nod. 'I hated it. Couldn't wait to leave.'

'Well, I'm not so crazy about this school, to be honest, but

I did like my last one . . .' And then I realise what just slipped out. Not information, but it's dangerous ground. I need to be more careful. Joe kicks my ankle lightly under the table. Nothing much slips past him.

'Teachers there still the same miserable pains in the ass they always were?' Matt asks.

Joe and I look at each other. 'Yup,' we say together.

There's a scratch at the door. Joe makes to get up but Matt says, 'I'll get it,' and whizzes his wheelchair out and around the table. Kip trots in, tail wagging madly as the old dog realises just who has let him in.

'Ah, you forgot I was back, didn't you? Getting old, lad. Memory's not what it was.' Matt fondles Kip's ears.

'Get away with you,' his dad says. 'That dog's as sharp as when he were a pup.'

I watch, smiling, hoping I'm not staring, but I've never seen someone with no legs before. There's a uselessness about the way his trousers just . . . end . . . in a fold that was never designed to be there.

And I suddenly think back to that English lesson with Joe. It's *obscene*. Wilfred Owen used that word in his poem. I understand now why that was the right word to use.

But Matt's zooming around in that wheelchair like he's been in it all his life. And Joe watches him and smiles. And I understand that too.

We leave after brunch. Joe's mum's invited me back for the party tomorrow. Katie would be welcome too, she says, but it'll be past her bedtime. I'm to tell my mum that they'll drive me back at the end of the party so she knows I'm not walking home alone in the dark.

'I'd walk her back,' Joe protests and I hear his brother splutter a laugh that makes Joe glare at him.

'Whatever Holly wants,' his mum says, giving him a funny look, and I make my exit quickly before it gets embarrassing.

Chapter 35

Matt's party is already in full swing when I get there on Saturday night. Dad drops me in the yard outside the house and waits until I've gone inside before he drives off. There's a crowd of boys in the kitchen, around Joe's and Matt's ages, eating home-made sausage rolls and drinking beer. Matt's in the thick of it and Joe's standing off to one side watching his brother, rather like Kip watches Joe when they're out together. He waves me over to his side and gets me a Coke, while I help myself to a plate of food.

'There are loads of people here,' I whisper in Joe's ear.

'Yeah. Once Mum convinced Dad to have the party, she told my Aunty Jenny, who is like the village tannoy system.'

Matt's laughing with the others as if he'll be back on his feet in a week or so. That's still puzzling me.

'How is he so . . .? Oh, I don't know how to describe it.' I ask Joe.

'That's just Matt. This is how he deals with difficult stuff. And, like he said to me, it's just his legs. The guy who was standing next to him came back in a body bag.'

I go cold all over. I don't know how Matt can be so pragmatic about it. And I realise that scares me about him. Especially when I wake so many nights in a cold sweat dreaming there's a gun pointed at my head again.

I finish my plate of food quietly and listen to the others talking. Joe stays next to me, but he gets dragged into the conversation, reluctantly at first as I guess he doesn't want to be rude when I have no one else to talk to. But pretty soon he's laughing along with the others about stupid stories they're swapping.

It isn't so bad being here and just listening to them talk. I smile occasionally at someone's joke and they don't seem to expect more.

'So, Joe, where've you been the last few weeks?' one of them asks. 'You fallen down a hole to Australia or something? Because it's like you vanished on us.'

'Is it now?' Matt says, grinning hugely. I've decided by now that Matt is a wind-up merchant, possibly of the highest order. 'Why's that, little bro?'

Joe narrows his eyes at him. 'Been busy with the cows.'

They all fall about laughing and I wonder if I've missed some in-joke. Joe's flushing a bit and laughing in a self-conscious way.

'That'll be the same cows we've always had? Those cows?' Matt says, sniggering at him. 'Or have we suddenly got five hundred head more that I don't know about?'

'OK, and busy with revision!' Joe adds, causing more raucous laughter, for some reason. He pulls a face. 'You're a comedian. You should be on stage.'

The others shove and jostle him, laughing, and he has to take it.

It's all a bit testosterone-rich for me and I'm relieved when a bunch of girls come and join us.

'Come on,' Joe mutters in my ear and he sneaks out for a cigarette.

'Who're the girls?' We stand in the shadow of the barn as Joe lights up.

'Couple of people's sisters or girlfriends, or friends of the family. They left the lads to it for a while so Matt could acclimatise a bit at a time.'

I nod. 'He looks like he's enjoying himself.'

'Yeah. Maybe Mum was right about this taking his mind off what he can't do, but equally he just likes seeing his old mates again.'

'You said he was your best friend before he went away. Has he changed much?'

Joe takes a drag on the cigarette and thinks about it. 'No. He's just as ready to rip me and all his mates as he always was. And he always was confident and sure of what he wanted. But there are changes too. He's more tolerant since he joined up. I noticed it even before he went out on tour. Last time he came back to visit, my granny was here. She drives us all crazy with her nagging when she comes to stay and he put up with her way better than the rest of us could. And he's not as quick to be down on people as he was. He told you he hated school and he gave the teachers a hard time back then, but I don't think he'd be like that now.' He pauses and takes another drag. 'But since he lost his legs? I think he's trying really hard to be who he was before it happened and I can't tell yet whether he is or whether he's pretending. So much of who he is was wrapped up in being active and able to do physical things that I can't see how he can ever be the same. But he'll fight to be the person he was before – that's what he's like.'

The back door opens and Matt shouts out into the yard, 'Come on, slacker. Dad wants you in the front room now.'

Joe groans.

'What's up?' I ask as I follow him back in.

'You'll see. Just don't laugh too much.'

The front room turns out to be a large rectangular room

with sofas and chairs and not much else. I think there's a TV in the corner, but if there is it's tiny and my view is blocked by some men about Joe's dad's age who are sitting on wooden chairs. One of them has a violin under his chin and as soon as I see it, I have eyes for nothing else.

He's tuning it and I watch as he twangs the strings and makes the minute twists to the pegs, then runs the bow across the strings to check the tuning has held. I listen as he warms his fingers up in a quick scale and feast my eyes on the curves around the chin rest, on the coils of the scroll. I'm dying to touch the sleek wood.

Joe's dad is organising people into a group near the violinist. I tear my eyes away to see that the man next to him has a flute, and another has a tin whistle. A younger man is strumming a guitar; Joe's mum is tuning a mandolin. Another woman is positioning herself as if she's going to sing. Joe perches on the edge of a wooden kitchen chair with some kind of drum and a little wooden beater.

The man with the guitar plays a few chords and then nods at the others and they break out into some kind of folk song. I don't recognise it, but after a few bars it's surprisingly infectious. The crowd from the kitchen have come in to listen and I'm drawn to the violinist's fingers flying on the strings, although I should call him a fiddler really.

Then I hear it . . . a soft drumbeat, like a heartbeat at first.

Missing every few beats and picking up on the fourth.

Soft and slow, soft and slow.

Then faster as the tune picks up pace and the drummer hits more of the beats.

When the singer – who actually isn't at all bad – moves into the main rhythm of the song, the drumbeat speeds up into a pace so fast I can't believe there's only one. I look at Joe, whose hand is flying so fast I can't see how he's hitting the drum, except his wrist is flicking the double-ended beater back and forth so quickly that it's a blur.

People's feet are jigging in time now, mine too even though I'm not generally into music like this. But hearing it played live is different and the beat catches at my breath, especially as the singer pauses and the fiddle plays a solo and Joe backs it up with the little drum. I begin to realise this is really a duet between the fiddle and the drum. And Joe's hitting the beater on the skin, on the wooden rim, and a couple of times for comic effect off the chair leg beside him, as the duet turns into a duel of who can play fastest. The fiddle wins in the end and Joe laughs as the crowd breaks out into applause. Then he goes back to the gentler beat as the vocalist takes up her part again.

The group play another song after that with the tin whistle taking centre stage this time. The fiddler makes that instrument sing and I wish I was him. I realise I miss playing my violin so very much. And the drumbeat makes me jig my foot and tap my hand against my leg like I'll never stop. The vibrations hum through the wooden floor and up through my feet, making my heart go, 'Play, play, *play*.'

When they stop, the fiddler grins at me and holds the fiddle out.

I shake my head and take a step back, surprised.

'Ah, go on,' he says. 'I think you know how to play this thing.'

'Yeah, go on,' a voice shouts from behind and I turn to see Matt wink at me. 'Give it a go. Even if you're bad, the view'll be better than watching that old goat.'

'Oh, I don't think I know anything —'

'You can't refuse a wounded man now . . .' He's grinning like it's just a scratch again.

But he's right. I can't. How do you say no to him when he's sitting there laughing at himself like that with no legs, and looking so like Joe.

I take the fiddle and think desperately what I can play. Then Joe hums a few bars of something I recognise from a film and raises an eyebrow in question . . . *What about this? Yes*, I nod.

He smiles and settles back to his drum. He beats a few soft strokes to lead me in. I tuck the fiddle under my chin and feel it become part of my arm, my shoulder.

It's been so long.

And then it's like yesterday.

I find the tune and my fingers know where to go and the bow glides on the strings, and I'm home.

How did I ever give this up? Why did I ever think it was a good idea to let this part of me go? Let it die?

As I get more confident, and I can hear the audience liking what we're doing, I pick up the tempo. Joe matches me and works up and down the drum. It's that subtle change in the drum's tone that makes what he's doing special and I begin to appreciate how much skill that takes. He catches the drum on the rim to make a clack that's perfectly in time with my up-bow. Matt yells some appreciation, and I get lost in what we're doing until the last bars of the song.

When I stop and open my eyes, the fiddler is beaming at me. 'Well, that was worth listening to and then some!' And he pats my arm as he takes his fiddle back.

Now Joe's on his feet waving at Matt to come forward. He shakes his head until Joe yells something that makes him laugh then he moves his wheelchair alongside his brother. He grabs the tin whistle and launches into a fast jig that has Joe biting his lip in concentration to keep up.

I've never met a family like this.

I smile to myself, looking at the two of them – so alike and yet so different. This music gets to you in the right atmosphere and I guess this is how it was always intended to be played, by amateurs in crowded rooms. That's where it has magic.

At the end of this piece, Joe passes the drum to his dad and beckons me out of the room. He goes to the fridge and hands me a can of Coke, popping the tab on one himself. They're playing again in the other room, but we sit on the kitchen table and listen from a distance.

'I didn't know you played the drum.'

I don't quite understand his reply and repeat what I've heard.

'Bough-ran?'

'That's what it's called. Spelt B-O-D-H-R-A-N. My dad taught me. And I didn't know you played the fiddle.'

I swig some Coke because my mouth's suddenly dry. 'I gave up.'

He looks at me, puzzled. 'Why? You looked like you love it.'

'It's complicated.'

'I can cope with complicated.'

'I lost my violin.'

He stares at me. 'Don't treat me like an idiot.'

'No, I did lose it. And afterwards I lost myself too so I decided to live without another violin because it was easier not to be me without the music.'

'But you miss it. I could see that when you were playing.'

'Yes. I didn't know how much until I saw that man —'

'Uncle John.'

265

'Oh, until I saw your uncle playing, and . . . yes, I missed it. A lot.'

He frowns at me. 'Start playing again then.'

'I don't know. Maybe after the exams.' *After the trial . . .*

People begin to leave at half nine. Matt's trying not to yawn. His eyes look heavy, reminding people that he's not long out of hospital. Joe gets his own way and walks me back home up the footpath. He doesn't talk much and there's a moment when we get to my front door where he pauses and gives me a strange look.

Before I have a chance to wonder what's up, he mumbles, 'See you tomorrow then,' and hurries off.

I feel . . . disappointed?

Do I?

Why?

Maybe I do know the answer . . .

I don't finish that thought, but I'm surprised by the flutter of *something* inside my stomach.

It takes me a while to drift off to sleep. The ghost of the fiddle haunts my hands – I can still feel it there, the smooth wood and the curves, the rub of the metal strings on my fingertips, which are slightly tender from playing again after so long.

Yes, maybe after the trial I can get another violin. Start to play again. Because I realise now what it was that stopped me

– fear, plain and simple. Not disguising my identity, or making it easier to be Holly. But stupid, illogical fear. I dropped my violin the night *They* took me and I've been too scared to pick one up since. In case somehow it brought them to me.

But after the trial . . . yes, then . . .

Chapter 36

Lucy alerts me to it — she texts me the link to the Facebook page. Maybe she felt guilty or something or maybe she just didn't like what Camilla did. Or they all wanted me to know because it was less fun if I didn't and this was part of Camilla making sure I found out. Yeah, that's her style — I'll vote for that option. All the same, when I open the Facebook page and see what Camilla's done, I don't care why. I just want to kill that little *bitch*.

It's a hate page called 'Holly Latham is a Ho'. She left it open for anyone to view, answering one question — she wanted me to see it.

I taste acid in my mouth as I read it.

At first there's only posts from Camilla. Stuff like how

I love myself and what a bitch I am. Then other people join in. Gemma's one of them. Fifty-three people have 'liked' it. Fraser's one of them, Lucy tells me, though he hasn't posted anything.

I throw the laptop down on the bed and run to the bathroom. Leaning over the sink for support, I splash cold water on my face with shaking hands.

Why?

I mean, I know she hates me, but why do that? I don't get in her way. I don't talk to her or her friends. There has to be another reason.

I dry my face and walk back to my room slowly. The page is still open. I don't look at it, but I sit carefully on the bed first, back against the pillows, and get myself ready. Then I pick up the laptop again and take a closer look.

As I saw at first, her opening posts are about what a stuck-up bitch I am with nothing to be stuck up about, and how weird I am too: how I've got no Facebook or Twitter, how none of my old friends seem to keep in touch with me because I never mention them, so everyone where I used to live must hate me too. And then, like a joke, but I'm not sure she is joking, there's a post: 'Reward for information – can you dish the dirt on Holly? Post what you know. Virtual cookies for the juiciest.'

It's pathetic. I stop feeling sick and just feel angry. Stupid, pathetic girl. What is her problem?

I read on. There's a bunch of answers saying how strange it is that I don't talk about old friends, and more speculation. It's after that the photos start.

She's been stalking me around the village and taking photos on her phone when I'm not looking, and getting other people like Gemma to do the same in school. They've got some kind of uber-loser competition going on for bitchiest caption for the photos.

Well, Crudmilla, you picked the wrong girl to bully. Because all this? I just don't care. It shows just how sad you really are. And when I count, I see there's only about six people posting with her. Even her best friends can't be bothered with it.

I ring Joe and tell him to look online . . . and then there's a volley of swearing down the phone.

'Yeah, I know, I know. No, I'm not upset. I mean, I was shocked, but it's too . . . oh, I dunno the word . . . to get upset about.'

'Puerile!' he spits down the phone.

I laugh. 'Yeah, that. Anyway, what do you think I should do?'

'Nothing. She'd just get off on that. I'll report it as abuse and it'll get taken down. It'll bug her more if you don't say or do anything.' And then there's another torrent of swearing while he rants.

I grin, despite it all. He's just what I needed.

'Why she's so bothered by me anyway?'

'Your loser ex, that's why. She's obsessed with trying to get into his pants.'

'Yeah, but I'm not seeing him any more so what's the problem?'

'He's obviously not taking her up on it. Maybe she thinks he's still into you.'

I shake my head. 'I just don't get it.'

'I know,' he answers and I can hear a smile in his voice — weird.

It's only afterwards, when we've made each other laugh and bitched long and hard until we've put it all to rights, and he's rung off, that a cold little chill creeps up my spine. A thin, icy shiver along each vertebra in turn, deathly slow.

My picture is out there on the internet, along with my new identity . . . This isn't supposed to happen. Ever.

I ought to call witness protection . . . but Joe said he'd report it, get it taken down. And the thought of telling Mum and Dad, and them seeing how someone hates me so . . .

They'll care. Mum will cry, I know she will.

So I choose the most dangerous option. I turn off the computer and try to forget about it.

I gamble.

Please, you up there, whoever you are, let me win . . .

Chapter 37

Hey Tasha,

This is going to be my last message. I've been thinking about it and I'm really not supposed to be doing this. I'll miss talking to you massively and one day I hope I'll be able to get in touch again, but right now I'm risking too much. I should never have started this. Please promise me you'll delete my messages. Don't mail me back as I'm not going to open my Facebook account any more.

   Love you xxx

It kills me to close things off with her, but right now it's too dangerous. I said I'd do anything to stop them finding us. No matter how much I try to justify it to myself by saying it's Tasha and she'd never tell etc, I've still put us at risk and that's so wrong. I have to stop it now while no harm's been done.

The thing with Crudmilla brought me to my senses. I was lucky – two days later the page disappeared. My gamble paid off. But I'm not taking any more chances so shutting Tasha out is the only thing I can do.

The doorbell goes and I shout to Katie. 'Come on. Time to go.'

Joe's dad is driving us to a nearby country park for an Easter egg hunt. Apparently it's an Easter Monday tradition and Joe and Matt always went when they were kids. They thought Katie might like it too and I think Matt wants to get out and about from what Joe said.

We hop into the Land Rover. Matt's in the front and we squash in the back with Joe and the wheelchair. It's not too far.

Maybe we all need a day doing something like this.

Their dad drops us off and tells Matt to text when we want to come home. Matt sets off towards the registration stand, propelling himself in the wheelchair. I shake my head – it's as if he took off in a rush before we could push him. I'd never attempt to push Matt. I'd be too scared. He's so together it's not real.

He fills the entry form in and we hover behind. Katie's

hopping on one foot with excitement. The woman at the counter takes the form back. 'Thank you, dear,' she booms at him.

He scrunches his face up at her. 'I'm in a wheelchair, love, I'm not deaf.'

I wince for him. He doesn't appear to be anything other than slightly irritated and turns his chair round to hand us the maps. Joe's scowling at her from under his fringe of hair and I pull him away before he has an outburst. 'Stupid bitch,' he mutters in my ear as we follow Matt towards the start.

Katie's looking at her map, though she doesn't understand it, so she hasn't seen Joe's blacker-than-black expression as he takes in how many people are staring at Matt as we pass. 'They don't mean anything,' I whisper to him.

Joe snarls suddenly.

I follow his line of vision and I see Camilla standing at the start, staring at Matt. She's with Gemma, who's also staring with her mouth open. Matt stops the chair a few metres from them. Cam looks lost for words. She doesn't notice the rest of us at all. Her eyes are fixed on where Matt's legs aren't and revulsion spreads slowly over her face. Gemma's almost in tears.

'Hi,' Matt says tonelessly to both of them and then he turns to Katie. 'Are you ready? Fastest one to that tree over there! Come on, race you!' He sets off before he's finished speaking and Katie squeals, taking off after him. Cam turns and walks quickly in the opposite direction, with Gemma following, sniffing and wiping her eyes.

'What was that about?' I ask Joe, who's looking like he might explode.

'Last time he was home on leave, Crudmilla tried it on with him. She was all over him, even though she knows that mate of hers had a crush on him. Matt blew her out. She's not his type. But I think she just made it clear to him that he isn't hers any more.'

'Let's catch him up.' I tug Joe's sleeve and he nods.

We jog up to the tree where Katie is jumping up and down because she won the race. Matt's laughing at her, but when he thinks no one is looking I see the first hint of pain in his eyes. He can't count on everyone any more. He knew that already, I guess, but being confronted with it is something else. I look at Joe and he's staring into space with his jaw set in an effort to keep his temper.

Chapter 38

It's the end of the holidays and Joe and I are sitting on a grass bank in the sun enjoying our last afternoon of freedom. Matt went back to the hospital on Tuesday, but only for a short while because he's expecting to be moved to a rehabilitation place called Headley Court soon. He said he was looking forward to getting prosthetic legs and being able to walk on two feet again. Even if they were plastic and metal, he added. Again, I winced inside at his bluntness. And I felt ashamed that I was still having nightmares most nights while he was so adjusted.

The sun's shining and I've just seen the first bee of the year buzzing lazily around some wild flowers a few metres away.

I'm also secretly watching Joe reading as he squints when

a beam of sunlight catches him in the eyes. He's got a silver ring in his eyebrow and I'm looking at the contrast of his straight black brow with the curved metal. I follow the line of his sharp cheekbones to his pointed jawline. His fringe is flopped off his face for once as he lies on his back holding the book above him. His forearms are bare and all smooth skin and sinew beneath. Yes, they're surprisingly attractive. I've never thought of forearms as being attractive before.

I wonder what he thinks of me. Does he find any parts of me attractive or doesn't he think of me in that way at all? I sometimes suspect he does, but he's so hard to read. Those eyes can be unfathomable most of the time.

He catches me looking at him and smiles lazily up at me.

And I'm struck by the maddest desire to lean down and put my lips on his.

I smile back vaguely and quickly turn over and pretend to concentrate harder on my maths paper. But I can still feel the pull, like gravitational attraction, between my mouth and his.

We're both kind of dreading going back to school and also eager to get it over with too. It's three weeks now to the start of exams. This is it, the vibe in every classroom says, no putting it off. It's now.

Joe's jittery. He gets stopped about his uniform on the first morning before we even reach class. The teacher is the same one who hassled him about his piercings on my very first day. She huffs and puffs about his trousers being slung so low and his Converses, which 'are strictly not allowed as you well know'.

He snaps, 'So what are you going to do about it?' and she gasps, looking around for another teacher to support her. I drag him away before he gets into more trouble.

We don't have any lessons together in the morning. I look for him in the canteen at break although I'm fairly sure he'll be up the field smoking. But I'm hungry and I want some toast so I'm not going searching for him today.

Unfortunately the person I do bump into in the queue is Fraser. None of the usual crowd is with him. He hesitates and then nods at me. 'All right?'

'Yeah, you?'

'Yeah.'

We shuffle uncomfortably, two people with nothing at all in common. At one time he'd have been the right person for Lou, but as I discover more and more, Lou is gone and Holly has become a real person.

I don't know how or when it happened, but I am. I know who Holly is now. She's the girl who thinks this school is sucky, but a few people are OK. She's the girl who hangs out with Joe. She's the girl who loves Mum and Dad and Katie. And she's the girl who's going to get through the next few months and then the trial and have a future.

'So, you and that Joe, you're . . .?'

I raise my eyebrows because that's really none of his business.

Fraser shrugs. 'That's what everyone's saying.'

'What about you and Camilla?'

He shrugs again. 'She's a friend but I'm not interested in her in that way.'

The way he's looking at me tells me he's still interested in me, but he's puzzled too. I wonder if he knows we weren't working when we touched, when we kissed. We looked OK to each other, but there's nothing deeper. I laugh inside – I don't suppose *he* can ask his mum why.

But he's not done yet.

'That Facebook thing with Camilla, um . . .' Fraser shuffles uncomfortably.

'What about it?'

'I asked her to take it down.'

'Oh. Thanks.'

Did she take it down because she didn't want to look bad in his eyes? I wonder why he's decided to tell me this – does he think I'll see him as my rescuing knight now? Or is he even telling the truth about this at all?

And then there really is nothing more to say. I make some excuse to go and he nods and says, 'Bye,' and we go our separate ways again.

Joe might not be my boyfriend, but we're together a lot of the time. After school we have a ton of homework for tomorrow so we agree to meet at mine later to plough through it together. He runs off to milking. I grab a snack from the fridge when I get home then amble upstairs to boot up my laptop.

I have been logging on to my Facebook account, despite what I said to Tasha, just to check that Crudmilla hasn't posted any new stuff about me. When I log on today, there's three messages from Tasha. Although I know I shouldn't – and I really do pause for at least a minute – in the end I click to open them.

The first two sound worried but the third says she understands. It's OK. Contact her when I'm able. She loves me too. Oh and click on the link – it'll cheer me up.

She's sent me an attachment. It's a little animated cartoon strip thing that does make me giggle. That's so cute of her. I save it to my docs but I don't reply.

It's for the best. It's what the police said. No contact. Certainly not until after the trial.

Chapter 39

I throw myself into revision like never before. Joe and I spend most of our free time with each other, but it's all work. Katie's fretful because we're not doing anything together and Dad's trying to take her out of the house as much as possible, but he doesn't have much time either. I feel like I'm sleeping twice my normal amount, though my nightmares are worse. I'm perpetually tired and I've always got a slight headache lingering behind my eyes.

Katie wakes me up one morning by crawling into bed with me.

'S'up, Pops?' I mumble as I wrap my arms round her.

She snuggles against me. 'I dreamed about the white car,' she whispers into my shoulder.

I'm instantly awake at her words and my skin prickles with fear. I can smell the Cornish summer afternoon even though I'm tucked up here in bed, and in my mind's eye I can see the white car with the spoiler cruising down the lane.

'Boo-Boo, car!' Katie rushed to me and pointed. And yes, there was the car. It was back again. I squinted my eyes to see if it was the same driver – a young man with close-cropped hair.

And it was. Why did he keep driving up and down our lane?

Katya waved to me. I waved back. I hadn't noticed her there in the garden before. Her easel was out and she was painting. I wandered over to take a look – it was a picture of a child fishing from a boat on a still, still ocean. I wondered what it meant. I guessed she wasn't just painting a nice picture.

'Is that how you feel?'

She smiled her serene smile. 'Yes, it is today.'

'That looks like it's a better way to feel than last time.'

'I think so.'

She touched some paint on to the water to show the reflection of the sunlight glinting off the ocean. I looked more closely at the child. It was a small girl with two black pigtails.

'But why hasn't my little friend come over to see me?'

'Oh, she's watching the road for that car.'

'What car?'

'There's a white one that keeps driving past here a lot. Katie's just seen it again. She notices things like that, things you and I wouldn't.'

'No, I haven't noticed it.' She put her brush down and I thought her eyes began to look worried.

'I know, it's a bit weird.' I laughed. 'Or maybe what's more weird is that Katie has me looking out for the stupid car now too.'

I open my eyes and hold Katie tight, as if doing that now can stop what happened next. As if it can save Katya. And us.

She squeaks in protest but I don't let her go for a long time.

Chapter 40

I don't know how, but suddenly it's our last day at school before the exams start. Apparently they always ship the whole of Year 11 off to a theme park on this day. Dad went a bit mental when I told him and went off into another of his rants about state education, but Mum rolled her eyes and gave me the cheque for thirty pounds and signed my permission slip.

Joe says it's a bribe so we don't trash the school with graffiti and eggs and flour. He laughed when he saw my expression. 'Yeah, well, some people would.'

It isn't even a good theme park we're going to, like Alton Towers. It's some rubbish place I've never heard of and it's going to take nearly two hours to get there. We're not going to get that much time on the rides and everyone on the coach is complaining about that. Joe and I are sitting near the back sharing an earphone each from my iPod.

'Have you got any decent music on here?' Joe whines for about the tenth time, and we've not even got to the motorway yet.

'Beyoncé is decent. Shut up. I'm not listening to depressed people wailing this early in the morning. We can have your stuff on the way home. That was the deal.'

'This is causing me physical pain. It's like torture. Actually you could use this against the Taliban. They'd quit Afghanistan in minutes if you blasted this out in the mountains.'

'I'm sure they'd rather have Beyoncé than your Emo rubbish.'

'Nah, because she'd have to wear a burka, wouldn't she? And Beyoncé in a burka is a waste.'

I poke my tongue out at him and look out of the window, ignoring his chuckle.

When we arrive at the park, the teachers dismiss us with the instruction to be back by three for the buses or be left behind. Nobody listens — they're not allowed to leave us behind so there's really no point in saying that. Joe and I break off from the main group straight away. There are lots of other schools here, all milling around and shouting in loud, confident, streetwise voices.

I hear accents from home and they make me smile. Not in a homesick way, but it's good to hear them even so. Just listening feels a bit like putting on a warm coat on a cold day.

Joe and I go into a café to get breakfast – his second as he's been up since five with the milking. I never eat before a coach journey otherwise I feel sick so I'm starving now. I get two coffees and ham and cheese croissants. They're ridiculously overpriced, but Dad relented last night and handed me a wodge of spending money for junk food and fairground tat.

As I start eating my croissant, a terrible thought strikes me. I pause, with my croissant halfway to my mouth.

'What's up?' Joe asks.

It's ridiculous. There won't be anyone here I know. London is vast and you can go into the city day after day after day and never see a single face you recognise. My old school won't be here for sure because they don't do this kind of thing – and if they did, they wouldn't bring us to this place. But now I've thought it I can't stop that whisper of panic in my ear: what if someone here recognises me?

'Holly, what's up?'

'It's stupid.'

He gives me that look. The 'we've been through this before, now tell me anyway' look.

'Oh, OK, but I did tell you it's dumb. I just crazily, madly thought that I could bump into someone who knew me from where I used to live.'

He looks at me steadily. 'And would that be so very bad?'

'It's not going to happen. It's just a stupid thought.'

He reaches across the table and takes hold of my hand. His is warm from the coffee mug. The contact of his fingers, the pressure of his palm, they make my breath catch in my throat.

They say in books when a boy touches you it feels like electricity. It doesn't. It feels like every cell in your skin is more alive. You're aware of your hand in a way you've never been. It's not just in your skin either, but deeper, through the tissues, into your very bones.

At least that's how it is when Joe holds my hand. It's never been that way before.

I can't speak. I can only sit and stare back. That stupid thing in books about drowning in someone's eyes – I think I understand what that means right now.

It feels frightening and wonderful and addictive all at once. I don't want him to let go and I don't want to tear my eyes away. I want it to go on forever. I don't want more because this feels like too much already. I'm afraid of how incredible it feels right now, how connected with him I am. Right now, *this* is exactly what I want. And right now, all my other worries dissolve.

Too, too soon, he lets go of my hand and looks out of the

window. I think his cheeks are pink, but I can't be sure in the dim light. 'Want to check out the rides?' he says. I get up because the moment is broken and there's nothing more to say now.

We walk around and find some waltzers, but there isn't anyone to spin us around like at the fair. Joe does quite a good job on his own though, throwing himself around to make the car whirl. I don't scream. But then I don't any more.

After that we try a roller coaster, which is OK but nothing amazing, and then we go on a log flume where Joe attempts to souse me in water whenever we get to the slow parts. I get my own back on the last turn before the big drop, scooping up enough water to soak his hair.

'I want a smoke,' he says when we get off. 'Down there – avoid the teachers.' He points to a bank covered in thick rhododendrons and we weave through a narrow path to the centre. We sit there while he lights up.

'Are you ever going to tell me about what gives you those nightmares?' he asks, looking at me all serious-eyed, and I so wish I could tell him. I do wish a lot that I could tell someone but most of all I'd like to be able to tell him because . . .

. . . because I know he'd understand.

'I'm not supposed to tell anyone.'

'Why?'

'Because it could be dangerous if I did.' I said could, not

would. The police would have said it the other way round.

'How could it be dangerous if I never told anybody?'

And how can I not believe eyes that serious? 'I don't know.'

'Then it's not dangerous to tell me. Unless you don't trust me.'

But I do trust him. And I know I'm about to break the biggest rule the police gave me. And for what? Some bond between us that I can't even explain. Just because it feels *right*.

'I saw something happen to someone.'

His eyes widen as he realises I'm actually going to talk. But I'll only tell him about Katya, not about the forest. Not yet, not out here in the sunshine. I'll only be able to share that one in a place where I feel safe and snug.

'I was on holiday and I saw something bad happen to the girl who was in the cottage next door, and after that my life went crazy. You could say my life ended.'

He puts the cigarette out and turns to face me properly, skewing round on the bank, and he moves closer. 'Go on.'

I tell him a little bit about Katya and how Katie liked her, and how mysterious she was about her dad and other parts of her life. And I tell him about the white car and he stiffens as if he's sensing what's coming without really knowing what it is.

And then I tell him about what happened the night they came for Katya, and I feel myself go cold despite the sun.

Chapter 41

'The day after we saw the car come back, there was a quiz at the pub in a village about eight miles away. My mum and dad persuaded Katya's mum to go along with them. Mum told her it was a British cultural experience that she had to try out and practically dragged her with them. You could tell she wasn't happy about leaving Katya and she was trying to talk her into going round to ours and spending the night there, but Katya was painting and said she wanted to finish what she was working on. She told her mum she'd stay in my place until the quiz was over, but she didn't. After dinner, she went back home. She said the desire to finish the painting was like a burning inside and it got so bad it actually hurt her not to do it. I had to stay at mine to look after Katie of course and

I'd just put on *The Lion King* DVD so there was totally no way she would have moved. She's watched that at least a hundred times but it's her favourite film ever.'

Joe nods at me and I go on.

'Katya told me the painting was about her dad and painting it made her feel as if he was there with her, and I understood. Her eyes were like the definition of sadness again and I guess painting that picture was the only way she could escape the pain of missing him. What I didn't know at the time was how scared she was for him. I only found that out later. It turned out she'd have been better off being scared for herself.'

I take a deep breath because the next part is something I see over and over again in nightmares.

'I got a call from Mum at about nine to check I was OK and she asked me about Katya. I could see the light in her little window through the twilight, and the shadow of her at the easel, so I said she was OK too. Katie was being awkward about going to bed so I let her have the end of the film on again because she wanted to sing along. It was about half nine before I managed to get her upstairs to her bedroom.'

I can feel my heart starting to beat faster, as if I'm there again.

'As I went to draw Katie's curtains, I noticed a pale-coloured car coming down the lane. Maybe if Katie hadn't noticed that white car, I wouldn't have lingered at the window to look, but I did and I saw that this car pulled up for a moment, then it slowly and quietly drove through the five-bar gate into the drive. I knew there was something odd, but I couldn't work out what. I could hardly see because it had got so dark by then, but I knew it wasn't our car. I thought it might be the one Katie kept seeing, but I also wondered if it could be Katya's dad at last.

'But then I realised what was weird – it was nearly fully dark outside and this car was driving with no lights on.'

Joe's frowning and chewing his lip. He would have been suspicious, I can tell. If only I'd been more suspicious. If only I'd rung Mum instead of standing and watching.

'I squinted through the window, and Katie was nagging me and pulling at my sleeve to know what was going on. Four men got out of the car – three with balaclavas on and one with his still in his hand. The security light at the side of Katya's cottage was on and I got a good look at him before he pulled his balaclava on like the rest. They stood talking for a moment and looking up at the light – I think they were trying to decide whether to break it or not.

'I froze. I didn't know what to do and I didn't have a clue what was going to happen. The awful thing is, even if I had known I think I'd still have stood there rooted to the spot like a fool.'

He rubs my arm slowly. 'What did happen next?'

'The one who put his balaclava on last went to knock on the door while the others hid at either side of the porch. I just stood there watching. Katya's shadow disappeared from the bedroom and then just after, the light came on in the hall and the front door opened. I guess she thought it was probably me.

'As I watched, the guy grabbed her and I saw him shoot something from a syringe into her arm. The police told me it was a knock-out drug. She didn't have a chance to fight. I saw her pull back, but the man stepped inside and pushed her against the door, and the other men followed him to get hold of her and she went limp. I saw her head lolling as they lifted her out of the porch and bundled her into the car.'

'You saw that guy's face before he put his balaclava on — you can identify him!'

'Yes.'

His face appears in my dreams all the time. The short brown hair, the wide, fleshy face with its slightly pitted skin, almost good-looking in a rough way, but not quite because the expression is too hard and cold for that.

'So that's why you're here. You saw them and you're in danger,' he says grimly. 'So what happened next?'

'They carried her to the car. One of them turned off the hall light and closed the door. It was so fast, Joe, and nobody made a sound.'

'You couldn't have done anything. Those guys were professionals, weren't they?'

'Yes. The police said they were hired by enemies of her dad and they kidnapped her to hold her to ransom. I don't properly understand what he was involved in, but he made some bad enemies because of some business deal and they were after money and revenge. I don't think what he did was illegal, but he upset the wrong kind of people. People he should never have messed with, one of the detectives told me.'

'You see, you couldn't have done anything.' He puts his arm round me consolingly.

I pull back a little to look at his face, all worried and upset for me. 'Oh, but I did. I did do something.'

Chapter 42

Joe's taken aback. 'What did you do?'

'I stopped them.'

His mouth drops open. 'You did what?'

'When I saw them bundling her into the car, I kind of unfroze. Suddenly I got really mad. I ran downstairs and grabbed the first weapon I could see – my dad's big metal torch. Then I ran outside. The strange thing is I was mad, but somehow mad *and* logical like a part of my brain I didn't know existed took over and acted for me.'

He looks thoughtful. 'Hmm, I think I know what you mean. Go on.'

'So I ran towards the car, squinting to see the number plate – and I could only just make it out in the darkness, but

I've never forgotten it. One of the men saw me and shouted, and the one getting into the car with him pulled something out of his pocket. I knew it was a gun even though I couldn't see. It didn't stop me though. He fired into the grass near me, to scare me, I guess.'

'Shit, Holly!'

'Yes, I don't know what came over me. I just kept going. As the car whizzed around, I smashed the torch through their windscreen. The back door flew open and I could hear them yelling inside and I knew they'd shoot again so I ran for the road. I don't know what I thought I was going to do. I remember thinking, *Please let Katie stay indoors, please!* and hoping the noise would keep her away.'

'Where was she? Still in her bedroom.'

'No, she'd followed me downstairs. I'd left my mobile on the table and Katie picked it up when she heard the yelling and the shot. She rang Mum on speed dial and said, "There are bad men here, Mummy, and Boo-Boo needs help."

'That was all Mum needed. They ran for the car and Dad phoned the police en route. Because Katie would never say anything like that normally. She mightn't understand everything, but she knows that guns are very bad.'

'So you ran for the road?'

'Like I said, I didn't know what I was doing. But you know how sometimes you just come up lucky? My guardian angel must have been working overtime that night because I hurtled out on to the road as all the commotion was going on and there was a row of tractor things coming down it – those big harvesty-type machines – you would know what they are – four in a convoy. The first one stopped when I ran into the beam of its headlights and the man was leaning out to yell at me when the gun went off again behind me. I must have looked pretty freaked.'

'Hell, yes, Holly! Who wouldn't?'

'He waved and yelled at me to get into the cab with him so I ran up, scrambled in and screamed, "Block the gate!" He slewed the tractor thing round in the lane and drove it at the gate.'

Joe punched the air. 'The lights of course! Clever girl!'

'Yes.' I allowed myself a smile. 'They dazzled the guys in the car.'

'They would. If you put a harvester on full beam it'll blind anyone in front of it. They have to be bright so you can see in the fields at night.'

'The guy with the gun started shooting at the tractor. I yelled to the man in the cab that they had my friend and he drove the tractor straight at the gateway and wedged them in. Then he pulled me out of the cab with him and told me to run. The men behind were bailing out of their machines and running too. I could hear the kidnappers shouting from behind the hedge and I was praying Katie didn't come out of the house. One of the farmers was calling the police as we ran down the lane.'

'Holly, that's . . . it's . . . you must have been terrified.'

'I just kept going without thinking.'

'They'd obviously had Katya under surveillance – that's what the white car was about, right?'

'Yes. He'd been watching and waiting and feeding information back to them. Anyway, once we got halfway down the lane I realised I had to go back for Katie. I couldn't leave her there. And then I heard one of them shouting, "I'm going to blow her brains out in front of you, bitch, and then I'm going to finish you." He meant Katya, but of course at the time I thought he meant Katie so I started to run back. One of the farmers tried to stop me but I dodged him – I was desperate to get back to her even though I didn't know what I was going to do.'

'Aw, babe.' Joe pulls me into a tight hug and I realise I'm close to tears again, but this is the first time I've talked about it since I told the police and I remember it so well. The noise and the terror that they had Katie and how scared Katie would be and what they were doing to her . . .

I lean against Joe's shoulder and despite what I'm feeling I find myself breathing *him* in again and it slows my racing heart down a little.

'I ran back down the side of the hedge until I could see the car. All the men were out of it – I could see them really clearly in the tractor lights but they couldn't see me. Two of the men had jumped into the tractor to try to get it started while the one with the gun was standing on the drive screaming at them to move faster. He was waving the gun about, threatening to shoot them if they didn't get it started in the next five seconds.'

'They didn't have Katie though?'

'No.' I snuggled my head round out of his shoulder so I could speak better. 'No, and when I looked, the front door of our cottage was closed and I'd definitely left it open when I ran out, so she'd hidden inside. That's when I realised it was Katya he'd been yelling about and she was still in the car.'

He hugs me again. 'No wonder you have nightmares.'

'Everything went even more insane then. There was this massive noise from above and lights in the sky and the men were yelling even more, but I couldn't make out what they were saying over all the racket.'

'What was it?'

'A police helicopter looking for a stolen car when the call came about us. It got scrambled to assess the scene before any other officers got there. The kidnappers finally got the tractor started and backed it up enough to get their car out, then they all piled in again and shot off down the road with the helicopter in pursuit. Mum and Dad got back a few minutes later. I'd run into the house to find Katie – she was hiding behind the sofa with the mobile phone and was totally hysterical. The tractors were still blocking the lane so Mum and Dad had to abandon their car to get to us. It took forever for a police car to reach us, and then even longer for news to come about what had happened.'

'About Katya? She was still in the car when they took off, right?'

'Yes. The police officers who got there first stayed with us. They got the news from the helicopter radioed through as it happened. It followed the car into Devon and the kidnappers went up on Dartmoor. When they got right out on to the moors, they stopped the car and threw Katya out, then drove off again. The helicopter couldn't follow because they had to stay to help her. They couldn't leave or the cars on the ground might never have found her in time.'

'I suppose the kidnappers knew that.'

'Totally. The police said that's why they went up there with her. By the time the helicopter guided in someone to help her, they'd got away and abandoned the car. The police said they got picked up in another car. Perhaps it was prearranged, or perhaps they phoned for help.'

'So was Katya OK when she came round from the drug they gave her?'

I can see her face again in the police photos. Eyes closed, face white, the trickle of blood by her ear, all captured in the lights they shone on her while she lay unconscious on the moorland grass. 'No, she wasn't OK. She never came round.'

I see the shock on his face. 'She's dead?'

'No, not dead.' I hate saying the words. I hate it because it makes it true all over again. 'She's in a coma. She has brain damage. She was pistol-whipped before the kidnappers threw her out of the car. They say she might never come out of it. Maybe it was revenge because they got interrupted. Maybe they did it because of what I did.' I bury my head in his shoulder again to see if having him so close can make it better a second time.

'You think they hurt her like that because you stepped in?'

'Yes.'

'Babe, they would probably have done it anyway if they wanted to get back at her dad. They don't care what they do to anyone. It means nothing to them. They've lost what made them human. So did the police catch them?'

'Not the guy whose face I saw, but the police did link him to two of his accomplices and they got arrested. They squealed on their bosses when they knew how long they were facing in prison. I think they get a reduced sentence and witness protection too when they get out. But the police said they still need me to testify because my statement's more reliable than a criminal's.'

I'm exhausted by going through the story. I feel drained and empty and I want to feel something else.

I don't want the past.

I want the now. And I know who I want.

I reach across and tilt Joe's chin around. His eyes widen as he realises what I'm about to do. But he doesn't pull away. That's the important thing.

He leans in. My lips brush his. I've never kissed a boy first before. I hear his intake of breath when our mouths make contact. His fingers touch my face softly, like I'm precious.

I feel something. I don't know what it is, but it's new and so strong that I am engulfed by it. I don't want this kiss to stop. Every cell in my body hums with life, with awareness of me and of him.

It's . . . beautiful.

I feel stupid for being so . . . *mushy* . . . but it . . . he . . . is so different to how it's been with every other boy I've kissed.

It's that rightness thing again.

He pulls back and looks at me with dark, dark eyes. How could I not notice how amazing his eyes are? And it seems like he's just as amazed by me.

'I thought this was never going to happen,' he whispers.

'Did you want it to?' I whisper back.

'Yeah,' he says with a snort. 'Of course.'

'Since when?'

He flushes red. 'Since I saw you outside your house that day you were moving in.'

'You gave me evils then!'

He grins at me. 'Yeah, but I still wanted you.'

I give up attempting to understand and kiss him again, and again, and again.

Chapter 43

So the coach was buzzing about me and Joe all the way home from the theme park. Well, it was pretty obvious. I was snuggled up to him for the whole journey. He even stroked my hair while I fell asleep on his shoulder at one point and he didn't care who saw.

He walked me home and kissed me goodnight on the doorstep and it was as awesome as it is in the old films they put on at Christmas.

Tasha would shriek if she could see me with him. I'd get so lectured about not letting him get the upper hand and thinking he had me where he wanted me. But for the first time I don't care. I want us on an equal footing. No games. I like it like this.

'What really scares me,' I told him as we walked home, 'is the trial. It's in August and I'll have to stand up and testify against them and go through it all again.'

'And after that?' He held me tight as if he was afraid of the answer.

'After that, I'll still be in witness protection. It's a forever thing for us all. But it'll be better after the trial because that won't always be at the back of my mind. I can move on but I'll always be Holly now and never who I was before.'

'What was your name?'

I hesitated for just a fraction of a second before I said, 'Louisa.'

He stroked the hair off my face and looked at me. 'I like Holly better.'

And I smiled at him. 'So do I. Now.'

Once the exams start, it's pretty heavy going from day to day. They're broken up by half-term, but that's not a holiday, just an extended last blast of revision before the final slog. I have 17th June, my last exam, circled in red on my calendar and the 19th is in purple because that's when Joe finishes.

Mum comments on how we're hardly apart, but she's not complaining because we're working so hard. Although I have to admit, hourly revision breaks have got more interesting lately and I haven't at all changed my opinion of how he kisses.

If I was mailing Tasha now, I'd tell her that being with him is so easy; he makes me happy; I like being his girlfriend. I'm pretty close to liking everything about him. Except the music. I'll never like the music. He's still not feeling the love for Beyoncé either.

When an exam feels like it didn't go too well, he's there with a hug to make it better. When I'm so tired my head hurts and I can't keep my eyes open any longer, he takes the English book off me and reads it to me because I won't give up until I've been through it one more time for tomorrow's exam.

He's awesome.

And when I remember what I thought the first time I saw him, I have to laugh. How screwed up wrong can you be?

When we finish our exams, Dad pays for us to go out for a meal at the newly opened Chinese restaurant in the village, and he buys us a bottle of champagne to share later.

Joe makes me laugh in the restaurant by pulling my chair out for me and holding my coat for me to put on when we leave. He ignores me when I giggle – he doesn't care and he's doing it anyway because that's how he wants it to be between us.

We take the champagne down to his place and lie in the orchard on a rug, looking at the stars and swigging from the bottle. I don't care if champagne's supposed to be drunk from the right-shaped glass etc. Drunk like this, it tastes of starlight and happiness and Joe.

'You know what?' he says, twisting a strand of my hair round his finger, 'I kinda think I love you.'

'You know what?' I say back, 'I kinda think I love you too.'

Chapter 44

We're curled up in Joe's bedroom and it's dusk outside. He's going through his music collection to find something I'll like, which is really an impossible task, but he's trying anyway.

And that's when I decide to tell him the rest of my story. It's the end of June and so there's only one more month standing between us and August. And the trial.

I need to have talked about this before the trial.

'I never told you what happened to me after Katya.'

He puts his iPod down and looks at me. 'You mean the witness protection stuff.'

'Kind of. There's a bit more to it, but I didn't feel up to talking about it before.'

He turns over and settles his head on the pillow, looking at me expectantly. I'm gathering myself to tell him when an owl hoots outside and makes me jump. He laughs at my nervousness and puts his arms round me. That's better — I should have known it would be easier to tell the story nestled up against him.

'After the kidnapping, we went home to London. I went back to school and pretended everything was normal. I didn't tell anyone what had happened, not even Tasha, my best friend. I just couldn't. The police didn't have any idea who they were dealing with at that stage. Katya's dad had gone into hiding and it wasn't until he finally tried to get in touch with his family that he found out they weren't safe in Cornwall where he thought they'd be. Then he was too scared the men after him would do even worse so he wouldn't tell the police anything at all. I carried on as if nothing had happened and waited for them to catch the men who did it. But the police didn't and then *They* found me instead.'

I tell Joe about the night I walked home from my violin lesson, how the man dragged me into the car, and then what I heard them saying about shooting me. He's tense against me and I can feel his anger through my body.

'I pretended I'd passed out against the seat. They didn't talk much as we drove out of London. I knew we were in the countryside when the amber glow in the car from the street lamps changed. You know?'

I glance up and he looks a bit blank. I kiss his mouth.

'Trust me, you do. Eventually we turned off down a bumpier lane. The driver slowed the car down to a crawl and I heard a click as he turned off the headlights. And I knew we'd not got far to go. And it was like when they came for Katya – headlights off. I knew I had to be totally focused on getting away, to be open to any chance I could take because I wouldn't get a second.

'I shut down and I was like a robot or something. I don't remember feeling anything other than this determination to get out of there and it was . . . I dunno . . . kind of cool and logical. I guess I'm weird.'

'Yeah, well, don't knock it because if it hadn't been for that you might not be here now and that would be . . . I don't even want to think what that would be,' Joe whispers.

But I don't want to stop and think about that either. I just want to get this story finished because this is the part that really haunts me at night.

'When the driver pulled the car up, I knew this was it. The guy in the back jerked me upright as his boss in the front pulled a gun and leaned over the seats. "We'll get her out here and you're going to do the business. Time to prove yourself!" he said and then got out and came round to the rear door to drag me out of the car. There was my one chance. He began to open the door and I twisted my legs around and I kicked the door as hard as I could. He swore and something crashed to the ground and then I heard him scrabbling in the dark, swearing.'

'Did he drop the gun?'

'Yes, and I think he might have broken some fingers from the way he was cursing. The guy next to me went to grab me back so I slammed the heel of my hand up into the base of his nose – my uncle taught me how to do that.'

'What does that do?'

'Smashes the nose up completely. Ask Matt – I bet he knows about it. My granddad and uncles are in the forces. Dad was an army brat – he and his brothers grew up moving around bases. Uncle Nick thought I needed to know some self-defence to look after myself living in London so he taught me when I was about thirteen. And thank God, it worked. So then I ran for it before the driver had a chance to join in. I shot out of the car and I just ran and ran.'

'But it was night. How did you see where you were going?'

'I couldn't, but they couldn't see me either. I hid in the undergrowth at one point and they almost walked over me and I thought they were going to find me for sure, but they didn't. And then they went off in another direction. I guess they gave up in the end and just got out of there. I was bumbling around in the dark when they'd gone and didn't see I was coming to a steep bank. The leaves were slippy on the ground – it was November – and my feet slid from under me. I went crashing down the bank and hit my head on a tree root at the bottom. A dog walker found me in the morning.

'When I came round, I was in hospital and my mum and dad had already agreed for us to go into witness protection. I had to wait until they discharged me to see them.'

'You're incredible, do you know that?' And Joe looks like he really means it.

But I don't feel incredible when the nightmares come night after night. I feel useless, helpless, weak . . . I don't tell him that though. I want him to keep thinking I am incredible. Nobody's ever said that to me before and I want to keep that feeling for a little longer. Maybe if somebody does think you're incredible then you are just a little bit.

Chapter 45

Summer. A long summer of freedom from exams and revision and work. OK, not free from stress due to the great big *thing* hanging over my head in August. The thought of the trial makes GCSE results seem pretty unimportant sometimes.

I say as much to Mum when we're in the garage sorting out the laundry.

'But those results *are* still important to you, darling. They're about the rest of your life, not what happened in the past.'

'I suppose so.'

'How are you feeling about the trial?'

'Nervous. Stressed. But strong.' Joe told me I sounded strong about it, and until he said that I hadn't realised I am.

He said it was because I was so sure that testifying was the right thing to do and I wasn't going to let them get away with what they did to Katya. That made me strong because I have belief.

'We'll be there for you.' Mum drops the washing and hugs me. 'Don't forget Dad and I will be with you the whole time.'

Tim W-P told me that they'd given my family the option to send me into witness protection without them. They'd told him no straight away – I was not going alone. At times I forget how lucky I am to have them.

Sometimes I lie in bed and think about how I would deal with this if I didn't have my family. If I'd had some other set of parents who weren't as good together, who weren't as devoted to me and Katie, how would I have coped? I don't think I would.

The weather's rubbish at first, which is typical. Joe and I hang out at our houses in between his farm jobs. Mum and I take a day together to go shopping and I spend all the pocket money I've been saving on a blitz of new clothes. Mum buys some new stuff for herself and decides to smarten Dad up too. She doesn't get anything for Katie, who hasn't grown out of her current clothes yet. New clothes are another of those changes Katie doesn't like.

I learn about strange farm stuff like milking machines and castrating bullocks and slurry pits while hanging out with

Joe. I can't say I ever wanted to know about these things, but he never fails to make me laugh when he shows or explains something farmy. It's the little grin he gives, like he knows I have absolutely zero interest, but he's making me suffer it anyway.

The weather improves eventually and by late July my summer tan is coming along nicely. I'm lounging in the garden while Joe is off milking when Katie comes home from school one day and rushes straight over to tell me something.

'There was a van outside school today.'

I squint into the sun to look at her. 'What kind of van?'

'It was a white Transit van with letters on the side. They were pretty and red.'

'What did the letters look like?' I don't really care. She does this all the time. It's part of her obsession with all things moving vehicle.

She traces the shapes on the grass.

'Lindop Joiners Ltd,' I tell her. 'That means they make and fit things out of wood, like doors and windows.'

'Oh. It was a very clean van.'

'That's nice.'

'It was there yesterday too.'

'They're probably going to be doing some work in your school over the summer holidays. You break up in a few

315

days – they'll have people in painting and making it nice for September.'

'Three days until we break up. We're having a party on Friday.'

'That'll be fun. Now do you want to go and play on Joe's swing?'

'SWWWIINGGG!'

'That's a yes then.'

The following day, I'm lying on my bed reading, because the weather's turned icky again, when Dad gets home from work. 'Where's your mother?' he asks, poking his head round the bedroom door.

'Gone to pick Katie up.' I glance at my watch. Half four. 'Oh! She should be back by now!'

'Yes.' He frowns and disappears downstairs.

When I slip on my trainers and follow him, he's reading through the messages on his phone and checking his missed calls.

'Anything from her?'

'No, I'm going to give her a call.' He speed-dials and the phone rings . . . rings . . . rings before Mum finally picks up. I can't make out her words exactly when she speaks, but I can hear the note of panic in them. 'Clare, where are you? . . . Still at the school? . . . I'll come down there now. Yes, call the police. I know she might turn up, but call them anyway.'

He's halfway down the hall before he says to me, 'Your sister's gone missing. I need to look for her. Stay here in case she's already wandering home or someone finds her and brings her back.'

'What's happened?'

'They don't know. School said she was there one minute and gone the next. She's probably got some crazy idea and wandered off on a mission by herself. Don't worry, we'll find her.'

And then he runs out of the house.

Where's she gone? If another kid had disappeared with her, I'd be less worried because they'd probably have cooked up some adventure together. But Mum didn't mention anyone else being gone, just Katie. Has someone upset her? I think of how stupid she can be near traffic sometimes and I start to get scared.

I sit by the phone and stare at four walls for what seems like an hour, but when I check my watch it's really only fifteen minutes. Fifteen minutes where the tick, tick, tick of the clock on the wall in the living room echoes through the house to the kitchen to torment me. Every tick marks a second where my sister is out there alone.

When the phone goes it makes me jump. I grab it with trembling hands.

'Dad?'

The voice on the other end laughs. 'Not quite.'

'Who is this?'

'I have your sister here. Do you want her back?'

'Yes, of course! Where is she? I'll call my dad to come and get her.'

'I told you. She's with me. And if you want to see her alive again, you'll have to come and get her yourself.'

All the blood in my body freezes.

'Did you hear me?'

'Yes.'

'Good. Now listen carefully and don't do anything stupid. We're watching your house. Take a walk outside – don't rush, don't look suspicious – and turn up the street through the bungalows. There's a footpath that takes you across some fields to a lane. Do you know it?'

'Yes,' I say dully.

'There's a white van parked on the lane. Get in the back.'

The line goes dead.

I can't breathe. I drop the phone and catch the back of the chair for support.

He's not lying. He has her. She'd be home by now otherwise.

This isn't some random psycho snatching her. I wouldn't have been called like this if it was. It's *Them*. They've found us.

I have no idea what to do. I don't know how to make my legs work, to make me brave, to make me suddenly have a superplan to rescue Katie. Make me anything other than a quivering jelly standing here and gripping the chair with white knuckles.

What do I do?

I get up. It feels like my knees won't hold me, but I get up.

I put on a waterproof jacket.

I walk to the door.

I open it and go out into the street. It's drizzling slightly and the sky is dark with cloud.

I go up the street through the bungalows, forcing myself to take one step at a time. It feels like a long walk.

Joe said I was brave. Tim W-P said I was brave. I'm not. I want to be anywhere but here. I don't want to even think about what's going to happen. I don't want to be there for Katie. Some better, far braver person than me should be in charge of this.

I'm not brave at all. I'm just too stupid to know how to do anything other than walk to the van like the man on the phone told me to.

At the end of the houses, I take the path that leads across Joe's fields, but this time where it splits into two, I take the upper fork to a lane up on the hill above the farmhouse.

What's Katie thinking? Have they hurt her? I feel sick and clammy all over at the thought of how terrified she must be now.

My phone vibrates in the pocket of my jeans. I'd forgotten it was there. Are they watching me? Will they see if I look? I daren't use it to make a call for help.

I ease the phone out of my jeans under my sleeve and glance down at the screen. It's a text from Joe.

What's going on?

A lump forms in my throat.

I wish I could tell him. I don't know how he knows something's wrong unless he's heard somehow that Katie's missing. I can't answer – they could be watching. Will I get to see him again?

I realise I don't believe I will. My eyes are prickling with tears.

But there's no time for this self-pitying stuff. Katie's with those men and they could be doing anything to her. She'll be so frightened. Surely they can't mean to kill her? She can't testify against them. She's nothing to them. Maybe they *will* let her go. It's me they're after.

I have to keep walking.

The sick feeling in my stomach makes my skin shiver.

It's like even my skin is retching at the thought of what I've got to do.

What I'm doing.

This is it. My luck's run out.

My knees are shaking so much that I don't think I can stand up much longer.

I finally get to the lane and climb over the stile. The van is waiting for me.

Chapter 46

I thought we were safe here. I thought they wouldn't find us.

How stupid.

I open the back door of the white van as *he* told me to.

Stupid, dense Holly. How am I going to get out of this?

The short answer is – I can't.

'Get in,' a voice says, and I obey.

I wish Katie had a better rescuer than me. I wish there was someone who was up to this job who could be here for her.

But there isn't. Just her dumb-ass sister.

The man sitting on the floor of the van closes the door behind me and we drive off. He hasn't got his face covered. I know what that means.

'Where's my sister?' I ask.

He looks at me contemptuously and doesn't answer.

I could make a move for the door and try to dive out. I could still get away . . . but there's Katie. I'm no closer to knowing where she is now. Or how she is.

The van keeps moving. Maybe when they stop I'll find out. Or maybe they'll just shoot me before I do get to find out and they'll leave my body here in this van, and I'll never know if they let her go.

But what choice did I have other than to be here? I know what they're capable of.

'Where's my sister?' I scream at the man opposite me.

He just laughs and stretches his legs out.

A minute later, the van pulls up and the man finally speaks. 'Get out and don't try anything. If you do, it's your sister who'll suffer.'

When he opens the door, there's another man waiting. A face I recognise and one I've seen in my nightmares over and over again. The man whose description I gave to the police. The man with so many aliases no one knows his real name. Whose photofit picture I helped the police artist construct. The one they've been looking for and never managed to find.

As his hate-filled eyes stare down at me, I know this man will never let Katie go. I've walked into his trap for nothing.

All I can possibly do is stall him for as long as possible and hope I can come up with a plan. It's a stupid, desperate hope, but no hope is worse.

'Where's my sister?' I hope my voice isn't shaking.

He ignores my question like I'm beneath notice and high-fives his accomplice. 'Nice work.'

The other man nods back at him. 'Do I go deal with the other one now?'

Katie? They must mean Katie.

'Where's my sister?' I scream as loud as I can.

He backhands me across the face. 'Shut up, bitch!'

My ears are still ringing as rage boils up inside me. I launch at him to claw his eyes, shred the skin on his face, make him hurt like he's made me hurt this past year.

He punches me hard on the side of the head and I drop to the ground, limp.

I think I'm unconscious for a moment because I don't remember being hauled up, but someone is holding my head off the ground and checking me over. I play dead. I'm frisked briefly. They find the phone in my pocket and toss it away.

'She's out cold, Zach. Do you want to finish her now?'

'Nah, this wasn't part of the plan,' Katya's kidnapper replies. 'Wait for the little bitch to come round. I want her to suffer. Tie her up and chuck her back in the van.'

It's an opportunity, I tell myself, so when they tie the bonds on my wrist and ankles, I don't wince. And I don't let them see how it hurts when they toss me in the back of the van.

They slam the door and tramp away. There's a barn on the other side of the track. Is Katie in there? Please don't let them hurt her . . .

I'm trussed so tight that the rope's cutting into the bare skin of my wrists and ankles. How did I think this was an opportunity? I can't move.

I can't tell how long I'm left lying here. It feels like ages and I can't hear a thing outside, though I strain my ears for voices or the sound of a car. But we're in the middle of acres of fields and all I saw before they tied me up was a black car, presumably theirs, parked beside the barn. Where are they? What are they doing out there? Oh, Katie, please be OK.

How did they find us? *How?* And why get Katie involved? Surely it was harder to lure her away than just to snatch me off the street again? Why did they take her? There has to be some reason.

But then there are footsteps coming back to the van. I collapse into a pretend faint just before they open the door.

They haul me out. I try to stay limp, but another ringing slap to the swollen side of my face makes me gasp in pain. I open my eyes to see the man who kidnapped Katya – Zach, they called him – standing over me, his hand raised again. He grins and lets me fall to the ground.

'You owe me payment on account, bitch. Time to settle it.'

The rope tying my ankles together is cut and I'm kicked hard. I pull myself on to my knees. He bends over me.

'Up!' he yells into my ear.

I wobble to my feet, struggling to balance with my hands still tied behind my back, legs stiff from being cramped up in the van.

He shoves me in the direction of the barn. 'In there, move it.'

His men follow behind, laughing at my attempts to walk on the uneven ground. Their boss sticks his foot out to try to trip me. I stagger but stay on my feet, just.

I hope they didn't do this to Katie. I can't stand to think about how terrified she must feel right now, wherever she is. Bad enough for a normal child, but for her . . .

Zach gives me a last shove as we enter the barn through a narrow side door and I go sprawling on the earth floor.

'I could just shoot her like that,' he says above me. 'Or we could untie her and get some practice on a moving target. Pump a few bullets at random and see who gets most hits. Then time how long she takes to die.' He laughs. 'Hey, I could turn my back and do it – that's how good I am.'

The bile rises in my throat. I swear if I had a gun now I'd shoot him myself.

I roll over and face them, on the ground, yes, but I still face them.

'How did you find us?'

He ignores me and nods to one of his men. 'Give me my gun.'

The man passes him a handgun. He points it at my head.

'Where's Katie?' I scream. 'What have you done with her?' I realise I *am* going to die without knowing what's happened to her. He's going to shoot me right here.

There's nothing I can do . . . nothing . . .

Will he kill her after he's killed me?

He smiles, and I know this is it.

CRACK!!!

But that's not his gun. The noise came from outside. I open my eyes.

The men are staring at the large sliding doors at the front of the barn. The noise came from beyond them.

'Check it!' Zach barks. 'And deal with it.' He raises the gun to my head again. 'I don't want interruptions.'

'Too late,' a voice says from our left.

Chapter 47

They spin around and I scramble on to my knees. It's Matt . . .

Matt? What . . .?

. . . and he's standing . . . *standing* . . . in the doorway of the barn, leaning on the door frame with a shotgun pointed right at my kidnapper's head.

'Who the hell are you?' the man growls.

Matt's face is expressionless. 'Drop the gun.'

Zach's hand remains in position, aiming right at my skull. 'You don't know who you're dealing with here, son. You've got two cartridges in that shotgun and there are four of us.'

'I've seen about five seconds of you,' Matt says in a flat, cold voice, 'and you don't strike me as the type men would die for. Two'll be enough. So drop the gun – last chance.'

'Do him!' Zach yells at the man nearest, throwing himself to the side.

It doesn't happen in slo-mo like in the films. It's a flash of action from so many directions that I'm not sure I've seen it straight until . . .

. . . a shot rings out, a loud crack, but it comes from the back of the barn not from Matt, and the revolver the man is raising in his hand goes clattering across the ground. There's another shot a fraction of a second later, like a stutter effect after the first, and Zach yells out in pain. Matt's ahead of me with the shotgun smoking . . . and at the back of the barn . . . it's Joe with a matching shotgun. I get unsteadily to my feet.

'Get out!' Matt yells and I run for cover behind the hay bales at the rear. Joe grabs me as I pass him and throws me behind him. He dives back as a revolver bullet smacks into the metal post where his head was.

'Four cartridges, dickhead, not two!' Joe shouts in response. Then he takes my hand and pulls me towards another door at the back, hidden behind the hay bales. 'Land Rover, now!'

As I run through it, I hear a voice from inside, 'You stupid fuck, you let her get away!'

Another shot rings out from the revolver . . . there's a dull thud. I look at Joe.

'Shit, he just shot his own man.' He shoves me hard. 'Move!'

We run for the Land Rover parked a few metres from the back door.

Matt's backing up towards it, covering us and himself. 'Get in and stay in,' he barks. 'He's a lunatic.'

I scramble into the Land Rover, remembering how Zach shouted at the men trying to move the tractor that night, shouting how he'd blow their heads off.

Matt gets into the jeep as Joe scrambles into the driver's seat. 'Floor it,' Matt yells as a bullet smacks into the door near Joe. 'Now!'

Joe starts it up and slams his foot on the accelerator. We shoot off down the steep bank back towards the lane.

Behind us, the men are making for a car parked further up the track. Zach's clutching his gun arm and there's blood all over him, but the revolver's still in his hand. The man he shot is limping badly at the back, but still following.

'They're going to come after us,' I cry out.

Matt's focusing on the track in front and barking instructions at Joe. 'Police are on their way,' he says, eyes on the road. 'I called them as soon as Joe told me what was happening, but I knew they wouldn't get here in time to get you out of there. Armed response takes forever.'

My head's almost shaken off my body as the jeep passes on

330

to the tarmacked lane with a violent lurch and Joe speeds up.

Matt leans over the seats. 'Turn around.' With a penknife he cuts through the cords still anchoring my wrists. I shake my head as I wiggle my fingers to get the blood flowing again.

'How did Joe know what was happening?'

'Tell you later – it's complicated. He saw you get in the van and we worked out where they were headed and came after you.'

'They've got Katie.'

'Yeah, I figured.'

The car's gaining on us, but Joe's speeding back down to the main road. Can he get there before they catch us up? And what do we do about Katie? I open my mouth to ask when Matt interrupts with a, 'Keep your foot down!'

His eyes are fixed on the car getting closer and closer, getting within range where they could easily take us out with bullets one by one.

Joe keeps his foot stamped on the accelerator. Just as we're nearly at the main road, the hitmen's car pulls up by the open gate to a field and I see the boot pop.

'What the . . .?' Matt's looking too, leaning over the seat. 'Joe, slow down.'

One of the men gets out and goes around to the back of the car. I hear Matt's sharp intake of breath before the man pulls something . . . no, *someone* out of the boot. Matt guesses what's happening before I do. He's reloading the shotgun.

They take my sister out of the boot and stand her in the middle of the lane. They cut the ropes on her hands and feet, but the gag's still over her mouth.

'K-K-K . . .' I try to say her name but the word won't come out. I'm opening and closing my mouth like a stupid drowning fish. Joe stops the car, leaning back to see.

'Reload,' Matt snaps at him.

I expect the men to shoot Katie. I only realise that when they don't, and instead push her through into the gateway of the field, I can hardly breathe with relief.

They shove her hard. Tears roll down my face as she stands and looks at them in confusion. Her face is streaked with salt and snot like she's been crying for hours and I'm surprised she hasn't choked herself on that gag. Zach shoots at the ground next to her feet and her mouth strains to shriek out, but she can't. Matt swears violently. I . . . I can't move . . .

Katie!

It's a silent scream like hers.

'Run, little girl,' Zach yells at her, and Katie finally understands. As she turns away, they shoot into the ground beside her. She breaks into a trot.

They get back into the car and for a crazy moment I think Zach's had a moment of compassion, that he's leaving her behind to come after us.

'Spin us round,' Matt shouts. He's there before me, guessing again, and Joe is already turning the wheel.

Even after everything I've seen Zach do, I still can't quite believe my eyes at what he does next. This time when he gets into the car, it's into the driver's seat. The others pile in the back, squashed up. It's only afterwards I wonder if it was because they didn't have the stomach for what he was going to do.

He drives the car into the field and he aims it straight at Katie. She runs faster as she realises the car is coming towards her, as fast as I've ever seen her go, but it won't be fast enough. Joe spins us round and then speeds towards them while they play with her like a cat after a mouse.

Zach revs up and zooms at her, then veers and slows just before he hits her. And I know, I just know, he's just waiting for us to catch up so we can see properly. See her die.

'What do we do?' Joe shouts.

My stomach is retching as I watch my sister run down the field like a hunted animal.

'Get out,' Matt replies grimly as Katie turns, running down the field parallel to us, herded by the car.

This time it nearly doesn't stop and almost catches her before Zach slams the brakes on.

I scream.

The boys are out of the jeep and Katie's hurtling in a

diagonal down the field. Zach's whooping from the car window as he pursues her. Matt steadies himself and Joe props the second shotgun against his brother's legs. They say something to each other, but I can't take it in because I'm still rooted to the back seat watching as Katie almost falls under the wheels of the car.

Matt fires a shot at the car, while Joe sprints forward, yelling to Katie to turn towards him.

She sees him and at first I think she's too scared and confused to obey. But he's yelling, 'Katie, come here now,' so loud that it must get through to her and it makes her change direction.

Zach turns the car round and stops it for a second, revving the engine again loudly, and then, with a screech of the wheels, he puts his foot down and heads the car straight towards Katie.

Faster and faster, speeding towards her.

There's no way Joe can get there. And nothing he can do if he does.

Katie's running as fast as she can.

Joe's at full speed down the field towards her. I remember what Gemma said about how he runs. She's right – he's fast, very fast. But he's not as fast as a car.

The tears are flowing down my face because I'm about to see my sister die in front of me and there's nothing I can do.

I get out of the jeep without knowing I'm doing it, and I can hear myself screaming . . .

And then Matt shoots.

One shot.

Into the wheel of the car. The driver's side.

The car veers wildly and Zach fights to keep control. His foot comes off the accelerator – I see the car slow – and the tyre hangs flabby around the wheel, falling apart, blown out by Matt's shot.

Zach's arm is injured, I remember, and I see one of the men struggling to reach over from the back seat to get control of the wheel.

They're still speeding towards Katie under their own momentum.

Matt fires again, through the window of the car, and then he grabs the second shotgun and fires a third round at the back wheel. He misses but the car careers so violently I know he's hit the driver. His fourth round buries itself in the rear wheel.

Joe puts on a last burst of speed. I can't believe how fast he sprints, except that I see him do it right here in front of me.

He dives at Katie . . .

. . . taking her down . . .

. . . and the car rockets forward out of control . . . straight at them.

Chapter 48

The car hurtles past the spot where I saw their bodies hit the ground and I scream again – one long, frantic note.

For a moment I think they're dead, but then I see Joe's rolled Katie out of the way. He lies over my sister and holds her on the ground as the car spins past to slam head first into a tree in the hedge. I watch it rebound and flip. It goes clear over the hedge to crash into the field beyond. Finally it comes to rest upside down, the shot-out wheels still spinning.

I stare and stare . . . at Katie on the ground, with Joe slowly unpeeling himself and getting up . . . at the car broken and smashed in the field of corn . . . at Matt, standing there with the shotgun, another by his feet. His face is ashen and he wipes his sweaty forehead.

'My brother can't half run when he wants,' he says, his voice shaking, and I sink to my knees on the grass.

Later we're sitting round my kitchen table drinking hot tea and I'm wrapped up in a sweatshirt and pyjama bottoms. The doctor said I'm feeling cold because of the shock. He's sedated Katie and she's asleep upstairs. No lasting damage, he said. A bit dehydrated, but she'll do better at home than in hospital after all she's been through, so he leaves us with the instructions to wake her for drinks, but otherwise to let her sleep through. Dad sits with her. He'll be there all night.

Tim W-P has been scrambled out to see us and we're waiting for him to arrive while the local witness protection are covering our backs with extra security and a total media blackout of the incident so news doesn't get out. The crash killed the men in the car. One of them was alive when the ambulance got there, but they pronounced him dead when he arrived at the hospital. Zach had been shot in the head and died instantly.

The police were all over Matt until the witness protection information got through to them and then their attitude changed. Full investigation under way and all that business, but they didn't arrest him. Joe's still here with me and he explains to one of the officers how they found me.

'My Aunty Jenny rang my mum to tell her to keep a

lookout. They were searching in the village for a little girl who'd gone missing from the special school, and she might have wandered off on to farm land. When she told Mum the girl's name was Katie, I went straight out to go round to Holly's to see if I could help. You know, looking for Katie or something. Matt wanted to come too but,' – and he grins ruefully here – 'he'd only just come home today, only been back a few hours, and I didn't think he was up to it, so I told him I'd call him if we needed him. Dad was out at a cattle auction or I'd have got him to help look too.'

'Did you know Matt was coming back today? You never said.' I interrupt.

'No, typical Matt – he never told us. Just turned up on the doorstep in a taxi, grinning his head off and showing off how well he could walk on his new legs. We all thought he was going to be at the rehab centre for at least a few more weeks, but he'd been leading us on so he could surprise us.' He laughs and goes on with his story. 'When I went out to head over to Holly's, I saw her going up our top field to the lane. I shouted at her, but she was too far away and couldn't see me, so I sent her a text and when she didn't answer I ran up there after her. I thought she might have seen Katie or something at first, but then I saw her get into the back of a white van. And I saw her face as she did. That's when I guessed what was going on.'

Tears sting in my eyes because if he hadn't been so smart neither Katie nor I would be here now.

'I saw the van driver too, you see, and his hood was up so you couldn't see his face. I hid behind the hedge and watched the direction the van took and I called Matt. He got Dad's shotguns out of storage and made the 999 call while I ran back to the farm. We were lucky – from the lane they turned up, I had an idea where they might be going and the ground was wet after the rain so they left tracks when they went off-road. It's been dry for days before today so theirs were the only tracks up on the hill.'

'Your father's shotguns –' the officer begins.

'He's licensed. They're for game shooting, but he doesn't use them much, though he taught both me and Matt to shoot when we were kids. Obviously Matt learned properly in the army so he's a way better shot than me.'

They ask me if I have any idea how the hitmen found us. I tell them about the Camilla Facebook hate page and wonder if they could have seen that, even though it seems like a remote possibility. Then they ask me if I've had contact with anyone. I go red and I know I can't hide it. I tell them about Tasha and they take my laptop away to look at it.

Just when I think I'll fall asleep with exhaustion at the table, Tim W-P arrives. He's already been briefed on what happened. He tells me I'm brave again, and I tell him I wasn't. At crunch time, when it came to saving Katie, I stood there screaming and crying. But he says I was brave when it counted and nobody could watch their autistic little sister go through what Katie did and stay as focused as somebody who isn't related to her. Especially as focused as someone who's fought in a war zone. And then Tim says something strange. He says, 'It's the same attitude as those hitmen really. Same thing — trained to kill. But your friend there is operating for the right side.' His words keep repeating in my head. They feel horrible and wrong. To think of Matt and those men as being the same in any way . . . no . . . that's just wrong! But then a tiny part of me sees how it's right too. And I want to close my mind off to that part.

One thing I still don't understand is why they took Katie, not just me. And Tim says very gently, 'Your kidnapper was a sick man. He'd do that to make you suffer more. Even his own men — the ones from the Chernokov incident — turned on him as soon as they got the chance. Even they were afraid of him.'

It's nice of Tim to try to make me feel better, but it's not until I'm lying on my bed with Joe curled round me that I begin to calm down. Mum says he can stay over until I fall asleep. That would surprise me if I had the energy, but I'm too tired.

His arms are round me and I feel safe within them, like he can keep the bad dreams away.

He kisses my ear and I lie still and breathe him in.

I don't let myself think that without him, and Matt of course, Katie and I would be dead.

It's not a time for that now. It's a time to let him hold me and keep the bad stuff at bay.

Chapter 49

In the days that follow, Tim W-P is torn between trying to persuade us to move, with a distraught Katie who keeps having nightmares, and being patient while the police track our kidnappers' trail. Although they never could find the man the other hitmen called Zach when they searched for him after Katya was taken, this time he left an important clue — his phone. When the police took it from his body, they found a route map programmed into it from his home location to our village that allowed them to track him back to base. And there they found the final answers they were looking for.

It was my fault he'd found me.

He'd hacked into Tasha's Facebook account and used it to watch our messages, hoping it'd lead him to me. When

I'd sent her the farewell message, it was him who sent me the final response with a little animated cartoon . . . one that carried a tracking cookie that embedded into my laptop and fed back information on my location. He'd traced me to the approximate area and then it was easy – a special school for autistic kids only a mile away . . . yes, wait and follow whoever picked Katie up from school. Very clever.

But what the police found also gave Tim the reassurance he needed that our cover wasn't blown. Zach or whoever he really was hadn't told his bosses where I was – he'd sent them an email to say he'd located me and he'd be bringing them back my body in a bag. But he worked independently and it seems they trusted him to do that, or too much information from him would incriminate them . . . no one was quite sure which.

So the only people who knew where we were died in that car. Tim said we could take a chance if we wanted and stay. They'd keep a heightened police watch until after the trial, which was only a couple of weeks away. Like I said to Mum and Dad, if they were going to find us here now then they'd find us anywhere, so why move again. Fortunately they agreed with me. I don't think any of us could have stood to start over another time.

On the day I give evidence in the trial, they clear the court of members of the public. The prosecution team tell me that's essential for my safety and I'm entitled to it being an under-eighteen in the witness protection programme. I would have been allowed to use the video link, but I want to give evidence in court. It feels important to actually be there and not hide away. They shield me from view with a screen. The judge is a woman and much younger than I expected her to be. That makes me feel better.

All this time I've built the trial up to be some huge spectre of awfulness in my mind, but I guess what happened in July changed that. The worst has happened and Zach Alias-Whatever can't ever hurt anyone again. Telling my story on a witness stand is nothing compared to that. Besides I keep remembering what Matt said.

The night before we left for the trial he came round with Joe to see me. While Joe played with Katie, he took me aside for a chat.

'How're you feeling about testifying?' he asked.

'Nervous. I hope I don't screw up. I don't want to let anyone down.'

He smiled wryly. 'That's exactly what I said before I got deployed for the first time.'

'I guess it's not as scary as that.'

'Not necessarily. If that's how you feel then –'

'No, Matt, it really is not as scary as that! I'm not stupid. I see the news. Standing in a courtroom talking is not as bad as going to war. It's not as if I'll be in any danger there with police everywhere.'

Katie was making Joe burp her baby doll and Matt struggled to keep his face straight when I pointed to them.

'I'm going to take the piss out of him so bad later,' he said, before turning back to me. 'But it's OK to be scared, you know.'

'I know.'

'Just imagine them all naked on the bog and you'll be fine.'

Joe turned round in surprise at my shout of laughter. He grinned at me. 'Did he just tell you the naked on the bog thing? He always says that to me.'

'Yeah, your brother is gross.'

'Ah, shut up, it works.' Matt leaned back in the chair and stretched out his prosthetic legs like he still had flesh and blood there that needed to be stretched. Was that habit? Or was it really more comfortable?

I wondered if he knew that I'd think of him when I was on the stand and then I'd just have to be brave even if I didn't feel like it. Because some people had to face far worse than me and they could still grin about it.

He looked at me and his eyes narrowed. Had he guessed what I was thinking? 'Did Joe ever tell you what I was like when I woke up in hospital?'

'No, what were you like?'

345

'I woke up screaming. I thought I was still out there. When I found out I had no legs, I mostly lost it again. The medical team had a hard time with me, and the poor sods paid to sort my head out had a worse one. The way I saw it, I'd never be a real person again without my legs, and definitely never a man again.'

'I wouldn't have known any of that when I met you.'

'Yeah, well, the family don't want to see you like that so you man up and don't let it show.'

That's when I swore to myself that I would not lose it or break down on that witness stand. I would not. I would think of Matt and hang in there.

'The thing is, you helped with that.'

'I did? How?' I couldn't see how anything I'd done could possibly have helped him.

'Because coming and dragging yours and Katie's asses out of that mess was the best thing that could have happened to me. It showed me I was still a man. One with a couple of limbs missing, but still a man. And it showed me I didn't have to be a defeatist, self-pitying crock of shit. When I had to do something like getting you two out of there, I could still do it. I just have to do it a bit differently to before.'

Katie waved at us and he beamed at her and waved back.

'So you see, I got to thinking after all that business . . . I shouldn't be giving up on anything I want to do. If I want to help my old man out with the farm, I will. I just have to do it like I did it back there and think around the problems. And whatever it is, I'll find a way. I'm already back doing the milking again.'

'Really? That's amazing . . . no, totally it is.'

Joe looked over. 'You're right, it is totally amazing. Considering how often he used to duck out of it when he had both legs.'

Matt threw a sofa cushion at his head. It hit hard – there was spin on it – and Katie made a face at him as Joe rubbed his head. She stomped over and picked up Matt's hand and bit it hard.

'YOWCH! She's vicious.'

Joe gave him a sickeningly smug smile.

'You wait till she's not around, little bro! I'll get you back. Anyway, Holly, what I was trying to say, before my brother stuck his nose in, was thank you, in a way, because if it hadn't been for you I don't know if the penny would have dropped for me yet.'

I think about Matt as I give my evidence and I get to the difficult parts where I start to shake and my eyes sting. His quick, sly grin flashes through my mind and I blink back the tears and hold myself steady. He's doing the milking today while Joe's down here with me, and I'm manning up.

I guess we both gave each other a helping hand.

Later, we're in a Thai restaurant that Mum and Dad promised me we'd go to after the trial – I love good Thai – and Joe whispers in my ear, 'You were mega brave today.'

It's not bravery, I want to tell him. *It's just getting on with it.*

And that's how I'll manage day after day. They could still come after me, the friends of all the guys who'll get sent down as a result of what I did. I guess they could try to trace me and keep trying until one day one of us messes up again. We'll never be able to come out of witness protection. But I'll keep on keeping on. I'm not going to spend my life worrying someone will find me one day and put a bullet in my brain. I could just as well get run over by a bus.

I've got Mum and Dad and Katie and Joe. And I've survived so far. I just have to keep on doing that.

Katie takes us all aback after the trial. She suddenly starts sleeping without any trouble again, no more bad dreams. She must have overheard us talking or something because when I tuck her in one night and say, 'Sleep well, Pops,' she answers, 'I will because the bad men can't get us now.' We hadn't explained to her about the trial because we didn't think she'd understand, but I guess we never will be able to predict what Katie will or won't grasp. Then she smiles and makes me lie back on the bed with her while she points out her star constellations on the ceiling above by name.

'Love you, Boo-Boo,' she says sleepily just before she drifts off. And I promise her that in the morning we'll go to Joe's and play on the swing. She holds my hand as she falls asleep. I lie beside her for a long time, happy I still get to hold her hand and happier still that she's smiling in her sleep.

Chapter 50

I visit Katya after the trial. It's a special arrangement set up by Tim W-P after I beg and beg him. The nurse leaves me alone with her. I sit by the bed on an orange plastic chair. Katya's face is as pale as the last time I saw her, her cheekbones even more pronounced. Her beautiful hair is dull.

'I want you to try to wake up, Katya,' I say softly to her. 'Come back to us. I'm so sorry you got hurt and I know you're trapped inside somewhere, but I think you can hear me. I hope so anyway.'

She breathes, attached to machines controlling that for her.

'I hope it's beautiful where you are, I hope that so much, but I came here to tell you something. Your mum and dad thought it might help if I did tell you. The man who did this to you, he can't get you now, Katya. He's dead and his bosses are locked up for life. They're never coming out.'

The machine breathes on.

'So I want you to know that, even if it is beautiful where you are, it's beautiful sometimes out here in this world too. Remember those sunsets over Treliske Cove, and the sea in the dawn light? It's safe for you here now. Those men can't hurt you any more. Your mum and dad have a new name like me and my family, like you can have if you come back to us. A whole new life, Katya, where you'll be safe. Your mum and dad miss you so much. They want you back.'

They say it'll take a miracle now for her to come out of the vegetative state after this length of time, but you have to hope, right? You have to try.

'I'd like to hang out with you again. I'd like us to do stuff like we would have planned to do if we'd had the time. I'd like us to get to be best friends. Because I think we would have been if you hadn't got hurt. I'd want you to know what real friends are like. I didn't know that when we first met, but I do now. Real friends are there for you. They watch your back and save your skin when you need them. I'd like you to meet Joe and Matt — I think you'd like them. Katie would love to see you again too, I know she would. I tried to make it better for you, Katya. I made sure they paid for what they did. Please come back to us. Please.'

There's no flutter from her eyes. No answering miracle. I sit and watch her for a while.

'I'm not going to give up on you, do you hear me? I've got to go now, but I found something out while you've been asleep and it's that I'm really good at not giving up. So you see, you have to wake up because I won't give up until you do.'

I stand up and give her hand a last squeeze.

'One day, you're going to come back to us, you just remember that. And we'll go swimming again together.'

Chapter 51

It's the fourth of September and Joe and I are lounging on a couple of easy chairs in the corner of the sixth form common room, filling in our signing-up papers and arguing over subject choices. We're taking French of course, and English Literature, but Joe's rubbishing my choice of media.

'You want to pick a proper subject like maths.'

'Two things – first, I don't even like maths, second, practically our whole lives are affected by the media. It's the subject of the future.'

'No, it's a doss.'

'Well, it could be my future career choice so suck it up.'

All over the room, people are chewing the ends of biros and agonising over making the decision that will influence the rest of their lives. Me, I'm just grateful I still have a life to make decisions over. And one of the people responsible for that is sitting right next to me, sticking out his tongue – complete with new silver stud – and wiggling it in my face before he grabs me and kisses me.

I kiss him back and I don't care who is watching.

I still choose media though, whatever he says. Maybe I'll be a TV journalist. That would be cool. Or a film producer. Or work in magazines, like Mum used to.

The thing is, I have so many choices. And every day I am thankful for that. I have a future. I have a past now too, just one that's shorter than most. But it's still a past.

Matt and Joe had a fight after the GCSE results came out and Joe got a string of A-stars. Matt told his dad how Joe really wanted to go to sixth form and uni, and Joe got mad at him for putting pressure on his dad when he was needed on the farm. Apparently Matt told him very bluntly that he was not in any way needed now as *he* was there so to 'get back to sixth form and stop being a martyr'.

I didn't take the fight part seriously, or Matt's words. That's just how those two are with each other over important things.

But Matt got his own way and Joe's dad duly backed him up and told Joe to get his backside to sixth form too. Then Matt made us all laugh the day before we went back to school by saying he had a plan too: he'd got hooked on watching the Paralympics. 'I could do that,' he said excitedly. 'Four years' time, I could be in Brazil!'

'Doing what?' Joe asked him.

'Not exactly sure yet, but I called a few of the lads I met at Headley Court and we're going to meet up and try a few things out when I've got some spare time. Got to be focused though – only four years to get to national standard!'

Joe shook his head and laughed. 'Crazy fool,' he said to me. 'He means it, you know. And I wouldn't bet against him making it either.'

So here we are in the common room. I've got a violin case at my feet. My first lesson in ages is booked for today straight after school and my fingers are already itching to get back to playing for real.

I look round the room again, at the now-familiar faces. Some I like and some I don't. Some I ignore, like the Crudmilla Cronies. I look at the boy sitting next to me, flicking his tongue stud as he debates whether he really should take further maths. And I smile.

My name is Holly Latham and I'm sixteen years and eight months old. My boyfriend is an Emo freak and he's awesome. There are two things about me worth knowing: I'm happy now and I'm a survivor.

Acknowledgments

Firstly thanks to my wonderful agent, Ariella Feiner, who gave me the idea of a story involving someone in the witness protection scheme and was my first reader, and who continues to look after my career with consummate skill. Further thanks go to Jane Willis for representing me so well in the foreign rights market.

A very important thank you to my editor at Egmont UK, Stella Paskins, whose wise advice and skilful editing made *By Any Other Name* so much better than I could have made it alone. Thank you for knowing where to cut when I didn't! Additional thanks to all at Egmont UK and Australia.

Thanks to several members of Authonomy:

• To Dutch for his technical help with the kidnapping plot, and to T L Tyson for her support, and thanks to both of you for making me laugh on my writing breaks – the balaclavas are there just for you!

• To Michael D Scott, for bouncing ideas around with me until I came up with Katie's role in the book, and also for the advice on tracking IP addresses

• To Shoshanna Einfeld for all her support and common sense

• To Berni Stevens for her cheerleading and for giving me information on London locations, and for travelling up for my wedding x

Final thanks to Paul, for taking over everything else so I had time to write this book, for teaching me unarmed combat and practising the fight scenes with me, and for solving my plot hole at the eleventh hour by having more common sense about communications devices than I do. Oh and, 'Reader, I married him.'

If you liked *By Any Other Name,* you'll love . . .

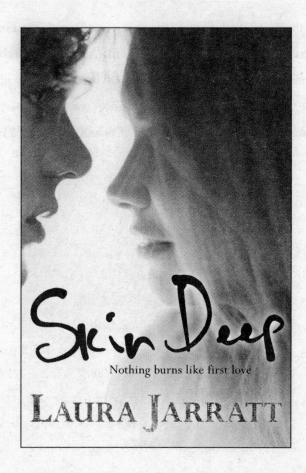

Skin Deep

Nothing burns like first love

LAURA JARRATT

Rewind

The stereo thumps out a drumbeat. Lindsay yells and reaches into the front of the car to turn the volume up – it's her favourite song. The boys in the front laugh and Rob puts his feet up on the dash. I smile like I'm having a good time, squashed in the middle of the back seat with Lindsay dance-jigging around on my knee and Charlotte and Sarah on either side of me. I wish Steven would slow down because the pitch of the car round the country lanes makes my stomach lurch and I don't think he should be driving this fast.

Charlotte's giggling and rubbing Rob's head over the back of the seat. She likes him, I can tell. He rolls a joint and takes a drag, then passes it to her. She inhales the smoke right down. I shiver inside. Mum and Dad would go crazy if they knew I was in a car with people taking drugs, and if they saw me in Lindsay's halter-neck top and short skirt. Charlotte passes me the joint and I shake my head. She shrugs, her face scornful, and Lindsay grabs it and takes a few puffs before passing it on.

The car careers round another corner like we're on a track ride at the funfair.

I sort of wish I was at home, tucked up on the sofa with Mum and Dad and Charlie watching TV. But when the bottle of cider goes round the car, I drink as much as the others so they don't laugh at me for being the youngest. For being a stupid little girl. My eyes feel funny and heavy with the mascara Lindsay brushed on them earlier. I don't know who this girl is. It's not the me who stacks the dishwasher every night for Mum and helps Charlie paint his Warhammer figures at the kitchen table.

I drink more cider, but that doesn't give me any answers, just makes me feel a bit more like throwing up.

Lindsay leans forward and kisses Steven on the neck. Open-mouthed. Sucking hard. He'll have a bruise there tomorrow.

Rob laughs. 'Get a room!'

And Steven waves to him to take the wheel while he cranes round to catch her mouth.

The car swerves and my stomach clenches.

Sarah's quiet, probably miffed that Charlotte's after Rob and there's no one for her.

Lindz whoops as Steven takes the wheel again and floors the accelerator. The car surges forward and hurtles faster and faster down the road.

We hit a straight stretch and Steven spins the wheel from side to side, hands in the air, steering with his knees. Us girls scream and laugh all at once. I force my giggles out.

Something white swoops low in front of the car. Steven

shouts out and the car veers towards the hedge.

An owl!

He grabs the wheel and we shriek with relief. My heart steadies again though I feel sicker than ever.

'Fairy!' Rob jeers at him and Steven's face sets harder in the rear-view mirror. His eyes glitter and he slams down on the accelerator.

We're moving rally-car fast. The January frost coats the hedges in the headlights' beam as we flash past.

We wheel round another bend into the dip down to Harton Brook. Another twist in the road, and another.

The needle on the speedo reads 70 mph and the girls and I are really screaming. Steven's knuckles are white on the wheel and even Rob takes his feet down off the glove compartment.

We shoot over the bridge into the bend straight after it.

The stereo bass batters my ears.

And then . . . then the car feels different underneath me. The wheels . . . they glide and spin.

Bumps in the road . . . I can't feel them any more.

We're floating.

And I remember. Remember how Mum always nags Dad to slow down here. 'It's a frost pocket. There's black ice here,' she always says.

Suddenly Rob starts to yell and Sarah shrieks. And I know why the car feels funny. Why it's skating on the road.

Steven cries out, 'Shit! Shit!'

The car spins off the road, crashes down the steep bank into the field below.

We're not gliding any more and my bones shake like they're falling to pieces.

Thump . . . thump . . . thump from the stereo.

Screaming.

So loud.

I'm thrown upwards as the car turns over.

Then sent slamming down again.

The car rolls once more and my head hits the roof.

Blackness.